WISH YOU WERE HERE

Victoria Connelly was brought up in Norfolk and studied English literature at Worcester University before becoming a teacher in North Yorkshire. After getting married in a medieval castle and living in London for eleven years, she moved to rural Suffolk with her artist husband and ever-increasing family of animals. She has had three novels published in Germany – the first of which was made into a film.

To find out more about Victoria Connelly please visit www.victoriaconnelly.com

By the same author

A Weekend with Mr Darcy
The Perfect Hero
The Runaway Actress

VICTORIA CONNELLY

Wish You Were Here

AVON

This novel is entirely a work of fiction.
The names, characters and incidents portrayed in it are
the work of the author's imagination. Any resemblance to
actual persons, living or dead, events or localities is
entirely coincidental.

AVON

A division of HarperCollinsPublishers
77–85 Fulham Palace Road,
London W6 8JB
www.harpercollins.co.uk

A Paperback Original 2013

1

First published in Great Britain by
HarperCollinsPublishers 2013

Copyright © Victoria Connelly 2013

Victoria Connelly asserts the moral right to
be identified as the author of this work

A catalogue record for this book is
available from the British Library

ISBN-13: 978-1-84756-283-8

Set in Minion
Printed and bound in Great Britain by
Clays Ltd, St Ives plc

All rights reserved. No part of this publication may be reproduced, stored in
a retrieval system, or transmitted, in any form or by any means, electronic,
mechanical, photocopying, recording or otherwise, without the prior
permission of the publishers.

MIX
Paper from
responsible sources
FSC FSC C007454

FSC™ is a non-profit international organisation established to promote
the responsible management of the world's forests. Products carrying the
FSC label are independently certified to assure consumers that they come
from forests that are managed to meet the social, economic and
ecological needs of present and future generations,
and other controlled sources.

Find out more about HarperCollins and the environment at
www.harpercollins.co.uk/green

Acknowledgements

To the fabulous support team I'm so lucky to have: Deborah Wright, Caroline Mackworth Praed, Ruth Saberton, Bridget, Gael and to my husband, Roy, who puts up with so much when I'm writing a novel!

To the lovely Leah Fleming and Allie Spencer for tips about Greece.

Thanks also to Wendy Holden, Fiona Dunbar, Brin and Helen, Andrea Jones, Annette Green, David Smith, Caroline Hogg and the team at Avon.

Special thanks to Alexandra Galani for letting me use her name - again!

Thanks also to the fantastic team in Norwich: Simon and Lisa Ludkin, Roger and Anne Betts, Jane McInnes and Vicky Green and Robert Welton at Jarrold's.

And to my dear readers and friends on Twitter and Facebook who send me such lovely messages – you're amazing!

To Bob and Anne with love

Prologue

On a tiny Greek island in the heart of the Mediterranean Sea sits the Villa Argenti, clinging precariously to a cliff that plummets into the aquamarine waters far below. It's a strange, rambling, tumbling sort of a building. Parts of it date back to the fourteenth century and it's been added to and extended by successive generations which have included one Italian prince, two Greek tycoons and three rock stars. There are towers and turrets, great wooden doors, and windows that would look more at home gracing a Venetian palace. The overall effect is slightly bemusing but very pleasing.

But it isn't the villa people come to see but the gardens. It is said that they are the most beautiful in the whole of the Mediterranean. Perhaps it's because they are so unexpected. They don't scream and shout their presence like some tourist destinations – rather, they whisper enticingly and people find them through serendipity or word of mouth.

Have you seen the gardens at the Villa Argenti? You haven't? Then you must. You really must!

There are long, shady avenues, sun-drenched terraces and lush green lawns. There are stone temples and urns spilling over with bright flowers, and fountains which cool the air in a musical mist. But it is most famous for the Goddess Garden

1

where beautiful statues are placed at respectful intervals, enticing the visitor to walk amongst them in venerable silence. There, beside a cypress tree, stands Artemis, goddess of the hunt, with two faithful hounds by her feet. Overlooking a pond is Demeter, goddess of the harvest, carrying a sheaf of wheat. And there are Athena, Hera and Iris too.

But it isn't until you reach the end of the garden that you find the most popular of the goddesses. In full sunlight, surrounded by roses, is Aphrodite, goddess of love and beauty.

There is something special about this statue – something that marks it out from the thousands of other statues of Aphrodite that can be found all over Greece. It's hard to spot at first because she looks very like the others with her curls tumbling down her back and the finest of silken garments only just covering her curves as her arms reach up to lift her hair away from her face. She holds the attention. She's mesmeric and, some even say, *magical.* Her eyes might be sightless but she seems to see so much and she appears to be smiling as if she can see into the future and knows what's going to happen.

Perhaps she does.

Chapter 1

Alice Archer would be the first to admit that she wasn't beautiful. Sweet, perhaps. But never beautiful. Beauty was a word far more at home describing somebody like her sister, Stella, with her blonde hair, sharp cheekbones and hourglass figure. Next to her sister, Alice faded away into the background. She was Alice the Gooseberry. Second-fiddle Alice. Alice – sister of Stella. She'd never been Alice in her own right. Not that she was complaining. She'd never really wanted to be the centre of attention. She was far happier just to watch life happen to other people.

So that's what makes what happened to her so hard to understand.

It all began on a perfectly ordinary day in February. Well, it was an ordinary day for Alice – Valentine's Day always was. She awoke in her tiny terraced cottage, shivering because the boiler had broken yet again, and got ready for work.

I will not look on the doormat, she told herself as she walked through to the kitchen for breakfast. *There won't be any Valentine's cards there and I will not let it bother me.*

Still, she couldn't help a sly little spy and, sure enough, the mat lay bare of all declarations of secret admiration and unrequited love.

3

It's wasn't that Alice didn't get to meet many men because she did. In fact, she was surrounded by men. But it was the *kind* of men she was surrounded by that was the problem and she couldn't help thinking about this as she left the house and saw Wilfred the postman ambling up the driveway as if he had all the time in the world and posting his letters was the last thing on his mind. He was in his mid-fifties and had the hairiest face Alice had ever seen, with great thick sideburns giving him a furry quality. He always reminded her of a half-metamorphosed werewolf.

'Morning, Wilfred,' Alice said with the brightest smile she could muster on a Monday.

'Morning, Alice. Just bills today,' he said. 'Gas and credit card.'

'Great,' she said. She didn't really mind that Wilfred knew all about her private business. If she was a postman, she'd probably make it her business to know too. It was one of the perks of the job, wasn't it?

'No Valentine's cards for you then?' he said.

'Well, I wasn't really expecting any.'

'Third year in a row now, isn't it?'

Alice sighed. Wilfred's memory was far too sharp sometimes. He stopped on the pavement for a moment, blocking Alice's way, and she knew she was in trouble.

'That cough of mine's back,' he said.

'Oh?' Alice said, knowing all about Wilfred's cough.

'Went to the doctor's again. Complete waste of time.'

'Oh, dear.'

Wilfred coughed loudly. 'Hear that?' he said. 'That rattle?'

Alice nodded.

'Exactly,' he said. 'Can't be right.'

Alice didn't like to point out that Wilfred's twenty cigarettes a day might not be helping matters because she knew he wouldn't listen.

'Oh, well. No rest for the wicked,' he said, and mooched on. 'Oh, look,' he added, 'a second red bill for Mrs Bates at number twenty-two. And a lingerie catalogue too. Bit old for that, isn't she?'

Alice rolled her eyes.

Wilfred was usually Alice's first male encounter of the day. The second one was Bruce at the bus stop and he was standing there in a long dark trench coat, his briefcase in his hand. She nodded to him and he nodded back. That was it, really. Alice had gone to school with Bruce but that was never worth talking about because they'd only ever nodded to each other there too. He was quite good-looking, she supposed, with short fair hair and hazel eyes. He had that mean and moody thing going on which had never really attracted Alice.

She turned the collar up on her winter coat and shivered. The Norfolk village of West Carleton was one of the prettiest places in summer. Surrounded by emerald fields, deep cool woods and more round-towered flint churches than you could shake a vicar at, it was like something out of a fairy tale but, in the depths of winter when the wind howled in from the coast across the great expanses of fields, it was a miserable place to be and Alice would wish that she hadn't had to sell her car and endure the bone-crippling conditions of February at the bus stop.

A half-hour bus ride took her into the centre of Norwich and to her job in the Human Resources department of a building society. She didn't enjoy her job but it did have its compensations for somebody who was as inquisitive as she was. Nobody suspected her of being nosy, of course. She was hard-working and quietly-spoken. In other words – completely above suspicion. Alice would often smile at the secrets she was privy to.

'Ah, Alice. Can you bring me Martin Kasky's file?' Alice's boss, Larry Baxter, asked as soon as she'd walked into the office. He was fifty-four, lived just off the Newmarket Road at the posh end of town, had had three sick days off last year and was a Sagittarius. That was one of the perks of working in Human Resources. Alice had all sorts of useful information at her fingertips.

'I'll just do a bit of filing,' she'd tell her colleagues when she wanted to find something out about a guy. Like last year when Philip Brady asked her out to dinner. He worked in the New Business department, had jet-black hair and was very charming. Before the date, Alice looked him up quickly in between filing jobs. She noticed he was on a very good salary, had had two jobs before taking this one and had nine GCSEs at grade A. What she forgot to look at, though, were his self-certified sick notes. If she had, she would have seen that he'd taken six separate days off for irritable bowel syndrome and that might have prepared her for the night ahead and the number of times Alice was left alone at the restaurant table.

She fetched Martin Kasky's file and handed it to her boss. He didn't bother to look up at her as he took it but Alice was used to that.

6

'We're still waiting for his references,' Larry said. 'Chase them up with a phone call.' He handed the file back to Alice without so much as an acknowledging smile or thank you and Alice returned it to its shelf and went to sit – invisibly – at her desk in the corner of the open-plan office.

It was then that Ben Alexander came in. He was the Accounts Manager and Alice didn't exist in his world although he did make some sort of an effort to acknowledge her.

'Hello, Anna,' he said without even looking at her. She didn't bother to correct his mistake. It wasn't as though he would ever remember her real name.

As Ben approached her boss's desk, she watched him from behind her computer. He had dark red hair and slate-grey eyes. He was wearing a navy shirt today which made his eyes seem even brighter than usual and Alice felt her heart do a little dance. She'd had a crush on him for longer than she could remember which was ridiculous because he'd never look at a girl like her. He went out with building society royalty like Pippa Danes who had platinum-blonde hair and catwalk legs. Still, there was no harm in dreaming, was there?

Actually, there was. Alice had lost count of the number of times she'd allowed herself to believe that maybe once – just once – a handsome man would turn round and look at her – *really* look at her. They'd see beyond the shyness and the plainness. They'd see *her*.

But Ben didn't see her even when he stared right at her to hand her a member of staff's sick note to file.

'Thanks, Anna,' he said before leaving the office.

Alice got up and walked through to the ladies' toilet. She'd just shut the cubicle door when two giggling members of staff came in.

'Did you see Alice Archer this morning?' one of them said.

'No – why?' the other replied.

'She was wearing that awful grey cardigan again.'

'Oh, no! Not the one with the bobbles on the front?'

'Yes! Classic Alice!'

They both shrieked with laughter.

'I like that old brown thing she wears with the funny belt.'

'The one that looks like a bear has died on top of her?'

They shrieked again, flushed toilets, ran some taps and left.

Alice waited a few moments before leaving the safety of her cubicle. She was very attached to her grey cardigan. It was a good practical one with a lot of wear in it yet but she had to admit that it probably wasn't the most attractive look for a young woman of twenty-eight with its overlong sleeves and baggy middle.

She looked at herself in the mirror above the sink. Her face was pale and her brown hair fell straight down to her shoulders, neat and unremarkable. Her blue eyes were the only feature really worth any notice but she never drew attention to them, choosing to hide them behind large dark-framed glasses when she was in the office and never bothering with the likes of eyeliner or mascara.

She often wondered what she would look like with a makeover. She liked to watch that programme on the television where they take a hopeless case with a terrible haircut and a baggy jumper and turned them into a glamour queen. She would probably qualify for that show, she thought, looking at the bobbly grey cardigan and her sensible, flat shoes.

As she returned to her desk, she couldn't help wondering what it would be like to be one of those women who knew what clothes to wear and how to have their hair. What was it like to have the ability to turn heads and make a man fall in love with you?

Alice sighed. Once – just once – she'd love to know what it felt like to be beautiful.

Chapter 2

'You know what your trouble is, Alice?'

Alice wasn't sure that she wanted to know but she was quite sure that Stella was going to tell her.

'You just don't make an effort. I mean *look* at you!' her sister said, pointing an admonishing finger at Alice's ensemble. '*Grey!*' She spat the word out as if it left a nasty taste in her mouth.

'There's nothing wrong with grey. It's very fashionable at the moment.'

'Not like *that* it isn't!'

Alice self-consciously pulled at her bobbly cardigan and watched as Stella flopped onto the sofa opposite her and stuck her spoon into a carton of ice cream.

'Anyway,' Stella continued through a mouthful of double chocolate chip, 'what are you doing here?'

Alice took a deep breath, knowing how the following conversation was likely to go.

'It's Dad's birthday in a couple of weeks and I wondered—'

'His birthday? Oh, I completely forgot!' Stella said.

'You forgot last year too.'

'I was busy.'

'And the year before that.'

'Don't be a bore, Alice. God, you're worse than a mother.'

For a moment, the two sisters sat in silence, remembering the mother who had been so cruelly taken away from them when Alice had been just twelve years old and Stella only eight.

'I'm sorry – I didn't mean—'

'It's all right,' Alice said. 'I shouldn't really nag you like that.' Stella stuck her spoon into the carton of ice cream again, thinking she'd got away with it, but Alice wasn't going to let her off so easily.

'So what are we going to do?' Alice asked.

'About what?'

'About Dad's birthday!'

Stella shrugged and kept her eyes down, resolutely refusing to meet Alice's.

'We have to do *something*. It's not every day that you're seventy,' Alice pressed.

'God, it's so disgusting having a seventy-year-old father,' Stella said. 'What was Mum thinking of?'

'She was in love with him,' Alice said, 'and it's just as well for us that she was or we wouldn't have been born, and he wasn't *that* old when he had us. Not for a man, at least.'

'I think it's horrible how men can go on having babies until they're ancient.'

'But Dad was only in his forties when he had us. That's not old these days and neither is seventy any more.' Alice paused and took a deep breath. 'Anyway, I was thinking we could visit him.'

'Oh, Alice!' Stella said. 'You know I hate that horrible place!

It smells of disinfectant and old people.'

'You'll smell like that one day too,' Alice said.

'Don't be foul!'

'Anyway, we needn't be at the home for long because I was thinking of taking him out somewhere.'

'Taking him out? What, in *public*?' Stella said, a look of shock on her face.

'He's still able to enjoy a day out by the sea and an ice cream. He's not dead yet, you know!'

'He might as well be. He's brain dead.'

'No, he's not!'

'Well, he is whenever I visit,' Stella said.

'And when did you last visit?'

'I don't know. I don't keep a written record like you obviously do. You always were the favourite, anyway.'

'How can you say that? You're the one with the house!' Alice pointed out, looking up at the lofty ceiling of the Victorian semi's living room.

'Oh, you're begrudging me the house, are you?'

'No, of course not.'

'I thought you said you wanted your own place.'

'I do want my own place, Stella. I just want you to see Dad once in a while. I thought we could take him to the seaside. He always loved the sea.' For a moment, Alice remembered the endless bucket and spade holidays they used to go on as a family. From Great Yarmouth to Blackpool, from Skegness to Brighton, they would laugh their way round the coastline of Britain, making wonky castles in the sand and eating mountains of candy floss. 'It really is the least we can do for him.'

'But it'll be so cold,' Stella said with a theatrical shiver.

'So, we'll wrap up!'

'How are you going to get there?'

'Well, Sam at the home has offered to drive us to the station.'

'The train station? With his chair?'

'Of *course* with his chair. He can't walk very far these days.'

'Oh, God! I *really* don't fancy it!' Stella said.

'I know you don't but can't you think beyond yourself for once?'

'What does that mean?'

'I mean, can't you think about Dad for a change and how much he'd love to see us both together and spend a day with us – a day *away* from the home?'

Stella wrinkled her nose.

'We really could use your car, actually,' Alice said. 'Dad did say we could share it, after all.'

'Oh, Alice! When are you going to get another car of your own? You really should, you know. You can't rely on other people to bail you out of awkward situations all the time.'

Alice baulked at the implication that their father was an *awkward situation*. 'When was the last time I asked you for your car?'

'I'm just saying that you should get your own.'

'I can't afford another car. I'm only just keeping my head above water as it is with the rent and bills.'

'I don't know what you do with your money, Alice, I really don't.'

Alice bit her tongue. If Stella had had to go out and find herself full-time employment and hadn't had everything handed to her by their father, she might realise how tough it was in the real world.

'It is Dad's car after all,' Alice reminded her.

'Yes, I know, and it's an old banger. He really should have bought me a new one. I can't believe he didn't think of that before he went into that home.'

'Buying his daughter a brand new car wasn't exactly at the forefront of his mind when he was in the process of losing it.'

'Well, what about going in Celia's car? She's got one of those big four by fours, hasn't she?' Stella said, thinking of Alice's oldest best friend.

'Yes, and it's always filled with her kids,' Alice pointed out. 'I hardly see her these days. She's always so busy running her boys around. Anyway, Dad wouldn't want to see Celia – he'd want to see *you!*'

They were quiet for a moment, their words hanging heavily in the air between them.

'Look,' Alice said at last, 'I didn't come round here to argue.'

'Good, because I'm not in the mood. I've had a horrible day, if you must know,' Stella said with a pout.

Alice looked at her sister. She was selfish and infuriating but she also looked a little paler than usual and Alice's sisterly genes kicked in.

'What's wrong?' she asked.

Almost immediately, tears welled up in Stella's big blue eyes. 'It's Joe!' she cried.

'What about him?'

'He broke up with me!'

14

'Oh, Stella!' Alice said, leaning towards her on the sofa and squeezing her shoulder. 'What happened?'

'He said I was too high-maintenance. What does that mean, anyway?'

'It means you spend a lot of time—'

'I *know* what it means! But *I'm* not high-maintenance! I haven't been to the hairdresser's for two weeks. Two *whole* weeks! And look at my nails!'

Alice looked at the immaculate scarlet talons her sister sported.

'Chipped and scuffed but I'm making do until tomorrow before getting them done. I ask you – is that "high-maintenance"?'

'Well—'

'And he said I didn't like the simple things in life just because I didn't want to go on some crumby camping holiday. I mean, what girl in her right mind would want 'to sleep in a tent? *On the ground?'*

Alice thought of Joe. He was the outdoors type with rock-climber's arms and an athletic build. She could think of any number of girls who'd give anything to spend a night in a tent with him. Not her sister, though. Nothing but a five-star hotel would do for her.

'He's a scumbag,' Stella said.

Alice sighed. Joe was most definitely *not* a scumbag. Alice actually quite liked him but she could guess what had happened. He'd probably grown tired of Stella's little ways as well as her constant flirting. For a start, Alice couldn't help noticing that there were no less than five Valentine's cards

15

lined up on the mantelpiece. *Five!* Who were they all from? Alice was guessing that Stella had flirted with every single one of the senders.

'We'd just booked a holiday to Greece together, too,' Stella went on with an almighty sniff, 'and I was really looking forward to it. He knew how much I needed a break.'

Alice blinked, wondering what exactly it was that Stella needed a break from. 'What are you going to do?' she asked.

'Well, I'm not going to waste it, am I? Joe gave me the tickets – probably so I wouldn't make a scene. Look.' Stella got up and retrieved a brochure from the dining table and tossed it into Alice's lap. 'Page eighteen.'

Alice flipped through the brochure until she came to the right page and gave a long, low whistle as she took in the picture-perfect white villa with the bright blue shutters. It had its own swimming pool and terrace overlooking the sea. It certainly wasn't your typical tourist trap Greek island with blaring nightclubs and bars. This looked quiet and exclusive – a real escape from the world. Joe certainly had good taste – it looked beautiful.

'You've *got* to come with me, Alice!'

'What?'

'You've got to come with me. I can't go on my own – it'll be so boring. And I've already asked Lily and Becks and they can't make it. I even asked Jess and I don't even like her that much and she said no too. So you've got to come. You don't have to pay or anything although you can buy me a present as a thank you if you like. I've seen this really beautiful cashmere jumper I really need. *Do* say you'll come!'

Alice bit her lip. What was there to think about? A week of glorious sunshine on a beautiful Greek island far far away from the bleak, Norfolk weather and the woes of office life. It was just what she needed.

'*Please*, Alice! I know you'd never forgive yourself if you thought I was going on holiday all by myself! You'd *never* let that happen, would you?'

Alice looked at her sister. She was so good at getting people to do exactly what she wanted and, of course, Alice was going to say yes but not because Stella was trying to make her feel guilty. Alice really wanted to go but it occurred to her that she could use this as a bargaining chip.

'Oh, Alice! I'll be so miserable all on my own!' Stella continued, her face as long as a bloodhound's.

Alice held her hands up in mock defeat. 'Okay,' she said. 'I'll come with you. On one condition.'

'What?' Stella said.

'You come with me on Dad's birthday and give him a really brilliant day out.'

Stella took a deep breath. She didn't look happy and, for a moment, Alice thought her bribe wasn't going to work. But it did. 'Okay!' Stella said at last.

'Promise?'

'I promise,' Stella said. 'I'll be there.'

Chapter 3

One of the pleasures of living in Norfolk was the extensive coastline to the north and east of the county. You were never far from the sea but, without a car, it was rather awkward to reach and Alice didn't get to see it very often but today was a wonderful exception.

'It was good of Stella to let us borrow her car,' Terry Archer said.

'It's *your* car, Dad,' Alice said.

He shook his head. 'No, no – it's Stella's all right,' he said, nodding to the pair of furry pink dice hanging from the rear-view mirror.

Alice groaned and took them down, chucking them onto the back seat. 'She was sorry she couldn't make it today,' she said. 'She really wanted to be here.'

She heard her father sigh. 'Alice, you don't need to lie on behalf of your sister. I know what she's like. In fact, I only expect to see her on special occasions like when she needs a cheque signing.'

'She's not still tapping you for money, is she?' Alice said, aghast.

'Only when I let her get away with it.'

'Oh, Dad!'

'I find it hard to say no to her sometimes – like your mother. I never could say no to her either.'

'But you'd say no to me, wouldn't you?' Alice said with a grin.

'You never ask in the first place, my dear,' he said.

Alice smiled at him as she took the turn onto the coast road but she was secretly seething because that morning, she'd got a phone call from her sister.

'Alice?' a little voice had squeaked at the end of the line.

'Stella?'

There was the sound of throat-clearing and then the squeaky voice began again. 'I don't feel so good. I think I'm coming down with flu.'

Alice had tried to believe her – she really had – but Stella was in the habit of crying wolf whenever it suited her and it was hard to know when she was telling the truth.

'Are you wrapped up in bed?' Alice had asked her.

'Yes,' the squeak replied.

'Good,' Alice said. 'Then I'll pop over and get the car.'

'What?' she'd shouted.

'I thought you'd lost your voice?'

There was the sound of throat-clearing again. 'I *have!* What do you want the car for?'

'For Dad's birthday. If you're ill in bed, you've no use for it,' she said and had immediately hung up.

When Stella had answered the door an hour later, she'd done a pretty good job of roughing her hair up but Alice could see she was wearing clothes underneath her housecoat and had a full face of make-up on, but she hadn't bothered to challenge her. One thing was certain – she wasn't going to let it spoil her special day with her father.

The little town of Bexley-on-Sea might not have Great Yarmouth's funfair or Cromer's pier but it was all the richer for that, Alice couldn't help thinking. It was an old-fashioned sort of place with its row of Regency hotels and its simple promenade lined with pretty wooden kiosks selling fish and chips and ice cream. It wasn't the first choice for the tourist venturing to Norfolk but it was a favourite with locals and Alice loved it.

Parking the car on the seafront, Alice shoved a woolly hat onto her head and, opening the car door, was greeted by an icy blast of salt-laden air. She got her father's wheelchair out from the boot, erecting it in record time and then helped him out of the car and into it.

'Just for a while,' he said, 'and then I'll have a little stroll.'

The sea was steely-grey under a matching sky. Great boulders of dark clouds banked up along the horizon and a chill wind was blowing from the north reminding Alice that there was very little between them and the North Pole.

'Not quite a day for a paddle, is it?' Terry said from his chair.

'I'm sorry, Dad! This was a terrible idea.'

His hand reached round and squeezed hers. 'A breath of sea air always does the power of good,' he said, 'even if it does try to blow your head off your shoulders.'

They followed the promenade along the seafront for a while, each lost in their own thoughts. The kiosks were in hibernation for the long winter months but Alice had spotted a café that was open and earmarked it for later.

'Park me here,' her dad said after they'd been on the go for about ten minutes, 'and sit down next to me for a bit. It gets lonely with you stuck behind me and I can't talk to you properly.'

Alice stopped the chair by a bench and sat down next to her father. The bench was wet with sea spray and the slats were cold and uncomfortable but it felt good to be with her father and she took one of his large hands and held it between her own.

'You're cold,' she said. 'We shouldn't stay here too long.'

Her father didn't reply and she saw that he was staring far out to sea and she wondered what he was thinking about, his eyes seeming to glaze over with memories of the past.

'Remember we used to come here with your mother?' he said at last.

'Yes, of course,' Alice said, thinking of how her mother would get up extra early to make up the most enormous picnic hamper you'd ever seen and then rounding up every blanket, towel and toy she could find, stuffing the car to bursting point. A day at the beach was a military operation but her mother loved every moment and she never lost her patience when Alice and Stella bickered on the back seat of the car or spilt ketchup or ice cream down their dresses.

'You used to love those holidays,' her father said. 'Give you a bucket and spade and you could create a kingdom that would entertain you for hours.' He shook his head and smiled at the memory. 'Stella, however, would be bored after five minutes.'

21

'She hasn't changed much, I'm afraid,' Alice said.

'No,' he said, as if accepting the fact.

'We're going away together in April.'

'You two? On holiday – *together?*'

Alice nodded and laughed. 'I know! It came as a bit of a surprise to me too but Stella was in a bit of a jam and didn't want to go on her own.'

'So, where are you going?'

'Kethos,' Alice said.

'Where's that?'

'Greece. It's a little island off the mainland.'

'What do you want to go there for? Our beaches not good enough for you?' Terry asked with a grin.

'Stella's boyfriend booked it but they broke up and now she wants me to go with her.'

'I didn't know she was seeing somebody,' Terry said.

'I don't think it was for very long,' Alice said.

Terry shook his head. 'Poor Stella,' he said. 'So, do you *want* to go on this holiday?'

'Yes, of course!' Alice said, feeling the weight of her father's gaze upon her. 'I do, really I do, only I can't help wishing you were going with me instead.'

He laughed. 'You won't get me out of the country now.'

'Never did, did we?'

He shrugged. 'There are them that's made for travelling and them that's made for home.'

Alice smiled, remembering her father's little motto from years gone by. It had usually been wheeled out when Stella made a scene about their holiday destination.

'Weston-super-Mare?' she'd complain. 'It sounds like an old horse. Can't we go to Italy? Jude's going to Italy with *her* family. Lake Como.'

'Let them get on with it,' their father would say. 'Lake Como has nothing – absolutely *nothing* on Weston-super-Mare.'

Alice tended to agree with her father but she was more easily pleased than her sister which was just as well as she'd never had the budget for exotic holidays – one of the reasons she was looking forward to Kethos.

She looked out over the grey waves of the North Sea and tried to imagine the aquamarine ones waiting to greet her in Greece. How wonderful it would be to feel warm, she thought. The last few winters had seemed to drag on forever, as if the White Witch of Narnia was back in business and had cursed the whole of the UK. Alice felt quite fatigued by it all and couldn't wait to shed her baggy winter layers and luxuriate in the feel of the sun on her skin.

'A penny for your thoughts,' her father said.

'Oh, I was just wondering if I'd be able to make it to that holiday in Greece or if I'd freeze to death first.'

Her father chuckled. 'Shall we go and get some lunch and warm up somewhere?'

'Good idea!' Alice said, leaping up from the bench.

They went to the tiny café Alice had spotted earlier and she pushed the door open into the welcome warmth before wheeling her father's chair through. She didn't need to ask what he wanted; it was always the same. So, she ordered two full English breakfasts with all the trimmings even though it was one in the afternoon, and they washed everything down with two mugs of piping hot tea.

'Do you want anything else, Dad?' she asked after everything had been consumed.

'Ice cream, of course,' he said.

'But we've only just thawed out!' Alice said.

'You can't come to the seaside and not have ice cream!'

Alice laughed. 'Two ice creams. In cones, please,' she said to the waitress who was hugely entertained by the idea but didn't mind in the slightest. 'One strawberry, one chocolate.'

Her father always had strawberry ice cream. You could offer him fifty different flavours from cherry chip to lemon meringue and you could guarantee that he would seek out the strawberry.

When the two cones arrived, they beamed at each other.

'See what your sister's missing out on?' her father said.

'Yes,' Alice agreed. 'It's like being on holiday.' And it really was. It felt wonderfully perverse to be eating ice cream in February with the wind blasting against the little café window and the great grey sea rolling malevolently towards the land. But it was even more wonderful being with her father. Not only did it remind Alice of her childhood when they'd all been together as a family, but she had his sole attention and Alice didn't often have anybody's sole attention. More often than not, people would talk through her or be looking over her shoulder or else they just wouldn't bother talking to her at all. It was something she'd grown used to over the years but it was rather lovely to be with somebody who gave her his undivided attention even if they were genetically predisposed to do so. Which reminded her, there was something she had to talk to him about and now was as good a time as any.

'Dad, I wish you'd rethink things,' Alice said.

'What things?'

'About the home.'

'What do you mean?' he asked, looking up from his ice cream.

'I mean, if we got a carer, you could come back and live in your own home.'

He shook his head. 'We've been through all this,' he said. 'Haven't we?'

'Yes, I know, but I just don't like the idea of you being there all on your own.'

'And you'd rather have me at the mercy of Stella?'

'She doesn't have to live there. She's big enough to get a place of her own. I can't believe she's never thought to do that.'

He took a lick of his ice cream. 'Alice – you mean well – I know you do – but you know my thoughts on this. I'm not having either of you worrying yourselves about me all the time. Carer or no carer, if I was at home, you'd be fussing around me all the time and you've got your own lives to live. I'm not going to do that to you. Besides, I like the home.'

'You do?'

'There's company there. I'm not on my own at all as you so often think.'

Alice narrowed her eyes. 'You've met somebody, haven't you?'

25

Her father smirked. 'I might have done.'

'Really?' Alice laughed. 'Tell me!'

Their matching blue eyes locked together but her father wasn't saying anything.

'You naughty man!' Alice said. 'I've been imagining you sat in a chair in a corner of some lonely room with nothing to do all day and, all this time, you've been flirting!'

He chuckled. 'I'm a wicked old man,' he said.

'What's her name?'

'I forget.'

Alice frowned. 'Oh.'

'I'm kidding, for goodness' sake!' he said with a chuckle.

'Oh, Dad!'

'Her name's Rosa and she's eighty-two.'

'Eighty-two?'

'Yup! Who would've thought your old man would be somebody's toy boy at seventy years of age?'

'You're incorrigible!'

'So, that's my love life up to date. Are you going to tell me what's going on in yours? Any nice young man on the horizon?'

'On the horizon? If there is, I think I need a telescope because I haven't spotted him yet.'

For a moment, Alice thought of Ben Alexander at work – his handsome face and lopsided smile that always made her heart flutter.

'There is somebody,' she said quietly, 'but he doesn't even know I exist.'

'Why not? Why doesn't he notice a pretty young girl like you?'

'Dad! I'm not pretty and I'm not that young anymore either.'

'What nonsense!'

'It's true! I'm just ordinary – I know that – you don't have to be kind. Stella was always the pretty one.'

Her father frowned at her. 'How can you say that?'

'Because it's true.'

'You are so beautiful, Alice. You have a pure and giving heart—'

'And the sort of face nobody looks at twice.'

'But nobody wants to look at a beautiful face if it hides a cruel heart,' he said and Alice couldn't help wondering if he was talking about somebody in particular. 'Listen,' he continued, 'Stella might get all the attention when it comes to the opposite sex and she might get her own way when it comes to you and me but just be careful.'

'What do you mean?'

'You mustn't trust her so wholeheartedly. She takes advantage of you.'

'Well, I'm used to that.'

'But you mustn't let her—' he paused.

'What?'

Her father shook his head and something inside him seemed to close down. The conversation was over; he wasn't going to elaborate.

They finished their ice creams and then drove home in virtual silence. The winter sky had darkened dramatically and Alice turned the car headlights on. Her father's eyes kept closing and she didn't prod him into wakefulness with conversation although she was desperate to know what he'd meant about Stella.

You mustn't trust her so wholeheartedly.

Of course, Alice knew that her sister wasn't completely honest all the time but she was used to all the white lies and Stella wouldn't be Stella without them. But was there something more sinister than that?

Alice turned into the tree-lined driveway and the south front of Bellwood House rose up out of the immaculate lawn to greet them. It was an imposing Georgian house which had been extended and modernised to provide more ground-floor facilities for its residents. Her father, though, despite his wheelchair, had insisted on having a first-floor room because he wanted a good view.

Alice pulled up outside the front door and one of the carers, Sam, was immediately there to help. He always had the uncanny ability to spring up out of nowhere when he was most needed and Alice watched as he helped her father into his chair, wheeling him up the ramp into the home.

'No need to come with me,' her father told her.

'Are you sure?'

'You've done quite enough for today, my dear.'

Alice bent down and kissed him on the cheek. 'Give me a call soon, won't you?'

'Of course,' he said, grabbing hold of one of her hands. 'Thank you.'

Alice smiled at him. 'Happy birthday, Dad.'

She watched as Sam wheeled her father's chair into the lift up to his room on the first floor and waited for him to return, peeping into the main sitting room which overlooked the front lawn and wondering if she'd catch a glimpse of Rosa. Would it be too intrusive to ask for her? she wondered. Yes, it would and what would she say, anyway? *Excuse me – are your intentions towards my father honourable?* No, she was quite sure that he was old enough to know what he was doing when it came to the opposite sex.

At last, after settling her father into his room, Sam returned.

'Did he have a good day?' he asked Alice, his young face beaming at her.

'He did,' Alice said, knowing that Sam was referring to the mental and physical state of her father rather than whether he'd enjoyed himself. 'He was absolutely fine. No problems at all. Just got a little tired at the end of the day.'

'Don't we all?' Sam said with a smile.

'You'll let me know if he has another turn, won't you?'

'Don't worry, we've got your number,' Sam assured her.

'My mobile *and* my home number?'

'Yes.'

'And the office one?'

'We checked them all last time, remember?' Sam said.

'Oh, yes,' Alice said.

'He's well looked after, Miss Archer,' Sam assured her. 'We've got him on the new dosage of medication for the MS and he's eating well, sleeping like a log and – well, everything is absolutely normal.'

'I know. It's just that I want to make sure,' Alice said.

'And the dementia – well, he has good days and bad days.'

Alice nodded. 'It's so unfair,' she said. 'Isn't MS enough?

Why dementia too?'

'Old age can be very cruel sometimes,' Sam said. 'I've seen so many of our clients battling no end of ills.'

Alice nodded, blinking fast so that her tears wouldn't spill. 'But he isn't old,' she said hopelessly.

'Well—'

'He *isn't!* Not by today's standards.'

Sam nodded. 'You just have to take things one day at a time with ageing. That's all you can do.'

Alice nodded and said goodbye, leaving Bellwood House for her sister's. It was dark now but there were no lights on in the house. Alice wondered if her sister really was tucked up in bed with a hot water bottle and a box of tissues but she quickly dismissed the thought as she popped the car keys through the letterbox.

Walking to the end of the road, Alice turned left and headed towards the bus stop. Fishing her mobile out of her pocket, she texted Stella.

Had a great day with Dad. Car returned. Hope you're feeling better. xx

The reply took only half a minute to arrive.

Hope you topped up the petrol. S x

Chapter 4

'We can't possibly go on using that room for interviews – it's far too noisy with them digging up half the street outside,' Larry Baxter told Alice without actually looking at her.

'How about the old filing room?' Alice suggested.

'What?' Larry snapped.

'The old filing room at the end of the corridor. It's only got one old filing cabinet in it and we don't really use it anymore. It's quiet in there too and has lots of natural light.'

Larry deigned to look at Alice for a moment but didn't really appear to see her. 'I'll have to think about it,' he said at last, scratching his bald head.

Alice shook her head. Ben Alexander had three interviewees arriving in less than an hour and they had nowhere to put them. The least Larry could do was listen to her perfectly decent suggestion or they'd end up interviewing the candidates in the canteen which would probably flout the all-important health and safety regulations.

Alice was just racking her brains for an alternative suggestion when Ben Alexander walked into the room.

'Hello, Larry. Hello, Anna,' he said, his all-encompassing gaze sweeping Alice oh-so-briefly. 'All set for the interviews?'

Larry cleared his throat. 'I suggest we use the old filing

room at the end of the corridor,' he told Ben. 'It's quiet and has lots of natural light.'

'*Excellent* idea!' Ben said, clapping his hands together.

'Yes, I thought so,' Larry said.

'Your boss is a miracle worker, isn't he, Anna?' Ben said.

Alice turned round and rolled her eyes, returning to her desk where she found Larry's empty coffee cup waiting for somebody to wash it. She sighed, thinking to herself that her situation might be more bearable if she had somebody in the office she could talk to but the only other woman who worked in her department was part time. Her name was Pearl Jaggers and she was about a hundred and twenty years old and was only interested in small talk if it was about her eleven grandchildren.

She wasn't sure how she managed to get through the next few weeks leading up to the holiday. She endured countless cold mornings at the bus stop, her neck retreating like a shy tortoise's into the woolly folds of her scarf. Bruce was his usual uncommunicative self and didn't even attempt to help when a speeding car splashed an icy puddle up her legs.

Wilfred the postman was as grouchy as ever, complaining about the conditions postmen had to endure during the cold months and then promptly sneezing on her and, at work, Larry continued to ignore her and Ben continued to call her Anna. Life was perfectly normal if far from perfect.

But, finally, the great day arrived. Alice had spent the final five evenings before the holiday packing. And unpacking. She just didn't know what to take. She'd looked up the temperatures in Kethos online and was assured that mid-April was mild but not hot. That meant you had to take absolutely everything: jeans and jumpers in case it was cool and dresses and swimsuits in case it was warm. Not that Alice had much in the way of clothes; she wasn't the sort of woman who had an excess of anything – unlike her sister who had once bought a favourite dress in three different colours. Alice thought of her sister's heaving wardrobe and the number of clothes which had been flung over their father's old bed. She couldn't help thinking that something was wrong when a person had more shoes than books in their home.

Which reminded her, which books was she going to take? She'd treated herself to a guidebook and a lovely paperback romance called *Swimming with Dolphins* as well as a funny little hardback she'd found in her favourite second-hand bookshop in Norwich. The book was called *Know Your Gods* and, as Alice didn't, she'd bought it.

Their flight to Greece left shortly after seven and Stella refused to drive to the airport so early in the morning and didn't want to pay the parking charges for the week either.

'You can pay for a taxi. You *are* getting a free holiday, after all,' she told Alice who swallowed hard, held her tongue and made a huge cash withdrawal from a hole in the wall.

Travelling with her sister was a trying experience. She had been the archetypal *are-we-nearly-there-yet* kid and she hadn't grown out of that with the passing of the years.

'I don't understand why we have to be at the airport so early,' she complained. Then came, 'There really isn't enough leg room for somebody like me. It's all right for you with your short legs.' Then, 'I can't believe we don't get a meal on this plane. Not that it would be edible or anything but it's the principle, isn't it?'

The world would never please Stella no matter how hard it tried, Alice thought, gazing out of the window and smiling at the intense blue waters far below them as they neared their destination.

The island of Kethos lay in the Mediterranean Sea just off the mainland of Greece. From the air, it looked rather like a squashed heart and Alice wondered if this had anything to do with the Aphrodite legend that was linked to the island.

She picked up her guidebook. 'Do you want to read this?' she asked Stella.

'No, I'm reading this,' her sister answered, holding up a copy of a glossy gossip magazine. Alice was just about to try and find out more about the famous Greek goddess when the announcement came that they were about to land.

'About time too!' Stella said, shoving her magazine into her handbag and reaching for her compact to make sure her face was still immaculate. Alice didn't bother reaching for hers.

For a moment, she was aware that her sister's eyes were upon her. 'You could've made an effort,' Stella told her. 'Were you in a rush this morning?'

'Pardon?'

'Well, just look at you!'

'We're travelling, Stella, not attending a party,' Alice said, noticing her sister's lacy dress with the plunging neckline.

'Yes, and you never know who you're going to meet,' Stella said, pointedly looking around the aeroplane. 'Take him over there – he's quite nice looking. In fact, I might introduce myself.'

'Stella, you've just broken up with Joe.'

'Oh, that was *ages* ago!' she said. 'And what's wrong with a bit of flirting, anyway? I'm totally up for a holiday romance and you should be too. Once you get a bit of sun on your face and do something with your hair, that is.'

Alice took a deep breath and counted to ten. She might be getting a free holiday but she knew that it was going to cost her dearly.

Chapter 5

Milo Galani had lived on the island of Kethos for all of his twenty-six years. His brothers – all three of them – had left for the mainland years ago but there was no life there for Milo. He couldn't imagine living anywhere that wasn't completely surrounded by the sea and the idea of a city gave him nightmares. He'd once stayed with his eldest brother in his tiny flat in Athens for a whole week and it had nearly killed him. He'd been kept awake all night by the sounds of the city: the police sirens, the drunken party-goers and the incessant mopeds.

When he'd returned to Kethos, he'd vowed he would never leave again. The bruising, bustling city might suit his three brothers but it didn't suit him. He would rather walk through an olive grove than a crowd and he preferred a rocky mountain track to a shop-lined pavement. The island was like an extension of himself and he knew every field and every cove and he loved them all, especially once the spring arrived, like now.

There were some islanders who objected to the arrival of spring because, just as the island was reawakening after its winter hibernation and the first of the year's flowers were emerging, the first tourists would arrive and the island would be wrenched from the residents and hauled back into life. There were some residents who lived up in the hills who had nothing to do with the tourists at all. They led solitary lives and were happy to do so. They believed that the island belonged to them and them alone and that the outside world had no business intruding upon it.

Luckily, the objectors to the tourists were in the minority and Milo certainly wasn't amongst them. He welcomed the new injection of life which the tourists brought – he liked talking to them and hearing about the places they came from and the lives they lived there. It was his way of travelling without actually having to leave his beloved island.

He loved watching the boats chugging across the sea from the mainland and he couldn't help but stare at the holiday-makers as they disembarked. What had brought them to his little island, he wondered? Were they in search of peace and solitude? Did they come in search of Greek myths and legends?

He was watching them today after doing a spot of shopping in Kethos Town. It wasn't a large crowd – they would come during the busier summer months – but there was enough to fill a couple of tavernas. He spied an elderly couple who were linking arms. The man looked a little pale after his sea crossing and the woman was patting his hand as if to reassure him it was all over. There was a young family with two children who were tugging their parents along as if they couldn't possibly wait a moment longer for their holiday to begin.

Then, his eye was suddenly caught by a young woman whose face was full of wonder as she stepped off the boat, her eyes large and searching as if she was trying to take everything in at once, and that made him smile. She looked so thrilled to be there – as she should, of course, but he'd seen some really miserable faces coming off that boat in the past. Like *her*, he thought, staring at a young woman who was following the smiling girl. She was beautiful with her shoulder-length golden hair and her perfect figure encased in a lacy dress but her face was as grim as a stormy day at sea. There was no joy to be found in it and Milo found his gaze returning to the smiling girl once again. She didn't have the golden hair or knockout figure of her companion but there was something rather special about her and Milo couldn't help but wonder if he would see her again. Maybe she'll come to the gardens, he thought. Yes, let her come to the gardens.

He didn't have time to hang around the harbour. He had to get to work and, for Milo, that meant a short moped ride to the Villa Argenti high up in the hills on the other side of the island. His boss was leaving the next day and wanted to go through some things with him and that always meant trouble. The sooner he left, the better, Milo thought, and then he would have the place to himself again.

Cedric Carlson was an American businessman who did something in technology. Milo wasn't quite sure what it was, exactly, but it was obviously something that made a lot of money because Mr Carlson had homes in New York, Los Angeles, London and Milan as well as the Villa Argenti on Kethos where Milo was the groundsman.

Milo loved his job at the villa. He had a team of three part-time gardeners working for him but, most of the time, he had the gardens to himself and that was exactly how he liked it.

When Milo clocked in for work, Mr Carlson was sitting on the veranda with an enormous newspaper obscuring the view and covering almost his entire body. How could he be bothered with such things? Milo wondered. Couldn't he sit back and luxuriate in the sun and enjoy the view for once? But perhaps that was the difference between the two of them – Milo might be able to enjoy the views that the Villa Argenti gave him but he'd never own them. Owning them took hard work, *endless* work. There was no time to just sit and stare at things.

'Ah, there you are,' Mr Carlson said as he spotted Milo.

'Yes, sir,' Milo said, running a hand self-consciously through his dark hair. He'd been told to address Mr Carlson as 'sir' on his first morning of employment seven years ago and woe betide him if he ever forgot.

'I'm leaving for New York in—' he paused and looked at the very expensive gold watch he was wearing, 'thirty-eight minutes precisely.'

Mr Carlson liked to be precise and his chauffeur would be fired on the spot if he ever failed to match his boss's precision.

'Yes, sir.'

'And I'll be gone for a fortnight.'

Milo nodded.

'I've left a list of things I want doing. It's all quite straightforward.'

Milo had no doubt that it was. He was used to the lists; his life was dominated by them. Not only would he be handed them by Mr Carlson each week but he would find them all over the gardens too: inside temples, taped to tree trunks and once on the inside of Milo's favourite wheelbarrow. That had been a classic. It had read:

1. Take this wheelbarrow to the tip.

2. Replace with new one.

3. Store new wheelbarrow away each night.

Milo had ignored it. What Mr Carlson didn't understand was that an old wheelbarrow was a good one. Its handles were almost a part of the user's hands because they had worked in perfect harmony for so long. It might not always move in a perfect straight line but that didn't mean it was ready for retirement. No. Mr Carlson should stick to things he knew and keep out of the garden whenever possible.

Milo listened to the rest of his instructions although there wasn't really anything new and he nodded politely. He said 'Yes, sir' wherever appropriate then wished his boss a good journey and got on with his day's work, walking down the long straight path lined with trees that was known as 'The Avenue'. He was going to get on with some work in the kitchen garden today. It was one of the few areas that wasn't open to the public and was hidden behind a large wall which harvested the best of the sunshine and produced bowlfuls of fruit on the trees grown against it.

Milo loved the kitchen garden because it was private and

he was rarely disturbed there. In the other parts of the garden, he was always at the mercy of the tourists with their questions and their cameras. If he had a euro for every photo he'd taken of tourists, he could probably afford to buy the Villa Argenti himself, he thought.

But, before he could reach his sanctuary, he saw a figure half-hiding in the shadows of a wall and he instantly knew who it was. Sabine – 'The Pushy French Girl' – as he had come to think of her. It wasn't really her fault. She was sixteen and was on holiday with her family and bored out of her mind. She'd been visiting the gardens with her parents one Tuesday afternoon and had taken one look at Milo and decided that she'd spend the rest of her time on Kethos trying to seduce him. It wasn't bad as fates went, Milo thought, and goodness only knew that he'd had his fair share of holiday romances with tourists. There was obviously something about being a gardener, he'd decided, that attracted women. Perhaps they liked men who worked with their hands in the great outdoors and it was certainly more original to fall for a Greek gardener than it was a Greek waiter.

He took a deep breath and walked towards her. Be brusque, he told himself.

'What are you doing here, Sabine?' he asked as he continued walking. He spoke in English in which she was also fluent.

'Keeping you company,' she said, running to catch up with him, her long blonde ponytail swinging about her bare shoulders.

'I don't need company. I'm very busy. How did you get in, anyway? We're not open yet.'

'I climbed over the wall.'

'Where?'

'I'm not telling you. You'll fence it off.'

'That's right,' Milo said. 'You shouldn't be in here.'

'But the gardens are open to everyone, aren't they?'

'Yes, but not you,' he said.

'Why *not* me?'

'Because you should be with your family.'

'Oh, they're so boring!' she said, puffing her cheeks out and sighing dramatically. 'They do nothing all day!'

'That can't be true.'

'But it *is!*' Sabine said. 'Dad sits around reading his boring books and Mum just sunbathes.'

'I thought you were going to the museum?'

'Oh, God! That was even *more* boring than sitting around the pool.'

Milo frowned. The little museum on Kethos might not be able to rival anything on the mainland but Milo was very proud of it and he objected to people who made fun of it. So it might only have two rooms but it housed a very interesting collection of coins and pottery.

'Well, what do you want to do all day?' he asked and then realised that he shouldn't have.

'I want to be with you,' she said, her green eyes large and wide.

'But I'm at work.'

'There's nobody around,' she said, still running to keep up with him.

'Sabine!' he said sharply, stopping in the middle of the path so abruptly that she crashed into him. 'Sorry.'

'It's all right,' she said coyly, fluttering her obscenely long eyelashes at him and smiling prettily. She really was very attractive. She was tall for her age too and her figure was full and—

Milo stopped. She was sixteen years old and, although that might all be legal and above board, she was still a child. She might have the body of a woman but she behaved like a petulant teenager and he didn't want to have anything to do with her. It was courting disaster.

'Sabine,' he tried again.

'Yes?' she said, tilting her head to one side and giving him her full attention.

'You have to go.'

'Oh, not yet!'

'Yes, you do. I really have to get on with my work and you can't come with me.'

She pouted at him. 'Okay,' she said. 'But say something in Greek first.'

'What?'

'Say something in Greek – anything! Go on!'

'Sabine!'

'Go on!' she pleaded.

'And then you'll go?'

'Yes,' she promised with a nod.

Milo took a deep breath and told her – in Greek – that she was a spoilt young girl who should really know better and that he didn't want her getting him into trouble.

'Oh!' she said once he'd finished. 'That's *so* romantic!'

43

He shook his head at her and then pointed towards the exit.

'All right, I'm going,' she said with a sigh. 'I'll see you tomorrow.'

'Sabine – *no!*' But she'd trotted off and pretended not to hear him. It was Milo's turn to sigh. Why, oh why, couldn't he meet a nice normal girl?

Chapter 6

One taxi, one plane, one boat and another taxi later, and Alice and Stella were finally holding the keys to their villa. The taxi had dropped them outside a large pair of iron gates and Alice looked at them in surprise.

'Are you sure we're at the right place?' she asked Stella.

'Joe obviously knew my taste,' Stella said, acknowledging the splendour with a brief glance. 'Come on, help me with my bags.'

Stella sauntered through the gates and Alice followed with the bags, smiling at the tree-lined driveway that led to the villa.

'This is beautiful!' she said, between short breaths as the luggage weighed her down. The villa was a dazzling white and its brilliant turquoise shutters couldn't fail to make you smile. Well, they failed to make Stella smile – she was frowning down at her dress on which a large beetle had landed.

'Ewww!' she cried, flicking the offending creature off her. 'What kind of a place is this?'

'A foreign one,' Alice dared to say, producing another key as they reached the enormous wooden front door. It opened with a long, low groan and the hallway that greeted them was large and echoey with a flagstoned floor which made everything feel wonderfully cool. Alice looked up at the lofty ceiling and then back down at the floor which could easily accommodate a grand ball. 'This place is huge!' she said with a whistle.

'Yes, well Joe always knew I never settled for second best,' Stella said, making her way to the sweeping staircase in order to choose the best bedroom for herself. 'Bring my bags up,' she said as an afterthought.

Alice stared at her, dumbfounded for a moment.

'Oh, you *know* how much stronger you are than I am,' Stella added with a tiny smile.

Alice rolled her eyes at the insincere flattery and then struggled up the stairs behind Stella, watching as she viewed all five of the bedrooms before picking the largest room for herself. It had an enormous four-poster bed draped with a white canopy, a gigantic en suite and a long balcony that overlooked the coast to the east of the property.

'Just put my things there,' Stella said, motioning to Alice whilst she flopped down on the immaculate white bed. 'It's probably best if you hang my dresses up before they're creased out of all recognition.'

Alice glanced at her sister. Was she serious? Alice had half a mind to tell her where she could stick her dresses when Stella stopped her.

'You know you do a much better job of it than I do,' she said.

Once again, Alice caved in. It wouldn't take her long and, if she didn't keep Stella sweet, there'd be all sorts of hell to pay, she was quite sure of that.

'I'm off to find a room for me now,' Alice said a moment later, having hung up her sister's clothes.

Stella groaned from the bed and swatted a hand in Alice's direction as if dismissing her. Relieved that she could have some time to herself at last, Alice walked out onto the landing and looked around. There were two large double bedrooms either side of Stella's and one small single at the end of the corridor. She headed to the single. Privacy, she thought, was more important than size.

Like Stella's room, the colours were soft and muted: the bed was a vision of white, and pale blue curtains fluttered in the breeze when Alice opened the windows. She didn't have a balcony but the room did have an unrivalled view down to the harbour at Kethos Town and Alice stood looking at it for a few moments, watching the boats bobbing about on the glassy, blue-green water.

'Am I really here?' she asked herself as she gazed at some distant mountains that rose and fell like the back of a sleeping beast. 'Am I really on holiday?' She couldn't remember the last time she'd had a proper holiday that involved going abroad. She hadn't been able to afford more than a couple of weekends away over the last few years and they'd been a very modest hotel break in the Lake District where she'd been rained on for an entire weekend, and a couple of nights in a youth hostel in Derbyshire where she'd had to share a room with a party of fifteen hyper schoolgirls. Not exactly the stuff of envy-inducing postcards. But here she was and it was a wonderfully sunny April day and the cold, grey days of the English winter that had seemed to drag on forever were now far behind her.

She glanced around her room again and then decided to do a bit of exploring, gasping at the enormous bathroom with walk-through shower and roll-top bath and the window looking straight out to sea.

Descending the staircase, Alice found an enormous modern kitchen with gleaming black worktops, a dining room with a table that sat twelve people and a living room filled with enormous white sofas. There were also doors out onto a terrace and Alice's eyes widened in wonder when she saw the swimming pool beyond them. It was a traditional rectangular shape with a mosaic of pale tiles around it. There were sun loungers, an umbrella, a scarlet hammock and a barbeque – everything the holidaymaker could possibly want. There was even a large table and chairs under the shade of a pretty pergola over which clambered a magenta bougainvillea, its flowers dazzlingly bright against the blue sky above.

Beyond the terrace was an olive grove before the land dipped down and headed steeply towards the sea, punctuated every now and then with the tall, dark spires of cypress trees. It was the stuff of fantasies and, for a moment, Alice felt guilty for being there. After all, Joe had booked this holiday and he must have paid an absolute fortune for it but Alice couldn't help thinking that maybe he'd thought it was worth missing out on it to be shot of Stella.

A huge bubble of excitement rose within her and, not wanting to waste a single moment, she decided that they should go straight down to Kethos Town and get something to eat, do a bit of shopping and stock up on supplies so they could cook at the villa.

Walking back upstairs, she popped her head round Stella's bedroom door. She was still on the bed and her eyes were closed.

'Do you want to get something to eat?' Alice whispered.

'What?' Stella croaked without opening her eyes.

'I'm going to walk into town and get some food.'

'Some *Greek* food?'

'I imagine so.'

'No thanks,' Stella said. 'I've brought some cereal bars with me.'

Alice wrinkled her nose. Her sister had flown all this way to fall asleep and eat cereal bars.

'Well, I'm going out, okay?'

'Knock yourself out,' Stella said before rolling over on the bed and burying her head further into her pillow.

Alice returned to her bedroom and changed from the jeans she had been wearing on the plane and opened her suitcase to reveal the summery clothes she'd optimistically packed. There were T-shirts in cream and navy and – Alice's hand hovered over a third – *grey*. She didn't dare wear grey in Greece. Stella would kill her if she did and, for once in her life, Alice didn't want to wear grey either. The brilliant colours of the island seemed to be whispering to her, persuading her to be a little more adventurous with her palette.

Ditch the grey, it seemed to say. Only she seemed to have an awful lot of it. Even one of her dresses had grey in it. It was only a background, mind, hiding behind the pretty pink roses but it was there all the same.

'Best to avoid,' she said to herself, her hands reaching under the layers of grey, white and navy and pulling out her one magnificent piece of colour. She caught her breath as she saw it because it was so un-Alice like. She remembered the day she'd bought it. She'd seen it on the sale rail of a shop she normally walked right by without even glancing at because it just wasn't the sort of shop someone like Alice went into but it had beckoned her in, urging her to take it home with her and now, holding the light folds of turquoise between her hands, she was so glad of her impulse buy. It was the one truly beautiful thing she owned and she was going to wear it right now.

First, she took off the rest of the drab clothes she'd been wearing on the flight and ran into the shower, washing away the weariness that comes from travelling. Then she combed her hair. Being fine, it would dry quickly in the sun.

Returning to her suitcase, she pulled out the turquoise dress. The little buttons down the front winked in the sunny bedroom and the fabric felt so luxurious against her skin, tickling her knees with its softness. If only she had some pretty piece of jewellery. If only she could borrow one of Stella's necklaces. She had heaps and heaps but, the problem was, Stella wasn't exactly a sharing sort of sister. Growing up, they'd never swapped make-up, and the idea of sharing or lending was abhorrent to Stella.

'But she never needs to know,' Alice thought, thinking that her sister must have packed a veritable treasure trove of jewellery judging by the weight of her luggage and Alice couldn't help feeling entitled to borrow a piece seeing as she'd carried it all.

With silent bare feet, Alice peeped round Stella's door. She was fast asleep on the bed and was snoring like an angry volcano. Alice spied the suitcase. She'd already hung up all the clothes on her sister's command but knew there must be a jewellery box or roll still hiding there so she crossed the room to where she'd left it.

The jewellery roll was easy to find and Alice sighed with pleasure as she saw the row of necklaces. There was silver and gold as well as all sorts of pretty costume pieces which one woman couldn't possibly hope to wear in a single week even if she had a dozen necks, and Alice's eyes fastened on a lovely blue pendant that was the colour of the summer sky. It would look beautiful with her turquoise dress and Stella wouldn't miss it if it was returned straightaway.

Folding the jewellery roll and closing the suitcase, Alice tiptoed out of the room and, once safely in her own bedroom, placed the pendant around her neck and dared to gaze at her reflection. Her newly-washed hair was clinging to her face in dark strands and her blue eyes were made all the bluer by the bright dress. She dared to smile. For once, she looked almost pretty.

She slipped on a pair of sandals. They were a simple brown leather with nothing really to recommend themselves. In fact, they looked a little at odds with the pretty summer dress and Stella would no doubt have a fit if she clapped eyes on them but they were the only pair Alice owned and they would have to do.

Grabbing her handbag which was a rather monstrous black affair in which Alice usually kept at least three books, she left the villa and turned right out of the gates, heading down the steep path that led to Kethos Town.

How wonderful it was to feel warm. She hadn't seen her limbs for months and they looked startlingly white in the Greek sunshine.

The road into town was quiet and Alice was soon down on the harbour front where they'd docked just a couple of hours before. She looked around at the pretty houses jostling along the water. Most of them were white and shaped like sugar cubes but there were some in brilliant colours too like Venetian red and sunset yellow and there, sat at the top of the hill overlooking the sea, was a beautiful church with a dazzlingly blue domed roof.

There were a few tourists about and Alice found a taverna overlooking the harbour and ordered moussaka, some salad and a glass of wine before closing her eyes and breathing in the salty tang of the sea and listening to it as it lapped against the harbour wall. Why couldn't life always be like this? she wondered. Why was life more about in-trays than outings? And why were there always more workdays than weekends?

How hard it was going to be to return to England and her job after spending a week in such a paradise, she thought. Maybe it had been a mistake to come on holiday. Maybe she would have been better off not knowing there were such beautiful places in the world.

Tucking in to her moussaka a few minutes later, Alice did her best to banish thoughts of the office waiting for her back in England. She wasn't going to think about the person she was there. Here, she could be anybody she wanted to be.

Nobody knew her here. Nobody would judge her or gossip about her in the staff toilets. She was just another tourist who had come to soak up a bit of sunshine and that realisation made her smile.

Finishing her meal and glass of wine, she paid at the bar and noticed a handful of leaflets on a nearby table. There was one about the island's museum and another about boat trips but one in particular caught her eye. It was for a villa set in acres of beautiful grounds which overlooked the sea at the south of the island.

'The Villa Argenti,' Alice whispered and the very name sounded like a promise. Its towers and turrets were mesmerising and its great Venetian-style windows seemed to hold secrets behind them, and the gardens rolled gently across the landscape before ending in cliffs which plummeted dramatically down to the sea.

She made up her mind then and there that she would visit it. Maybe it would even tempt Stella to leave the comfort of their villa. Yes, it would be the first of many wonderful adventures they would have together on the island. They'd laugh, relax and become closer than they'd ever been before, Alice thought, as she walked along the steep road that led out of the town and back to their villa. Stella couldn't fail to be charmed by such a place as the Villa Argenti, could she?

'I'm back!' Alice called as she closed the front door behind her. 'Stella?'

'I'm through here,' Stella said, her voice coming from the living room.

Alice found her sprawled out on one of the enormous

cream sofas, the empty wrapper of a cereal bar on the table before her. She sat down next to her sister, half-expecting her to ask her where she'd been but she didn't.

Undeterred, Alice took the leaflet for the Villa Argenti out of her handbag and handed it to Stella.

'What's this?' Stella asked.

'Somewhere I think we should visit.'

'What – some boring old house?'

'It isn't a house – it's a *villa*.'

'But we're in a villa already.'

'Not like this one – just look at it!' Alice said, her voice high with excitement. 'Anyway, the villa isn't actually open to the public but the gardens look so beautiful, don't you think?'

'It looks like somewhere they'd drag you on a school trip!' Stella said, handing the leaflet back to Alice.

Alice bit her tongue and returned the leaflet to her bag. There wasn't going to be any laughter on this trip, and they weren't going to become closer than ever either, were they?

'Hey!' Stella suddenly said, leaning forward on the sofa and staring at Alice. 'What are you doing wearing my necklace?'

Chapter 7

By the time Milo had tidied around the garden and put all the tools safely away, the sun was setting fast, leaving great violet streaks across the sky and turning the sea indigo. It was a time of day that he loved, especially in the spring when the air was balmy and one could get away with a short-sleeved shirt.

Leaving the Villa Argenti on his moped, he took a winding mountain road which first descended towards the sea and then climbed steeply. From the top, you could see across the water to a neighbouring island. Milo had been there a couple of times. It was about ten times the size of Kethos and had been heaving with tourists. It made his own dear island seem deserted. Certainly, there wasn't the notorious rush hour that some places were famous for; Milo practically had the roads to himself when he left work although the occasional stray goat would often force him to slow down and swerve. He'd heard his brothers complaining about their commute in Athens and he didn't envy them. He always looked forward to his ride to and from home, occasionally breaking into song as he rode, his voice filling the air – not always in tune, perhaps, but always happy. Life was good. He loved his island, he loved his job and he loved his home.

But he wasn't going directly home that evening because there was something he had to pick up first. Turning his moped into a narrow road, he drove through a tiny village which ended in a small courtyard where half a dozen hens were pecking around in the dirt. There was a simple two-storey white house that was typical of Kethos. Its windows were wide open and a pair of orange curtains fluttered in the evening breeze and Milo could smell something wonderful cooking.

'Hanna?' he called as he took off his helmet and got off his bike. 'Anyone at home?' he called in Greek as he entered the kitchen but there was nobody about so he went back outside again and spotted a portly woman in her sixties with a huge wicker basket full of white sheets. Milo ran across the grass and took the basket from her. Her round face was red from the exertion.

'Shouldn't Tiana be helping you with this?'

Hanna waved a fat hand at him. 'Oh, let the child be a child.'

'Where is she?'

'In the back room on that computer thing.'

Milo sighed. Slowly but surely their little island was being taken over by computers and hand-held gadgets. Even the most unlikely of people seemed to have them now and were connecting to the internet with alarming regularity.

'She knows I don't like her on that day and night. She's a kid. She should be outside, running up mountains and scraping her knees on rocks.'

They entered the kitchen and Milo put the basket of washing down on the tiled floor. Two large black cats were asleep on an old leather chair by the cooker and, once again, Milo inhaled the aroma of a fine dinner.

'You'll stay for something to eat?' Hanna asked.

'Oh, that's really kind of you but I've got to get back,' Milo said, thinking of the chores he had to do around the house if he was to keep on top of things. His eldest brother, Georgio, had threatened to visit and Milo wanted to be above reproach if he did show up.

'Suit yourself,' Hanna said and then left the kitchen and hollered, '*Tiana!*'

A few seconds later, a ten-year-old girl darted from one of the rooms at the back of the house, her long dark hair flowing wildly behind her as she launched herself into Milo's arms.

'Tiana!' he cried, wrapping his arms round her and kissing the top of her head. 'You okay? Had a good day?'

'She's had her tea,' Hanna said, 'and you look as if you could do with some yourself. Look at the size of you!'

'What?' Milo said.

'There's nothing of you!'

'I keep myself fit – that's all.'

'A working man needs a bit of meat on him,' Hanna said. 'Like my boys.'

Milo thought of Hanna's four sons. They were all as tall as Greek temples and about the same width too. By contrast, Milo and his three brothers were positively slender although he'd never have thought of himself as skinny. He was just well-toned, that was all. His job and his lifestyle made sure that there wasn't any surplus flesh on him.

'Now, are you sure you won't stay for a bit of dinner?'

57

As tempting as that offer was, he really had to get home. 'Another time, Hanna,' he said with a smile and she waved him from her kitchen.

'I've been on the internet!' Tiana said as they left the little house.

'Yes, Hanna told me,' Milo said. 'I don't like you spending all your time in front of a computer.'

'But it's *brilliant!* You never let me use ours,' she said.

'And for good reasons too.'

'Like what?'

'Your beautiful dark eyes will turn square and your brain will frazzle up and die.'

Tiana wrinkled her little nose. 'Don't be silly!'

'I'm being absolutely serious. You should be outside and running around like I was at your age.'

'Oh, you're so *old* sometimes!' Tiana said with a little laugh.

'Maybe I am,' Milo said, 'but you should take advantage of that and learn from me.' He shook his head. He was beginning to sound old even to himself now. 'Come on – helmet on!' Milo ordered as they walked towards the moped.

'Do I have to?' Tiana protested.

'You most certainly do.'

'But I want to feel the wind in my hair,' she said.

'If you want to feel the wind in your hair, it'll be a very long walk home.'

She pouted but then placed the helmet firmly on her head and Milo helped her with the strap. Then they both hopped on and took off. Milo took the roads a little slower when Tiana was riding behind him. He loved to speed around the island when he was on his own, careening around the bends a little too fast sometimes and speeding down the hills towards the sea but he was the perfect rider when Tiana was with him and he never took any unnecessary chances.

Feeling the tightness of her little hands on his waist, he smiled.

'You okay?' he shouted and he felt her squeeze his belly in affirmative response. They rode through another village, scattering a group of children who were kicking a football around and then they ascended into the hills before coming to a stop at last.

Their house was like most of the others on the island: small, square and white but, over the years, they'd put their own stamp on it, painting the three tiny bedrooms, living room and kitchen in cheering yellows and vibrant reds apart from Tiana's bedroom which – like the bedrooms of almost every other ten-year-old girl around the world – was a symphony of pink. Milo remembered the weekend they'd chosen the pots of pink paint together and had spent two whole days getting just as much paint on themselves as on the walls.

The furniture around the house was simple wooden hand-me-down pieces which weren't worth a lot of money but were good and sturdy. His favourite piece was a rather fine rocking chair by the fire which had been rocked by at least four generations of Galanis. He adored that old chair.

But it was the garden which was Milo's real forte. He'd planted it with flowers, fruit bushes and vegetables. One of the perks of his job at the Villa Argenti was that his pockets would often be stuffed with seeds taken from the garden he'd created there and he'd replicated some of the borders at the villa in miniature in his own back garden for Tiana. Even though he spent all day working in one garden, he couldn't resist tinkering around in his own once he got home, only he really didn't have time for that tonight. There were the morning dishes to wash, dinner to prepare, the ironing to do and heaven only knew that the little house hadn't seen the sight of a vacuum cleaner for a good many days.

Walking into the kitchen together, he watched as Tiana reached into a cupboard for her favourite pink glass before filling it with pineapple juice from the fridge. She took it to the table and sipped it thoughtfully. It was a routine that Milo observed every day and never tired of. What a little miracle she was, he thought, and how wonderful that she had come into his life.

She looked up at him with her large dark eyes and smiled. 'What is it?' She was at the age where he could no longer just stare at her without her asking him what he was doing or thinking or plotting.

'It's nothing,' he said.

She didn't look convinced. 'Tell me!'

He shrugged but then said, 'You *are* happy here, aren't you, Tiana?'

She sighed. 'Of *course* I am,' she said. 'Why do you always ask me that?'

'Because I worry.'

'What about?'

'Everything. I worry that you're not happy living with me.

I worry that you're not happy living here. I mean, are you sure you wouldn't want to live somewhere else?'

'Like where?'

'Like the mainland.'

She shook her head and took another sip of her pineapple juice. 'Why would I want to live there?'

'No reason.'

'You said it was horrible there. You said it was dirty and smelly and noisy.'

'It is.'

'So why would I want to live there? You're not going to send me there, are you? We're not leaving here, are we?' she asked, her eyes filled with anxiety.

'No, we're not leaving here.'

'Well, then,' she said with a little shrug before finishing her juice and leaving the table. 'I'm going on the computer,' she added as she left the room.

'No, Tiana! You've spent quite enough time on there already for one day.'

'But I need to. It's for my homework!'

'Well, I'm timing you. Make sure it's just your homework you're doing and remember I'll be checking up on you.'

'No, you won't. You'll go out in the garden and forget all about me!'

'I will not, you cheeky miss!' Milo shook his head. Honestly, his little sister could be so astute sometimes.

Chapter 8

The room was cool and dark and Alice had no idea what the time was when she awoke, fumbling for her travel clock on the bedside cabinet. Eight o'clock.

'Eight o'clock!' she cried, leaping out of bed. She didn't want to miss a single moment of her holiday and ran across the room to draw the curtains. Sunlight blasted into the bedroom and dazzled Alice's eyes, the vibrant colours of Kethos dancing before her. The sky was a perfect blue and the sea was a gloriously glassy aquamarine.

Showering quickly and pulling on a pair of beige cotton trousers and a blouse that was still new enough to look white rather than grey, she ventured downstairs, walking into the kitchen and fixing herself a light breakfast of toast and honey. She'd had to make a return journey into Kethos Town the night before to buy provisions for the villa. She'd meant to get them after eating at the taverna but the leaflet for the Villa Argenti had excited her so much that she'd forgotten to go shopping.

Alice had been up a full hour by the time Stella shuffled downstairs. She was wearing a pink satin bathrobe and her blonde hair was newly washed and blow-dried. Alice had noticed the enormous hairdryer and straightening tongs in her sister's suitcase.

In the spirit of sisterhood, Alice decided to try again and took a deep breath. 'It's such a glorious day. Have you changed your mind about a bit of exploring?'

'I'm going to work on my tan,' Stella announced.

'But you'll be out in the sun if you come with me to this villa. There's a wonderful garden. We can do a bit of sunbathing there.'

'It's not the same. I want to lie about the pool and *really* relax. You've no idea how stressed I've been recently,' she said with a dramatic sigh.

Alice watched as Stella untied her bath robe and let it fall to the floor. She was wearing the skimpiest of bikinis in a metallic gold material that managed to look expensive and cheap at the same time.

'Put some cream on my back,' she said, handing Alice a large bottle of coconut-scented sun lotion. 'Blimey! That's cold!' she complained a moment later. 'Can't you warm your hands up or something first?'

'No, I can't,' Alice said abruptly, 'or I'll be late for the bus. Are you sure you don't want to come with me?'

'To that boring old villa?' She made a funny huffing sound and waltzed out through the patio doors onto the terrace and took position on the sun lounger nearest the pool. Alice sighed. She couldn't believe that they had flown all the way to the Mediterranean and Stella wanted to do nothing more than get a tan. Didn't she want to see any of the island? Wasn't she the least bit interested in exploring some of its history and culture? Well, Alice wasn't going to just sit around, that was for sure.

'My friends are all going to be so jealous of my tan,' Stella said, stretching herself out like a cat. 'You'll have to get lots of photos of me,' she said, putting on her very large, very dark sunglasses.

It was such a relief to leave the villa and walk into town. Why did she always let her sister get to her like that? She was twenty-eight years old and she'd had to put up with Stella for all but four of those years – surely she knew what she was like by now. So why did it still hurt her so much?

Alice caught a little bus from the centre of Kethos Town which headed up a road into the mountains. She'd shown her leaflet of the Villa Argenti to the driver and he nodded in understanding and Alice sat on the back seat and prepared to enjoy the journey. As long as it took her as far away from Stella as was possible on a tiny island, that would suit her.

Alice took a deep breath. She was going to push all thoughts of Stella out of her head and enjoy her surroundings and, looking out of the bus window, she gasped as she noticed just how high they had climbed. The road had twisted its way high up into the mountains and the drop back down gave Alice goosebumps but the view was spectacular. She could see so much of the island all at once from this vantage point and she could just make out the large curve of the coastline that made up one part of the heart shape that the island was famous for.

It was about twenty minutes later when the bus stopped and the driver nodded and pointed along a little road. Alice looked down it but couldn't see anything.

'Villa Argenti?' she asked.

He waved his hand and nodded again and Alice hopped off the bus. She was the only one to do so and she watched as it rounded a bend in the road and disappeared.

Suddenly, she was alone and it was totally silent. She looked down the road the bus driver had pointed along but she couldn't see anything other than trees and hills. Was there really a magnificent villa tucked away there? She took the leaflet out of her handbag but it didn't help very much so she set off at a smart pace in what she hoped was the right direction.

The sun had climbed high in the sky and Alice soon felt she'd been walking for hours but consoled herself with the fact that you couldn't go far wrong on an island. Then, as she rounded a bend, she saw a large white sign with the words 'Villa Argenti' on it. She sighed with relief and followed a tree-lined driveway until she came to a pair of large gates which stood open in welcome.

What now? she wondered. There was nobody around to take her money and she suddenly felt shy about entering the garden but she had come all this way to see it and she didn't want to miss out now.

'Hello?' she called but there was no reply. She looked around. She really was the only soul about and, if that was the case, surely a quick look wouldn't do any harm.

She followed a neat brick path and descended some steps and, suddenly, it was there. The Villa Argenti. It was a large wedding cake of a building with pillars and balconies and enormous doors and sweeping steps. Alice had never seen anything like it in her life. Its honey-coloured stone glowed warmly in the sunshine and Alice had the peculiar feeling that the house was actually smiling at her and she smiled right back at it. It had every right to smile too because it had the good fortune to be in one of the most beautiful settings Alice had ever seen. Completely surrounded by gardens which Alice couldn't wait to explore, the villa was also positioned high enough to have one of the best views along the coastline of Kethos.

What a pity the house was not open to the public, she thought, although there was plenty to see in the garden.

Leaving the house behind her, Alice walked down yet more steps into a world of green. There was an immaculate emerald lawn that looked as if no human being had ever dared to walk on it and Alice was loath to now but there were no signs to tell her not to so she walked as quickly and delicately as she could, crossing to a little path lined with low walls which had been planted with flowering shrubs. It was one of those times when you needed at least three pairs of eyes to take everything in so Alice slowed her pace because she wanted to see everything: each tree, shrub and flower, and every pond, fountain and temple.

Alice had always wanted a garden. Their family home had a long strip of uninspiring grass which had never been very well tended and her little cottage only had a tiny enclosed courtyard. She'd bought a plastic chair and a terracotta pot in which she grew a rose bush but it wasn't the stuff of dreams.

But this garden *was* the stuff of dreams. It was laid out in wide terraces which ended in a large stone wall on top of a cliff which plummeted down to the sea. It was a dizzying vista and Alice stood on the terrace, daring to lean on the iron railings that were the only thing preventing her from tumbling onto the craggy rocks far below.

Gazing out across the coastline, she suddenly felt sad and couldn't help wishing that her dad was there with her. He would have loved to have seen the villa and the gardens. She would have to send him a postcard or two so that he could at least appreciate it all from afar.

Turning her back on the sea for a moment, she spotted an ornate white bench underneath a fig tree. Sitting down on it a moment later, she closed her eyes, her face drinking in the warm rays of the sun. She wasn't sure how long she was sitting there for or even if she nodded off for a few blissful moments but, when she opened her eyes, a young man was approaching her. He was tall and had dark hair and olive skin and he was wearing khaki trousers and a dark grey T-shirt. If Alice had worn such colours, her complexion would have drained away to nothing and her sister would have berated her for her bad taste but, on him, they looked wonderfully masculine.

'Hello,' he said in English as he pushed an ancient wheelbarrow in front of him.

'The gardens aren't closing, are they?' Alice asked, fearing she was being rounded up and pushed out. 'I've lost all track of time.'

'This place can do that to you,' the man said. 'But, no, they're not closing. Not for a few hours.'

'Good,' she said, liking his gentle accent. 'I don't think I'm quite ready to leave yet.' She looked up into his smiling face. 'Do you work here?'

'No,' he said, 'I just like coming and pushing a wheelbarrow around the grounds from time to time.'

She blushed. 'Sorry – it was a silly question.'

He grinned at her. 'No, I'm sorry. And, yes, I do work here. I've worked here for a very long time.'

Alice smiled. 'It must be a wonderful place to work.'

'It is, yes,' he said. 'I wouldn't want to work anywhere else.'

'You're very lucky.'

'I am,' he said simply and then he put his wheelbarrow down and sat on the bench beside her.

Alice shuffled up a little, not used to having handsome men sitting so close to her.

'And where do you work? You're here on holiday, right?' the young man asked her.

Alice nodded. 'I'm here for a week – with my sister.'

'And your job? You have a job back in England – right?'

'Yes, I'm from England and I do have a job but do you mind if we don't talk about it? I wouldn't like to spoil this beautiful place by talking about something so dreary.'

The man nodded. 'I'm sorry to hear that it is dreary. That is a great shame.'

Alice nodded again. 'I don't really know what happened. I mean, you never plan these things, do you? You don't grow up thinking, I want a really dreary job when I grow up. I want to be bored out of my skull and fill my days doing meaningless things that don't seem to add anything worthwhile to the world.' She gave a little sigh. 'But I said I wasn't going to talk about it and I wouldn't want to bore you.'

'You're not boring me,' he said, his dark eyes warm and

attentive and, all of a sudden, Alice was talking – talking like she'd never talked in her life because nobody had ever really listened to her before except her father. She told him about her job and her boss and how bored she was there and how nobody ever seemed to notice her or care about what she thought.

She told him about her father and how worried she was about him even though he always said he was all right and that she shouldn't worry. She told him about her sister and how cross she made her and how she'd thought this holiday would change things between them.

'Gosh,' she said once she'd finished, 'I didn't mean to say all that. I'm not quite sure where it all came from.'

'That's okay,' he said. 'You needed to talk it all out of you.'

She smiled at his funny phrasing but still felt horribly embarrassed at having unburdened herself to a complete stranger and so stood up and started looking for an escape route and then she remembered something. 'I – er – I haven't actually paid to get in,' she said. 'There was nobody at the gate.'

The young man waved his hand dismissively. 'There's no need.'

'But this place must cost a fortune to keep going.'

'Yes, but the owner has plenty of money. He doesn't need yours.' He stood up and followed her along a footpath and there was a moment of silence between them as their feet crunched along the gravel.

'Did you come to see Aphrodite?' the young man said at last.

'Pardon?' Alice said, surprised by his question.

'The statue of Aphrodite – over there by the fountain. Most tourists come here to see her. Perhaps you missed her.'

'I think I must have,' Alice said, annoyed with herself. She thought she'd seen everything.

'They say she grants wishes,' the man said with a little smile.

'Do they?' Alice said.

'If your wish is for love or beauty, it will be granted.'

'I don't believe in wishes,' Alice said.

'Just because you don't believe in something, doesn't make it less real.'

She blinked in surprise. 'Perhaps I'll make a wish another day,' she said, 'if I come back.'

'I hope you do,' he said. 'Goodbye.'

He turned to go and she watched until he was out of sight and then glanced in the direction of the avenue of statues. She'd walked that way earlier but now realised that she hadn't been paying attention. She'd been thinking about Stella and her head had been full of worries which meant she hadn't really seen the beauty of the place she was in.

She took out the leaflet from her handbag. She'd remembered reading something about the statues there.

The Goddess Garden is a place like no other, the leaflet proclaimed. *Travel back to Ancient Greece and meet Hera, Athena, Artemis and Aphrodite whilst enjoying the lush beauty of the garden with its fountains and sea views.*

It was, indeed, a beautiful part of the garden with its enormous urns spilling over with bright flowers and its fountains cooling the air with watery mist. Alice walked up to the first statue which was standing beside the protection of a cypress tree. Its figure was long and boyish and her hair was scraped away from her rather serious-looking face. She was reaching behind her shoulder to where she was carrying her arrows and her other hand was resting upon the head of a faithful hound.

'Artemis,' Alice said, 'goddess of the hunt.'

She walked on and found the next goddess standing by a small pool. She was carrying a sheaf of wheat, a gentle expression gracing her face.

'Demeter,' Alice said, 'goddess of the harvest.' She smiled because she knew that her knowledge would have intensely annoyed Stella had she been there.

Alice walked on by the other goddesses and then she saw her. Standing in full sunlight at the end of the walk was Aphrodite. Alice recognised her at once because she was quite unlike all the other statues in that she was smiling. Artemis had worn the expression of a head teacher and Demeter had looked dreamy but Aphrodite was positively beaming with happiness, her long curls tumbling down her back and the finest of silken garments only just covering her curves as her arms reached up to lift her hair away from her face. Alice couldn't stop looking at her.

'So you're the one everybody comes to see, are you?' She took a step towards her. 'Do you really grant wishes?' she asked, looking into the blank eyes. She reached out, her hand resting on Aphrodite's gown which was warm from the sunshine. 'Heaven only knows I could use a granted wish or two right now.'

Alice thought for a moment. What *exactly* would she wish for? The health and happiness of her dear father, of course. A better, more normal relationship with her sister. But what for herself? If she was being really selfish, what would she wish for herself? Aphrodite was the goddess of love and beauty and the young gardener had said that wishes to do with those would be granted.

What would I wish for? Alice wondered, looking up into the beautiful face of Aphrodite. Should I wish to be as beautiful as you?

The warmth of the stone statue seemed to seep into Alice's arm and she felt the strange tingling sensation that one feels after five minutes too long in the sunshine.

She shook herself out of her reverie.

This is silly, she told herself, and she quickly left the garden.

Chapter 9

It had been very remiss of Milo not even to ask the English girl her name. He should have found out a little bit more about her but, by the time he'd thought to do so, she had long disappeared.

He'd recognised her as one of the tourists he'd seen in Kethos Town the day before. She'd been with the beautiful blonde girl who had looked so moody. Milo now realised that this was the English girl's sister. He shook his head. He knew the sister's name but not the girl he'd sat with for half an hour. How absurd was that? He felt as if he knew everything about this girl's life from the father whom she obviously loved more than life itself to the job that seemed to be swallowing her whole.

He smiled as he remembered the way her past had tumbled out of her mouth with no regard for what he might be thinking. There was something curiously endearing about that. She'd had a certain sweetness and he'd adored her honesty when she'd tried to pay her entrance fee and she had the prettiest blue eyes he'd ever seen. He should have kept her talking at least until he'd finished work and then he could have got to know her better.

Perhaps she'll come back, he thought. Maybe he should make a wish on the statue of Aphrodite so that the English girl would return. He smiled at the thought. He didn't really believe in wishes even though he told all the tourists that he did. It was all just a bit of fun, wasn't it? Still, as he walked towards the statue before the last of the sun's rays dipped behind the villa casting Aphrodite into shade, he knew that he wanted this wish to be granted more than anything else.

Alice felt strangely flat when she returned to the villa, which was odd, really, because she'd had such a wonderful day. She knew what it was, of course. It was the gardener she'd met.

Why did she tell him those things, she wondered, blushing at the memory of having revealed so much to somebody she'd only just met. Perhaps it had been part of the magic that was the Villa Argenti. Perhaps it had woven its spell over her and had broken down her inhibitions. She'd certainly never behaved like that before in her life. She never expressed her true feelings to anybody around her because nobody ever seemed interested enough but this gardener had really listened to her.

He seemed to have cared too. She remembered the gentle look in his deep brown eyes and the expression on his face as she was leaving. But then something occurred to her. He was a good-looking young man who probably met and flirted with hundreds of impressionable tourists every year. Alice had been just another gullible young woman who would fall for his easy charm and handsome face, hadn't she? Only she hadn't given him a chance and she was glad of that now.

Are you? Are you really glad? a little voice inside her asked. *Why did you up and leave him so quickly when he was obviously interested in you? How many chances like that come along?*

Alice laughed. *No* chances like that ever came along in her life. She thought about Ben Alexander at work and how the only time he looked at her was when he was handing her a member of staff's sick note.

'Here you go, Anna. Another one for the collection.' His brief eye contact was what got her through whole days of boredom and that was a very sad way to live. But here, on this beautiful magical island, she'd held the sole attention of one of the most handsome men she had ever seen and she had batted it away as if she received such attention all the time. What had she been thinking of? And what was it about Kethos that was making her so reflective? She'd never really stood still and examined her life before but she was beginning to realise how unhappy she was and she knew that something had to change.

'Oh, there you are,' Stella said as Alice walked out onto the terrace. 'You've been gone for hours.'

Alice couldn't help but be surprised that her sister had even noticed her absence. Sitting down on the sun lounger beside her, she wondered whether to tell Stella about the young gardener she'd met but decided not to. For the time being, she wanted to keep him secret – a wonderful secret.

'What are you grinning about?' Stella suddenly asked, peering at her from behind her oversized sunglasses.

'Nothing,' Alice said.

'Don't lie – you've got a silly smile plastered right across your face.'

'Have I?'

'Yes, you have,' Stella said.

'I'm just happy.'

'Are you?' Stella said. 'Well, *I'm* bored.'

'I'm not surprised if you've just been sitting here all day doing nothing.'

'What was your villa like, then?'

'It was—' Alice paused. If she told her sister just how beautiful it was, Stella might decide to visit it for herself and Alice knew exactly what would happen then. She would be bound to run into the gardener and then he wouldn't even notice Alice any more. It was a pattern that had repeated itself since the girls had become teenagers and it had happened with at least two of Alice's boyfriends.

Alice took a deep breath. She didn't like telling lies but this was a time when a lie was definitely needed. 'Oh, the villa was deadly dull,' she said. 'You were right. I don't know why I went there.'

'I told you!' Stella said. 'Didn't I say?'

'Yes,' Alice said. 'I should've listened to you.'

Stella nodded. 'Nobody ever listens to me but I'm always right and I don't know about you,' she continued, 'but I'm going to spend the entire week right here.' She stretched out her long legs which were gleaming with sun lotion and settled back to soak up the rays.

'I thought you said you were bored.'

'I am but at least I'm getting a good tan.'

'You really shouldn't lie out in the sun all day,' Alice said.

'Oh, don't start!' Stella said. 'I haven't come to Greece to remain all pale and pasty like you.'

'I'm just saying that you want to take care of yourself.'

'Oh, lighten up, Alice. Stop worrying about everything and start *enjoying* life!'

Alice sat stunned for a moment. Not because of her sister's rude tone – she was quite used to that – but because perhaps for the first time in her life, Stella had actually given Alice some advice worth listening to.

That night, Alice couldn't sleep. Stella's words kept somersaulting around her head in a teasing chant.

'Stop worrying about everything and start enjoying life!'

Alice sat up in bed. Start enjoying life!

She couldn't remember the last time she'd enjoyed herself. Stella was right. She was always worrying about everything, wasn't she? Perhaps it was time to relax a little and have some fun.

For a moment, she thought about the dark-eyed gardener at the Villa Argenti. She didn't even know his name but she couldn't help wondering if he was somehow inextricably linked with Stella's advice.

There was something else too – an idea which Alice just couldn't shake from her mind.

'Aphrodite.' She spoke the name quietly into the silence of her bedroom. It sounded like a magical spell and seemed to weave rainbows in her mind. Lying back on her pillow, Alice closed her eyes. She knew it was ludicrous and impossible but, all the same, what did she have to lose? She would go back to the Villa Argenti tomorrow.

Chapter 10

The bus ride up into the mountains from Kethos Town was just as beautiful the second time. Alice had left around mid-morning and had tried to be as casual as possible when Stella asked her where she was going.

'I don't know yet,' Alice had said with a shrug. 'Probably a museum or something. Want to come?'

Predictably, Stella had declined which was a great relief to Alice who had made her escape into town and was now just about to get off the bus at the stop for the Villa Argenti. This time, a young couple got off the bus with her and they all walked together down the road that led to the villa. They were from Worcester and had just got married and Alice couldn't help but envy them their new life together. She saw the way that Tim looked so adoringly at his new wife, Janey, and the way that they held hands so tightly. *What must it be like to be so adored*, Alice couldn't help wondering?

There was a little old man by the gate today and he took their money with a polite little nod and Alice watched as Tim and Janey walked hand in hand towards a sunlit bench. She didn't follow them.

All of a sudden, Alice wondered what she was doing there and a coldness resembling fear chilled her whole body. It had all been very well imagining romantic scenarios with the handsome gardener whilst in the safety of her bed but Alice really wasn't the kind of girl to initiate something as wonderful and frivolous as a holiday romance.

She stopped by a little fountain and trailed her fingers in the cool water and sighed. Perhaps she was worrying unnecessarily. She couldn't see the gardener anywhere and it occurred to her that he might not be there at all. She couldn't help smiling at that. The one time she had allowed herself to be a little bit brave and the man in question had foiled her by having a day off. Besides, she had every right to be in the garden, didn't she? Not only had he invited her to come back but she was a tourist who was simply enjoying a beautiful place. That was all. She nodded to herself and determined that she would let things fall into the hands of destiny.

It was then that Alice remembered that she hadn't just come back to the garden in the hope of seeing Milo again but to see the statue too.

She walked down the neat path which led to the Goddess Garden, passing Artemis, Demeter, Athena and the others but she hadn't come to see them. She'd come to see Aphrodite.

Once again, the statue of the goddess of love was in full sunlight and the loveliness of her face made Alice smile. She placed her hand on the hem of the finely-carved gown and felt the magical warmth seep through her skin. What did she have to lose? She closed her eyes.

Concentrate.

What did she want for herself that the goddess could grant? What was it the gardener had told her?

'If your wish is for love or beauty, it will be granted.'

Love or beauty. The two words spun inside her mind until she had her wish.

'I wish,' she began, her fingers trembling against the warm stone, 'I wish men would notice me. I wish I wasn't so invisible to them but that they really *really* saw me.'

She thought of Stella for a moment and how much attention she got from the opposite sex. Her life seemed like one long joyous date and she was constantly showered in gifts and spoilt rotten. Just once, Alice wanted to know what that would be like.

'Yes,' she told Aphrodite, 'I want men to notice me at last!'

She stood perfectly still for a moment longer and then she opened her eyes and the sunlight dazzled her before everything settled back to normal. Alice smiled. The world looked exactly the same as before and she felt no different than she had a moment ago. What had she been expecting? It was silly to think anything would change. The statue couldn't grant wishes. It was just a piece of masonry that had been carved for the pleasure of a few tourists.

Suddenly feeling very silly, she walked away from the statue before anybody saw her. It was when she was back at the fountain that she saw him.

'Hello,' he called, waving a tanned hand at her and smiling as if he were greeting a long-lost friend.

'Hello,' Alice replied.

His pace picked up and he was beside her in an instant. 'You left without saying goodbye yesterday.'

'I'm sorry,' she said. 'I had to run for my bus.'

His eyebrows rose and she could feel herself blushing at her lie. He would know exactly when the buses ran, wouldn't he?

'I mean, I was scared I'd missed it.'

'I could have given you a lift back. I have a very fine moped,' he said, his dark eyes twinkling.

'Is it safe?' Alice asked and then cursed her question. This wasn't the new, carefree Alice she had determined to be the night before. 'I mean – that sounds fun.'

'You'd like a ride?'

'Oh!' Alice exclaimed, taken by surprise at the speed of his invitation.

'It can be arranged,' he added.

Alice smiled at the sudden image of her on the back of a moped with the handsome Greek gardener, whizzing along the mountain roads around Kethos, her hands clasped around his waist.

'Okay,' she said.

'Okay?'

'Yes.'

The gardener looked as surprised as Alice felt. 'I – er – I think I'd better introduce myself. My name is Milo,' he said, extending a hand towards her.

'I'm Alice,' she said, shaking his hand, and marvelling at how warm and strong it felt.

'So,' he said, 'did you come back to make a wish?'

'I might have done,' Alice said evasively.

'Ah,' he said. 'You do not want to say in case it doesn't come true, yes?'

'Maybe,' she said and then she did something curiously out of character and winked at him.

Milo's eyes widened and he grinned. 'Listen,' he said, 'it's my day off tomorrow and I was thinking of going to the beach. It's not far from here but tourists don't know about it. It has the softest, whitest sand in Greece and the bluest sea in the world. I think you'll like it.'

'You mean you want me to go with you?'

'Of course!' he said with a grin. 'It will be fun. It's my day off and you are on holiday. It's bound to be fun, yes?'

Alice bit her lip but then nodded. 'Yes,' she said. 'That does sound like fun.'

'Good,' he said.

Alice waited for him to say something else and, when he didn't, she spoke. 'You're not married, are you?'

He visibly blanched at her question. 'What?'

Alice shrugged. 'I mean, I don't want to get involved with anyone who has commitments elsewhere even if this is just to be a fun holiday thing.'

'I'm not married,' he said.

Alice nodded. 'I didn't mean to pry but – well – in your job, you must meet a lot of women and it must be easy for you—' she paused. What exactly was she trying to say?

'Easy for me to…?' he prompted her.

'I think you know what I mean,' she said, 'and I need you to know – right now – before this day at the beach – that I'm not one of those girls.'

'Okay,' Milo said, shoving his hands into the pockets of his rather beaten-up trousers. 'You're not one of those girls and

I am not married.' He smiled at her and she couldn't help but smile back. 'So we're still on for this day at the beach?'

Alice took a deep breath. 'Yes,' she said. 'We're on.'

'Good. Shall I come to your hotel and pick you up?'

'Oh – no,' Alice said quickly, imagining the scene if Milo arrived at their villa and Stella clapped eyes on him. 'I'll meet you in Kethos Town.'

'Okay,' he said. 'Are you sure *you're* not married?'

'No!' Alice said. 'I'm not hiding anything. It's just easier if we meet in town.'

He laughed and it was a delightfully warm and full-hearted laugh and Alice was instantly at ease. 'Good. Then I'll meet you at the harbour front where you got off the ferry.'

'All right,' Alice said. 'Is eleven o'clock okay?' She thought a late morning departure would be less suspicious to her sister.

Milo frowned. 'That is so late. Half the day is gone at eleven o'clock.'

'What about ten?' Alice said, thinking Stella might very well still be in bed by then.

He nodded his approval. 'Ten o'clock.'

'Do I need to bring anything?'

'No – no. This is my day to you. I will prepare it all.' His hands were out of his pockets again and waving about in the air as if conjuring up the day for her right there and then. 'You need do nothing but turn up, please.'

Alice couldn't help feeling charmed by his sweet enthusiasm. 'All right,' she said.

'Good. Then I will see you at nine o'clock.'

'*Ten!*' Alice corrected him.

'Okay,' he said, raising his hands in defeat. 'Ten o'clock!'

She watched as he sauntered away down the path with a little wave and then disappeared behind a high hedge. Had that all really happened, she wondered? Had she just promised a strange man that she would spend a whole day with him on some deserted beach? She had, hadn't she? And the thought of it made her feel so excited that she wanted to leap right into the fountain and do a zany little water dance.

Men like Milo just weren't interested in someone like her. It was a fact of life that she'd learned to accept years ago and yet he had asked her out. He wanted to prepare a whole day for her and take her somewhere that was special to him, and that really touched her.

She suddenly felt herself blushing at her forwardness when she remembered asking him if he was married. What had got into her? And where on earth had that wink come from? She'd been behaving like another person entirely and that made her wonder about something.

Had Aphrodite granted her wish?

Chapter 11

It was a perfect spring morning and, when Alice walked out onto the terrace after breakfast, she inhaled the sweet warm air and knew that this day was going to be special. In fact, it was going to be a blue dress day and she skipped back up to her bedroom and grabbed the dress from her wardrobe. She had already worn it once into town but Milo hadn't seen it yet and she hoped he would like it.

Looking at herself in the mirror before leaving, she couldn't help thinking that there was something different about her today. Was it really as simple as putting on a beautiful dress? She doubted it and yet she couldn't help acknowledging the fact that she felt so unlike her old self. Maybe it was because she was on holiday, but did it really matter? All that she knew was that she was happy to be her and that was a wonderful novelty.

As she walked into town, an old man raised his hat to her and a teenager on a bicycle waved to her and shouted something in Greek that she didn't understand. She watched as he cycled on down the road and then he did a double take.

'Just a friendly local,' she said to herself, putting all thoughts of it out of her mind as she caught her first glimpse of the sea between the steeply stacked houses. There was a row of men sitting on the harbour wall with fishing rods, the backs of their necks already dark with exposure to the sun, and boats bobbed about on the water, the reflected light making magical patterns on their sterns.

And there was Milo waiting for her at the harbour, his moped standing alongside him. He didn't see her at first and she had a chance to look at him properly. He was tall and slim with lean, strong arms and a head of dark curls and there seemed to be a nervous sort of energy within him as if it was difficult for him to keep still. His dark eyes were scanning the horizon and, when he turned and saw her and smiled, Alice felt as if she had been blessed.

Don't get carried away, she told herself. *This is just a bit of holiday fun. Don't go making anything more of it.*

'Good morning,' she said as she approached him.

'I like that,' he said.

Alice looked at him curiously. 'What?'

'The way you English say "good morning" – as if wishing the day to be good even if it is not so.'

'But today *is* a good day, isn't it?' she said.

'Today is *very* good,' he said, handing her a helmet and helping her with the strap. 'Right. We are ready to begin.'

Alice nodded, liking the way he phrased things. She was definitely ready to begin, she thought. Looping her bag over her head, she watched as Milo hopped onto the bike. She followed, placing her hands around his waist and giving a little yelp as they took off.

The speed at which they left the town made Alice feel quite giddy. She hadn't realised how much power a moped had even when loaded with two people, but it climbed the steep streets of Kethos Town easily and they were out onto the open road with the sea far below them in no time.

The sky was a brilliant blue above them and Alice felt a huge bubble of excitement inside her and she couldn't help wishing that her sister could see her now. Stella wouldn't recognise her boring big sister, would she? Alice had to admit that she barely recognised herself.

Being on a moped was such a freeing experience and Alice could see why Milo loved it so much. He kept half-turning round and shouting back at her to make sure she was okay which she was, of course. She was so much more than okay.

It was about twenty minutes and several miles of scarily twisting roads later when Milo began to slow down. This part of the island was a lot quieter. There was only a scattering of houses and there were certainly no tourists. The landscape was rugged and rocky and it was hard to imagine a perfect sandy beach nearby but that's what Milo had promised her.

They turned off the twisting main road onto a sandy track filled with enormous potholes.

'Hold on tight!' he called back as he skilfully negotiated the primitive track. It was obvious to Alice that he'd done so countless times before but she tightened her grip all the same.

The track was steep and went straight downhill and Alice gasped as she got her first glimpse of the beach. It was a tiny strip of sand between two hills covered with trees and was completely secluded from the world. Nobody but the most ardent of tourists would ever find it. This was a place for locals only and Alice felt honoured to be shown it.

'You okay?' Milo asked as they hopped off the bike. 'Not too dizzy?'

'Not dizzy at all!' Alice said as she took her helmet off and shook her hair free. A wonderful breeze from the sea lifted it away from her face and she inhaled deeply. 'What a perfect beach!'

'This is my very special place,' he said. 'I keep it to myself but – today – I share it with you.'

Alice smiled and watched him as he unpacked the secret compartment on the back of the moped and shook out a blanket for them to sit on.

'Let me help,' she said, as he reached inside and brought out two bags of food. Together, they negotiated their way down the boulder-strewn beach before reaching the perfect white sand.

'How did you discover this place?' Alice asked.

Milo shrugged. 'I used to explore a lot. When I got my first moped, I would be gone for hours – just riding the roads and looking, you know?'

Alice nodded. 'I used to have a bicycle and do the same thing.'

'And what did you find?'

Alice thought back to her bike rides around the Norfolk countryside. 'Fields and woods and lakes.'

'You still ride?'

She shook her head. 'No. There doesn't seem to be time anymore.'

'No time?'

'With work and things. I always seem so tired these days,' she said.

'But you should always make time for yourself,' Milo said, shaking out the blanket.

'It isn't always that easy,' Alice said. They put the bags of food and drink down and sat on the blanket.

'When I first got my bike,' Milo said, 'I couldn't get away fast enough.'

'What did you have to get away from?'

'A large family!' he said with a grin.

'You have lots of brothers and sisters?'

'Oh, yes,' he said.

'I only have one sister and that's *more* than enough!'

'Here,' he said, 'let's have some lunch.'

She watched as he opened the first bag of food and brought out a large white loaf of bread already neatly cut into slices. 'I made it this morning,' he said, 'so it's very fresh.'

'You made bread this morning?'

'You don't believe me?'

'Well—'

'I told you I'd give you a whole day and that day starts very early when I get up to make this bread,' he said.

Alice smiled. He seemed to do nothing but make her smile.

Following the loaf of bread was a great hunk of creamy yellow cheese, a container filled with shiny olives, and a bag of glossy green salad leaves.

'I feel so bad that I didn't bring anything,' Alice said.

'Don't feel bad. This was my wish. You are my guest. Now, please help yourself and I will pour the wine.'

'Wine?'

'Of course. You cannot have a picnic without wine.'

Alice looked up into the sky where the sun was shining so brightly. Sun, sea and wine – this was going to be a sensory overload. 'I think I'd better put my hat on,' she said.

For a while, neither of them spoke but got on with the business of eating good food and drinking good wine. In fact, Alice couldn't believe how good it all tasted. She'd forgotten the last time she'd eaten really glorious food. The canteen at work might have introduced a few new salads to the menu but most of the food was still school-dinner stodgy and, by the time she got home from work, she rarely had the energy left to prepare herself something wholesome but she promised herself that she would from now on. After all, what could be more simple than a loaf of bread and fresh produce?

She watched Milo as he ate, fast and merrily, glorying in every mouthful. This, Alice thought, was how life should be – taking the time to enjoy a simple meal in a beautiful place.

'You're having a good time?'

Alice nodded through a mouthful of salad. 'You really know how to live, don't you?'

Milo laughed. 'What a funny thing to say!'

'But you do. You really do and I envy you that.'

'But anyone could live like this,' he said, his dark forehead furrowed in bewilderment.

Alice shook her head. 'Not everyone. You have to have courage to live like this.'

'What do you mean?'

'I mean – you seem so free – so close to everything around you. Do you know what I mean?'

'No. I don't,' he said. 'But my English is not very good, I'm afraid.'

'Your English is almost perfect,' Alice said. 'What I mean is, you do what you like. You have a job you love in a place you adore.'

'That is true.'

'And not many people have that luxury,' Alice said.

'That's very sad,' he said. 'I mean, I can't imagine living anywhere else or doing anything else.'

'Have you always lived on Kethos?' Alice asked.

Milo nodded as he drank the last of his wine. 'Of course,' he said. 'There is nowhere else. At least, not for me.'

Alice looked at him and saw the light in his eyes as he gazed out to sea. 'That must be wonderful – to be so sure of your home.'

'But you have a home too?' he said, turning to face her.

'Yes, but I'm not sure I'm as attached to it as you are to yours.'

He looked at her for a moment and then nodded out towards the sea. 'Look at that,' he said. 'The sea is six shades of blue. I know – I counted. Yesterday, it was four and the Sunday before you arrived, it was a green-grey like slate.' He paused. 'The sea is alive. It is like a person that keeps you company. You get to know its every mood and you come to rely on it being there.'

'We have the sea too – where I live – but I don't get to visit it very often.'

'That's – *mad*,' he said. 'Why live near the sea and yet not go there?'

91

'I know! It's crazy, isn't it?' Alice said, shifting herself on the rug so that she was kneeling. 'I live in this beautiful county and yet I hardly get to see any of it.'

'Why not?'

'Because I'm working all the time!' Alice all but cried.

'Not *all* the time, surely?'

'Well, no, but there's my father too and I see him whenever I can.'

'He's ill, isn't he?' Milo asked gently.

Alice nodded. 'He's in a home and I know he has company there but it's not the same as family, is it? So I visit him at weekends and then there are all the usual things to do around the house and then it's time to begin the working week again.'

'Oh!' Milo said.

'I'm sorry,' Alice said. 'I seem to do nothing but complain when I'm with you but it's like you're helping me to see things clearly for the first time.'

'And what is it you're seeing?' he asked, leaning forward and gently tucking a strand of her brown hair behind her ear.

Alice flinched very slightly in surprise at his movement which caused his fingers to brush her cheek.

'What?' she asked.

'I said, what is it you're seeing?'

She looked into his dark eyes and swallowed hard. She'd only just met this man and yet here she was, once again, telling him everything about herself. 'Change,' she said. 'I need things to change.'

He nodded. 'You're unhappy, aren't you?'

His tone was gentle and she could feel tears vibrating in

her eyes and then something unexpected happened and he leant forward and kissed her. She couldn't move – didn't want to move. Instead, she kissed him back, and the sound of the sea in her ears and the warmth of his lips on hers seemed mesmeric for one beautiful moment and her tears were forgotten.

'I should not have done that,' Milo said at last when they stopped. 'But you looked so sad and I—'

'Wanted to take advantage of that?' Alice said.

Milo's face fell. 'No,' he said quickly.

Alice gave a little laugh. 'I'm joking! Sorry. I didn't mean to tease and it's okay.' She blinked hard, determined to get a grip of herself.

'You don't mind?' he asked, his eyes wide with concern.

'I don't mind.'

He cocked his head to one side. 'You are so lovely, Alice,' he said, 'and I hate to see you sad especially when today is such a happy day, yes? And you are—' he paused.

'What am I?' Alice asked, almost dreading hearing his response.

'I can't think of the word.' He seemed to be scanning the sky for a moment as if the right word might leap out of it and fall into his head. '*Irresistible!*' he said at last. 'That's it – you're irresistible!'

Alice laughed. 'Are you sure?'

He nodded, his face lit up with his smile.

Alice sat stunned for a moment, realising that she had the sole attention of a handsome man. Just like she'd wished for.

Chapter 12

'I'm sorry,' Milo said. 'I'm embarrassing you.'

'No, you're not,' Alice said. 'It was just unexpected.'

'But a good unexpected?' he asked with the tiniest of smiles.

She nodded, thinking it best if she didn't have any more wine that day. They sat in silence, both staring out to sea. Alice was just wondering what was going to happen next and hoping that Milo wasn't going to write the day off as a huge mistake and take her straight back to Kethos Town when he suddenly clapped his hands together.

'Well, there's only one thing to do when you live near the sea and that's to swim in it! Are you coming?' he asked, standing up and brushing sand off his legs.

'Oh, you didn't say we might be swimming,' Alice said, looking disappointed.

'We're on an island – swimming is always on the agenda,' he said. 'Come on!'

'But I don't have my costume.'

'What do you need a costume for? The sea will dress you!' he said.

She watched as Milo walked towards the water, shedding clothes as he went. At first, Alice averted her eyes but then she wondered why. If he was unabashed to strip off in front of her in broad daylight, why shouldn't she watch?

His body was lean and tanned and she really couldn't stop looking at it. This just wasn't the kind of thing that happened back home in Norfolk and Alice was jolly well going to enjoy it.

'You won't believe how good this feels!' Milo cried as he entered the water, beating it with enthusiastic arms.

'You're mad!' Alice shouted.

'Come on in!' he yelled back.

'I haven't got my costume,' Alice said.

'You are born naked,' Milo shouted across the waves.

'Yes, but you acquire clothes pretty damned quickly,' Alice replied.

'Why are you English girls so shy?'

So this was his ploy, was it? For a moment, Alice had a vision of him seducing half the women of England in this very way but then she thought, so what? So what if that's what this was all about – the picnic, the kiss, the swim. If it was nothing more than a bit of naked flirtation then she could handle that, couldn't she?

She stood up on the picnic rug, two words cascading themselves around her head. *Why not?*

'In your own time,' Milo said. 'I won't look!' She watched as he swam farther out to sea, his strokes strong and confident, and then she took a deep breath. She'd never done anything like this before in her life but something strange was happening to her – it was as if her shyness had been banished by some force much stronger than she was and she really didn't care any more. She felt empowered, confident, free.

Slowly, she stepped out of her shoes and unbuttoned the front of her dress. The turquoise fabric slithered down her body onto the sand and was soon joined by her underwear.

Walking across the sugar-soft sand, she looked out into the sea. Milo was still swimming towards the horizon but suddenly doubled back and started swimming towards the shore once again but he kept his word and was facing away from Alice so she was able to slip into the water without being seen.

As soon as she was in up to her knees, she took a deep breath and did the only sensible thing to acclimatise and threw herself straight into the water until her whole body was immersed.

Gasping, she broke clear of the water, blinking and laughing. Milo was right – it felt glorious, the sea enveloping her body in its cooling embrace. She floated on her back for a while, gazing into the blue depths of the sky and then turned to face the shore, marvelling at the rocky landscape and the deep dark greens of the trees. She hadn't been swimming in the sea for years and remembered how much she loved it. Seeing the land from the sea was one of life's little miracles.

Alice loved the sensation of the water all around her and the gentle bobbing motion of the tide that cradled her. The sea had the wonderful ability of making everything else disappear so that you really lived in the moment with its salt tang in your nose and its lulling waves in your ears.

When Milo spotted her, he waved across and then started to swim towards her, as beautiful and sleek as a sea lion.

'I told you!' he cried above the waves. 'It's the best place in the whole world!'

'It is!' Alice replied.

'I come here whenever I can in the good weather but it's never often enough,' he said, inching towards her in the water. Alice remained where she was, bobbing about in the little spot that was fast feeling like a second home. She was aware of how diaphanous the water was and wondered just how much Milo was able to see but his eyes remained fixed on the land as he drank in his beloved island. Well, that wasn't very flattering, was it? Here she was, naked in the water and supposedly 'irresistible' and he only had eyes for Kethos.

Alice bit her lip and her hand seemed to take on a life of its own because it was suddenly flicking water over Milo's head.

Milo turned around, stunned by her action and that's when the war of water began with great fat droplets flying through the air and mini waves cascading over them.

They splashed each other, dunked each other, raced each other towards the shore and back and then – finally – floated happily together, catching their breaths.

'Oh my God!' Milo said, closing his eyes for a moment. 'I surrender – you win!'

'Good!' Alice said with a laugh. She felt completely exhausted but wonderfully so.

'Come on,' he said a moment later, 'let's get out of here.'

They were just about to make for the shore when they saw an old man with a walking stick shuffling along the beach.

'Oh, no!' Milo said.

'Who is it?' Alice said, squinting against the sun.

'It's Old Stamos – he walks here every day and he likes to

– how do you say? *Talk a lot.*'

'But how on earth did he get down that steep track?' Alice asked. 'He looks about a hundred and ten.'

'He's fitter than I am,' Milo said.

'But how are we going to get out of the water now? We've got no clothes on!' Alice pointed out quite unnecessarily.

'Oh, Old Stamos won't mind that,' Milo said.

'Well, he might not but *I'd* mind!' Alice said.

Milo seemed to be mulling things over for a moment and then he pointed over to the left.

'We can hide behind those rocks until he leaves,' he said and the two of them swam off together, reaching the rocks just as the old man reached their piles of clothes on the beach. They watched as he used his walking stick to poke around amongst the garments.

'What *is* he doing?' Alice asked.

'Seeing what he can find,' Milo said and it soon became obvious what he had found because, hoisted on the end of his stick was Alice's bra which he proceeded to wave in the air like a flag.

Milo laughed.

'Oh my God!' Alice cried in mortification but she couldn't help laughing too as the old man looked out to sea and the two of them ducked their heads.

'I bet he's remembering his own past when he used to swim naked too!' Milo said.

'I wish he'd hurry up and leave. What's he doing now?' Alice asked.

Milo peeped over the top of one of the rocks. 'It's all right – he's going,' he said.

'Thank goodness,' Alice said. 'I'm getting cold.'

They swam towards the shore together and Milo waded out as unashamedly as he'd waded in whilst Alice bobbed about in the shallows.

'It's okay – I won't look!' he said, sitting himself down on the blanket with his back to the sea as he pulled on his clothes.

When she was quite sure Milo was thoroughly occupied in drying his hair, Alice walked out of the sea, the sun instantly warming her limbs. Milo's arm extended out behind himself, a towel for her in his hand and she quickly dried herself before slipping her dress on again and sitting down on the blanket.

'That was fun,' he said, shaking the last few droplets of water out of his hair.

'Yes,' Alice said, squeezing her own hair.

'Here – let me,' he said, inching forwards on the blanket, towel in hand.

Alice felt the firmness of his hands as they rubbed her hair gently with the towel and she closed her eyes, luxuriating in the experience.

'All done,' he said a moment later. 'The sun will do the rest.'

'Thank you,' she said, wishing he'd taken just a little longer over the job.

He looked at her, his dark eyes seeming to drink her in. 'You have beautiful hair,' he told her.

Alice laughed. 'No I don't,' she said.

He frowned. 'You do!'

'My hair is too fine and way too brown to be beautiful.'

'But it is soft and pretty and it just suits you,' he said.

She smiled. He was being ridiculous again, she thought. Was this all a part of his seduction technique?

'I know I'm not beautiful,' she said, 'and you don't need to flatter me.' Alice looked out to sea in an attempt to deflect his comments. She wasn't used to being the centre of somebody's attention and, although it felt nice, she wasn't sure she was completely comfortable with it. 'Tell me about Aphrodite,' she said.

Milo scratched his chin and looked thoughtful. 'Well, she's the goddess of love and beauty and was born right here off the coast of Kethos.'

Alice turned to look at him. 'Really? I thought she was born in Cyprus – isn't that what all the legends say?'

'*Cyprus!*' Milo said, spitting out the word as if it were a curse. 'What would Aphrodite be doing in Cyprus? She's a *Greek* goddess!' He shook his head, looking thoroughly disgusted by the idea of Cyprus having anything to do with his special goddess. 'Cyprus only made up the legend to get tourists to visit.'

'Oh,' Alice said, resisting the temptation to suggest that Kethos had had the same idea.

'There's a legend,' Milo began, stretching his long legs out across the blanket, 'that Aphrodite once seduced all the inhabitants of Kethos in the course of one night.'

'What – men *and* women?'

Milo nodded. 'And that everybody today is descended from her.'

'But she's just a myth, isn't she? She was never real.'

Milo shrugged and grinned. 'What do you think?'

'I don't know,' Alice said. She didn't really believe it but didn't want to say so in case Milo believed the legend but she had to admit that she'd never seen so many good-looking people before in her life than on the island of Kethos. *Could there be a grain of truth in the legend,* she wondered?

'Why are you so interested in Aphrodite?' he asked.

'Just curious,' Alice said.

Milo's eyebrows rose. 'You made a wish, didn't you? You made a wish and it's come true, hasn't it?' His bright smile was both mocking and delighted.

'I told you – I don't believe in wishes,' Alice said.

'Is Aphrodite the reason you came back to the villa?'

Alice turned to look at him. 'It might have been one of the reasons.'

He held her gaze for a moment and then he spoke. 'I'm glad you came back,' he said.

When Alice arrived back at the villa, there was no sign of Stella other than a mess of dishes in the sink. Alice peered into it and saw two cereal bar wrappers and four cups and spoons which had obviously been Stella's coffee quota so far that day.

'Stella?' Alice shouted up the stairs but there was no reply so she went to her bedroom and took a quick shower. It had been an amazing day. She had stayed on the beach with Milo for hours just sitting and chatting and swimming and – what was even better – she was going to see him again.

The ride back to Kethos Town in the afternoon had been like a dream from which Alice hadn't wanted to wake up. She kept trying to think of ways to delay their parting but he said he had to get back.

'I wish this day could last forever,' he said, 'and I'm sorry that it can't.'

She didn't ask him what he had to get back for and she'd waited for him to say if he wanted to see her again. Well, she'd waited about two seconds.

'Will I see you again?' she'd blurted before having a chance to check the rules of etiquette.

'Come to the villa tomorrow. My boss is away. I have to work but–' he'd paused, 'we can talk, yes?'

'Yes,' Alice had said with a smile of relief and delight.

Now, as she walked down the stairs after her shower, she couldn't help smiling at the thought of seeing Milo again. She couldn't remember talking to a man with such ease before but, with Milo, the hours had passed by so quickly and happily and the day had ended all too suddenly.

'Oh! *There* you are!' Stella's voice broke into Alice's thoughts and there, standing in the kitchen with her fifth cup of coffee of the day, was her sister.

'Hello,' Alice said. 'Where have you been?'

'Just out,' Stella said mysteriously, draining her cup and flinging it in the sink to join the others.

'Into town?' Alice probed.

Stella's lips twisted and then she nodded. 'I got so bored here that I thought I'd try and find you so I ended up going to the museum you said you were visiting but you weren't there and then I got stuck with this local man who insisted on showing me every single coin and piece of pottery that has ever been dug up on the whole of Kethos!'

'Oh, poor Stella!' Alice said in sympathy even though she was laughing inside.

'It was awful. Where *were* you?'

Alice swallowed. She hated telling lies but she couldn't risk Stella finding out about Milo.

'I just wandered around really,' she said with a shrug, turning her back on her sister and opening the fridge to pour herself some fruit juice.

'Wandered around *where?*'

'Well, I ended up getting a bus and I found this little beach. I spent most of the day there,' she said, happy that some of what she'd said was the truth.

'Maybe you can show me this beach,' Stella said.

'Oh, I don't think you'd like it,' Alice said.

'Why wouldn't I like it?'

'It's very stony and the sea's so cold,' Alice said without so much as a twinge at her lie. She was becoming bolder because the thought of not seeing Milo again was too much.

'God, it's so boring here, isn't it?' Stella said, walking through to the living room and flopping down heavily on one of the white sofas.

'I thought you were happy by the pool all day?'

'Only to begin with.'

'Haven't you brought books with you?'

'Oh, I hate books!'

Alice sighed. 'Well, maybe we can find something to do

103

together,' she said at last.

'Really?' Stella said, looking at her sister with hope in her eyes. 'Tomorrow? Can we do something tomorrow?'

'What about the day after?' Alice said.

'But I want to do something tomorrow!' she said. 'I can't bear another day in this place. I really can't stand it and you *did say* we could do something.'

'Yes but just not tomorrow,' Alice said.

'Why not? What have you got planned?'

'I haven't got anything pla—'

'What are you hiding from me, Alice?'

'I'm not hiding—'

'And you *did say* we could do something together!'

'ALL RIGHT!' Alice shouted. 'We'll do something.'

'*Tomorrow!*'

'Yes,' Alice relented, 'we'll do something tomorrow.'

Chapter 13

Milo hadn't wanted to say goodbye to Alice so early in the day. It was frustrating that they couldn't spend the evening together. He could have taken her to his favourite restaurant and they could have talked whilst watching the sun go down. That's what any normal guy would have done, he thought, but he wasn't a normal guy, was he? He had responsibilities. He had a little sister.

He'd picked Tiana up from Hanna's at the usual time and they'd gone straight home for tea together.

'Did you have a nice day off?' Tiana asked him when they were sitting at the kitchen table together.

'I did,' he said. And then she'd started. She seemed to know that it hadn't been an ordinary day off because she wouldn't relent with the questions.

'But you must have done *something* interesting because you took the picnic blanket and you never take that unless you're going somewhere really nice.'

Milo turned to where Tiana was looking. It was the little wicker chair by the door on which the picnic blanket lived. Of course, it wasn't there because it was in the back of Milo's bike.

'You would make a good detective,' Milo told her and she beamed a smile at him.

'I know. You can't hide anything from me. I always know *exactly* what you're doing.'

'But I'm not trying to hide anything from you,' he said with what he hoped was a deflecting smile.

'So where did you go?' she asked.

He sighed. The deflecting smile hadn't worked. 'Just to the beach.'

'Your favourite beach?' Her bright eyes were wide and inquisitive.

'Yes.'

'On your own?'

Milo clattered his cutlery onto his plate. 'What is it with all these questions?'

'I just want to know so I can picture it,' Tiana said innocently.

Milo pushed his chair out behind him and started clearing away the debris of dinner whilst buying himself some time. It was one of the problems he faced as a single man in sole charge of a little sister – what did he do with his girlfriends? Did he tell them from the outset? He'd tried that before and it hadn't worked out. He remembered one woman had just laughed at him when he'd brought his phone out and shown her a photo of Tiana.

Then there was the problem of what to do with a girlfriend if things did get serious. It wouldn't be right to bring them home because his home was Tiana's too and he couldn't very well have a normal healthy relationship without inviting them back to his. There were only so many times you could put such a thing off. And what about the long-term implications?

How many women would really want a man who came joined at the hip with a little girl?

His eldest brother, Georgio, was all too aware of Milo's predicament and had been quizzing him about it for years but Milo didn't want to think about that now. He turned to face his little sister. She was still staring at him with those huge eyes of hers. Milo thought of them as *truth detectors* because he was never able to lie when she looked at him.

'I didn't go to the beach on my own,' he said.

Tiana smiled at him. 'Who did you go with?'

'Her name's Alice.'

'That's a pretty name.'

'For a pretty girl,' he said and then wondered if he should have volunteered such information.

'Is she a tourist?'

He nodded. 'She's from England.'

'So she'll be going home soon?'

'Yes,' Milo said, and the sudden realisation of that made him sad. Whatever had happened today and whatever was going to happen next, it was only going to last one short week and then she would leave his little island and go home.

'Will I get to meet her or will she be like all your other girlfriends?'

'What do you mean?' Milo asked, surprised by her question.

'I never get to meet any of them,' Tiana said with a definite sulk in her voice.

'I didn't know you wanted to meet them.'

'Of *course* I want to meet them. I want to know if they're right for you,' she said and her face was perfectly serious.

'Right for me?' Milo frowned.

She nodded as she cleared her plate and drank down the last of her juice. 'You keep them all hidden away and I never get to meet them.'

Milo scratched his head. This had never come up before. He'd always tried to keep his love life separate from his home life with Tiana because that had seemed the right thing to do but he was now being chastised for doing so.

'Look,' he said, 'I can't bring my girlfriends home all the time.'

'Why not?'

'Well, because some of them don't last long enough.' He grimaced. That hadn't come out right.

'But I'd still like to meet them.'

'Why?'

'Because I don't get to meet grown-up girls,' she said and Milo felt a pang inside his heart at her words. She missed her mother, didn't she? She was crying out for a replacement but wasn't that enough of a reason *not* to bring his girlfriends home? Just imagine telling them at the end of a romantic dinner that they now had to be vetted by his little sister. That wasn't exactly the stuff of romance, was it?

'You should have taken me with you today,' Tiana said, pouting.

'But you had to go to school.'

'Oh, I hate school,' she declared.

'No, you don't.'

'Well, take me on your next date with Alice.'

'How do you know there'll be a second one?' he said.

'Isn't there?'

Milo grinned. He wasn't going to be able to get out of this one so he thought he might as well be honest. 'I might be seeing her again,' he said.

'Good,' Tiana said. 'I'll let you know what I think of her when you bring her home.'

Spending a whole day with Stella when she should have been with Milo was the last thing Alice wanted to do but how else was she going to stop her sister from becoming overly suspicious? She just had to hope that Stella would soon grow bored of spending time with her and would run back to the villa, allowing Alice to return to see Milo.

Alice was all too aware of the passing of time. She wasn't going to be on Kethos for much longer and she wanted to spend as much time as possible with Milo. She'd never met anyone like him and, although they'd only spent a few hours together, she felt as if they had a real connection.

The two sisters left their villa just after noon which was ridiculously early by Stella's standards.

'This had better be good,' Stella said, looking up and down the road as they left the villa. It was the first time she'd set foot outside the gates since they'd arrived.

'Of course it will be good. Kethos Town is beautiful,' Alice said.

'Well, I don't really care if it's beautiful or not. Are there any decent shops?'

'I don't think there are that many shops,' Alice said, 'but I'm sure there'll be lots to do.'

'Lots to do *without* shops?' Stella said incredulously.

It was then that the young lad on the bicycle from the day before passed them and, just as he'd done previously, he did a double take.

'Honestly!' Stella said in mock aggravation. 'He's *way* too young to be eyeing up somebody like me!' She flicked her blonde hair over her shoulder and her gait developed an exaggerated swing. Alice rolled her eyes. This was going to be a very long day.

Alice had been right about the number of shops in Kethos Town. There were a few that catered purely for the tourists, selling swimming costumes, suntan lotion, hats and postcards, but there was one little boutique that looked promising and Stella spotted it straight away. It was at the far end of the harbour and, to get to it, they had to walk by the row of men fishing along the harbour wall.

At first, Alice didn't think anything of it but, as each one turned round, their fishing forgotten as their eyes focused solely on Alice, she began to realise that something was wrong although she really did try to believe that it was Stella they were all looking at. That's what Stella obviously thought too because a coquettish smile suddenly filled her face and she sucked in her tummy and thrust her chest forward.

The boutique was tiny but packed with promising clothing from cool blues to vibrant oranges. There was colour everywhere and Alice instantly felt dowdy in her cream blouse and brown skirt. Why hadn't she ever noticed how plain she looked? Well, she had, of course, but it had never bothered her enough to do anything about it but – suddenly – here and now – she wanted to change everything about the way she dressed. She wanted to be bright and colourful – like a butterfly rather than a moth. She wanted fabric to whisper over her body rather than submerge it. In short, she wanted to be beautiful.

She caught sight of her reflection in one of the shop's mirrors and noticed the definite sparkle in her eyes. *Now* was the time. Now was the time to change.

'What do you think?' Stella asked Alice as she held up a beautiful violet-coloured dress.

For a split second, Alice was tempted to tell her what she really thought – that Stella was thoroughly spoilt and didn't need to buy another item of clothing for at least ten years – but she held her tongue and nodded instead.

'It's lovely,' she told her.

'Hmmmmm,' Stella said, pulling a face. 'I don't know.' She twirled the dress around on its hanger and then placed it back on the rail and Alice's hands flew towards it.

'What are you doing?' Stella asked.

'I might try it on,' Alice said.

Stella looked dumfounded. 'Are you sure it's your kind of thing?'

'Stella – you're always complaining that I look dowdy and that my clothes are never right. So aren't you the least bit pleased that I'm showing an interest now?'

Stella looked far from pleased as Alice took the dress and headed towards the changing room. Maybe it was because she'd never had to fear Alice as a rival before; she'd grown used to having all the attention for herself.

Alice smiled to herself as she disrobed and put the dress on. It looked gorgeous and she felt beautiful wearing it. She drew back the changing room curtain and stepped out for Stella to inspect her.

'What do you think?' she dared to ask.

For a brief second, Stella looked stunned but then she shook her head. 'It's not you,' she said.

'I know,' Alice said. 'But it could be.'

'Put it back. It's just *wrong*.'

Alice flinched and hesitated for a moment and then something awful happened – the new Alice was vanquished by the old one and she put the dress back.

'I'm going to get this one,' Stella announced, reaching for a glitzy gold gown that skimmed the knees and revealed plenty of cleavage. She didn't even try it on. It wouldn't matter if it didn't fit or didn't suit her. It would just go to the back of the wardrobe and be replaced by a dozen other new dresses.

They left the shop half an hour later with three carrier bags full of new things for Stella. Alice was carrying two of them and wondering how on earth her sister was going to fit the new clothes into her already stuffed-to-the-brim suitcase. But Stella's addiction to new clothes wasn't what was bothering Alice as she took a surreptitious look at her watch. It was lunchtime and Stella was showing no signs of the boredom which Alice had been counting on. She was never going to get to the Villa Argenti at this rate, was she?

'I'm hungry,' Stella declared.

Alice nodded and they entered a small taverna and chose a table overlooking the harbour.

'I don't think I like Greek food,' Stella said as she gave the menu the once-over.

'Just try some. It's fresh and wonderful. You can't spend all week eating cereal bars,' Alice said.

'I don't see why not. At least you know what's in them.'

'Yes, sugar and additives and all sorts of horrors,' Alice said.

'Oh, don't start, Alice! You can be such a bore.'

The waiter came over and Alice gave him their order in her broken Greek. He smiled at her.

'You are English?' he asked. He was in his late fifties but he still had a twinkle in his eyes.

'Yes,' Alice said, 'and my Greek is not very good.'

'Ah! It is excellent!' he said. 'And you are a very beautiful woman – if you don't mind me saying!'

He turned to leave and Alice could feel herself blushing.

'What was all that about?' Stella said. 'He didn't even notice *me*!'

'No,' Alice said, taking a sip of water from the glass on the table.

When the food arrived, Stella poked at it with a reluctant knife. 'It's not fish, is it?' she asked.

'No, it's not fish,' Alice said, knowing that Stella wouldn't touch it if she knew what it really was.

'Because I don't want to eat anything from the sea.'

'We're on an island, Stella. Ninety per cent of the food is going to be from the sea.' Alice watched as Stella took a forkful of food to her mouth and chewed. She was the only person Alice knew who could chew with her nose all screwed up.

'Do you like it?' Alice asked.

'I'm not sure,' Stella said as she took another mouthful.

Alice grinned. It was actually fried *kalamarakia* – squid. It was something Milo said she couldn't possibly leave Kethos without trying and it really was rather delicious if you didn't think too much about legs and tentacles and such.

They managed to get through another course of Greek food without Stella throwing too much of a strop and then Alice paid which was only fair, Stella pointed out because, of course, she *was* getting a free holiday.

They took a walk along the harbour wall. The sea was a dark sapphire and there was a cool breeze coming from it that had Alice reaching for a trusty cardigan from her handbag.

'Oh, Alice! You're *not* going to wear that, are you?' Stella said.

'Why not? It's chilly,' Alice said as they turned into a winding alleyway that was so narrow, they had to walk one behind the other.

'It's absolutely hideous,' Stella said, pulling at a lumpy grey sleeve. 'Just look at it.'

'I'll have to get a new one,' Alice said, shaking her sister's hand from her and walking briskly ahead.

'Yes, and I know exactly what you'll buy – a *new* grey one!'

'Look!' Alice stopped so suddenly that Stella crashed right into her. 'You're not happy when I wear my old clothes and you're not happy when I try on new ones either! Make up your mind, Stella!'

Stella's mouth dropped open at the outburst but she didn't get time to say anything because Alice had marched onwards. They spent the next couple of hours drifting around the backstreets. Alice admired the simple beauty of the architecture and took photos whilst Stella complained about her shoes and examined her burgeoning blisters.

It was the middle of the afternoon when they entered a tiny square surrounded by pretty white houses with shutters and doors open to the sunshine. In the far right corner were four workmen who were cutting lengths of wood, their sleeves rolled up. As soon as Alice and Stella entered the square, they downed tools and just stood staring. At first, Stella smiled. She always assumed that all male attention was directed at her but, as Alice walked ahead, it became obvious whom they were looking at.

'Oh my God!' Stella exclaimed. 'They're looking at *you!*'

'What?' Alice turned around.

'Those men – they're all staring at you! What are you doing?'

'What do you mean, what am I doing? I'm just walking.'

'Well, you must be doing *something!*' Stella grabbed her by the shoulders and stared at her face before scanning her up and down.

'Stella – I'm not doing *anything!*'

'Greek men are weird! They must go for dowdy women or something,' Stella shouted after her as she walked away.

They left the little square and walked up a flight of steps which wound their way up a hill, finally coming out at a walkway which overlooked the whole of Kethos Town.

Alice put the shopping bags down at her feet and gazed out at the view before them. 'It's so beautiful,' she said. 'Isn't it beautiful?'

Stella gave a great yawn.

'You look tired,' Alice said, trying not to look at her watch.

'I'm *exhausted!*' Stella said. 'You know, I think we should get back to the villa and catch a few rays before evening.'

Alice nodded. 'Good idea.'

'Come on, then.'

'Oh, I thought you meant *you*.'

'Who else is going to carry my bags? I can't manage on my own,' Stella said, her face suddenly very long and pitiful.

'Of *course* you can,' Alice said. 'Anyway, I want to stay in town a bit longer.'

Stella didn't look happy. 'There's something wrong with you, Alice.'

'What do you mean?'

'I mean, you're not right. You're up to something and I don't like it.'

'I have absolutely no idea what you're talking about,' Alice said. 'I'm not up to anything. Now, stop worrying and go home.' She picked up the two carrier bags she'd been in charge of and handed them to a shocked Stella. 'I'll see you later.'

Her sister made a huge show of struggling with her three bags and Alice shook her head, waiting until she was completely out of sight with no possibility of her returning. She then ran all the way back to the little boutique and bought the violet dress that she'd tried on that morning. She also bought a dress in cream, threaded with gold and even treated herself to a new handbag that was dainty and pretty and then she ran towards the bus stop.

She couldn't remember what time the last bus left but, when she got to the stop, she saw that she was too late. The last bus had gone and wouldn't have got her to the Villa Argenti in time anyway so Alice ran to the one place in town where she knew she could find a taxi.

The driver was absurdly careful on the mountain roads and Alice was desperate to tell him to take a few more chances and put his foot down. He also spent more time staring at her in the rear-view mirror than he did looking at the road, which was most unnerving.

She kept looking at her watch. They weren't going to make it, were they? She'd told Milo she'd be there and she hadn't shown up. What was he going to think of her?

Finally, they took the turn to the villa but, when they reached the end of the long driveway, Alice saw that the gates were closed. Milo had gone home for the day and she didn't even know where that home was.

Chapter 14

Milo had started the day with a spring in his step. He'd dropped Tiana off at school and kissed her smartly on the forehead even though he knew she hated such displays in front of all her friends but, this morning, he couldn't help himself and she didn't seem to mind.

'You're going to see her again today, aren't you?' Tiana asked.

'I might,' he told her.

Tiana had laughed and he'd definitely seen a little spring in her step too as she'd walked into the playground.

He'd driven to work that morning like a little comet tearing around the mountain roads, startling the local goats, the image of Alice constantly before him. He'd never been so excited in his life. What was happening? Why was she so different? He'd had plenty of girlfriends in the past but he'd never felt like this before.

He'd maintained his sense of excitement and anticipation for a number of hours too, rushing through his jobs around the garden with unusual alacrity. He normally took his time over things – luxuriating in each little task that brought him into contact with his beloved plants and flowers but his mind was in a different place today.

What was he going to say to her when she arrived? He'd been so calm and confident with her on the beach yesterday but, with each passing hour, he was becoming a nervous wreck. What if he became tongue-tied and ruined his chances? He shook his head.

'Stop worrying!' he said to the middle of a large geranium. 'You'll be fine.'

But the spring in his step had soon turned into a heavy plod and he felt as if his boots were great boulders upon his feet as the day dragged on with no sight of Alice. That's when his imagination had started to torment him. Maybe she was with somebody else today – skinny-dipping on another beach with another man. Or she'd taken a boat trip with one of the millionaires who occasionally moored their yachts in the harbour and preyed on pretty tourists.

Milo had never checked his watch so much in his life. He didn't need to, of course, because he could tell the time accurately from the position of the sun and the shadows in the garden, but he couldn't relax. He didn't dare leave the main paths around the garden for fear of Alice missing him if she did show up and he kept stopping what he was doing so he could look out for her, finding endless reasons to walk to the entrance gate whenever the bus from Kethos Town was due.

Finally, he stopped. She wasn't coming, was she? What he'd *thought* had happened on the beach the day before and what had *actually* happened weren't the same thing at all. He'd thought there'd been something between them but perhaps there hadn't been anything more than a little light flirtation.

What was he going to tell Tiana? She would be poised for news of his day and what did he have to tell her? That her big brother was a loser when it came to love?

Then, to make the day even worse, Sabine turned up. She had climbed a tree and hopped over a wall, scraping her knee on the way down and expecting him to clean her up.

'You're not a child any more,' he told her, as he cleaned the dirt away with dampened cotton wool.

'But you always treat me like a child,' she told him.

He'd walked into that one, hadn't he? 'You shouldn't be climbing over walls at your age,' he went on. 'It's not proper. It's not ladylike. Besides, the main gate is open.'

'But I wanted to fly over the wall like Romeo in *Romeo and Juliet*,' she said with a romantic sigh.

Milo rolled his eyes.

'You weren't here yesterday, were you?' Sabine went on.

'No, I wasn't,' Milo said bluntly.

'Where were you?'

'It's none of your business.'

Sabine pouted. 'Why won't you tell me?'

Milo sighed. What was it with all these questions? First Tiana and now Sabine. Couldn't a man enjoy a little privacy when it came to his love life?

Love life! He scoffed at the thought. He was getting a bit ahead of himself imagining that he had a love life to look forward to with Alice. One date had obviously been more than enough as far as she was concerned.

But what if it had all been some terrible misunderstanding? Or what if something had happened to Alice to prevent her from coming to the villa that day? What if she'd had some terrible accident, and here he was thinking the very worst of her when she was, in fact, lying in a hospital bed somewhere. He had to find out. He had to know the truth even if the truth was that she just didn't like him.

He had to find Alice before she left Kethos.

Alice knew that she had to get to the Villa Argenti as quickly as possible the next day and try to explain to Milo what had happened. What must he be thinking of her? She felt awful that she hadn't been able to keep her word. What if he thought she just didn't want to come? Perhaps he had forgotten her already and moved on to the next pretty young tourist to enter the garden.

She'd got up early the next morning with every intention of leaving for the first bus out of Kethos Town but Stella had soon put a stop to that. Alice had gone into her bedroom to let her know she was going out and had been met with the loudest of groans.

'I don't feel well,' Stella's voice complained.

'What's the matter?'

'I've got a headache.'

Alice grimaced. Stella had found a bottle of ouzo in one of the kitchen cupboards and had enjoyed rather a lot of it the night before with only a cereal bar to accompany it. She was obviously paying the price for it now.

'Take some aspirin and have something to eat,' Alice told her.

'Will you get some for me?'

'Don't you have any?'

Stella shook her head and winced at the movement. 'I thought you'd bring some.'

'Well, I don't have any.'

'Get me some!' the voice begged.

'That'll mean a trip into town.'

Alice's shoulders slumped in resignation, leaving the villa, and practically running into town. She was going to miss the first bus to the Villa Argenti, that was for sure, and she'd probably be a dishevelled mess by the time she walked into town for the second time but that couldn't be helped.

Alice found some aspirin at a little chemist and bought two packets and then headed straight back to the villa. She didn't see the boy on the bicycle with the neck-breaking double take this time but she walked by an old man who stared at her so hard that Alice actually stopped.

'Are you all right?' she asked.

He said something to her in Greek, his eyes misty with emotion, and then he shook his head and went on his way. Alice watched him go for a moment, wondering what he'd said. Maybe he didn't like tourists.

When she arrived back at the villa, she noticed that the French doors had been left open and she could hear voices out beside the pool.

'Stella?' she called. She could hear her sister laughing and she obviously had company.

'I'm by the pool with a friend of yours!' Stella called back.

'Milo?' Alice said as she walked out onto the terrace and

saw him sitting on the edge of a sun lounger next to her sister.

'Alice – you *are* a sly one!' Stella said, springing up from her sun lounger. Her tone was mocking but Alice could see that she was fuming inside. 'You didn't tell me you'd made friends with a handsome local.'

'I thought you had a headache,' Alice said.

'Oh, that's gone!' Stella said, waving the proffered aspirins away in irritation. 'Now, I've just been getting to know the gorgeous Milo here and he said you two spent a whole day together and you didn't go to any boring museum at all. Isn't that funny?'

'Hilarious,' Alice said.

'Yes,' Stella continued. 'He said you spent the whole day on a beach and it wasn't a stony beach and the water wasn't cold either.'

'Er – look!' Milo said, standing up. 'I didn't mean to get Alice into trouble. There's been some misunderstanding, that's all. Perhaps I should leave.'

'No – don't go!' the two sisters said in unison.

Milo halted and Alice walked up to him and placed a hand on his arm. 'I was coming to see you.'

'You were?'

'Of course I was!' she said. 'Look, shall we go somewhere we can talk?'

Milo glanced across at Stella who was standing with her hands on her hips and a frown on her face.

'Yes,' Milo said. 'Let's get out of here.'

'Where are you going?' Stella cried.

'Maybe back to the beach,' Milo said with a little grin.

'Can't I come?'

'No,' Alice said. 'I think you should take some aspirin and go back to bed.'

'There's only room for two on my bike anyway,' Milo said kindly. 'Perhaps another time.'

'When? *When* another time?' Stella asked.

'Goodbye, Stella,' Alice said and they left quickly before Stella got it into her head to follow them.

'I'm sorry about that,' Alice said. 'She can be a bit full-on sometimes. I hope she didn't make things awkward for you.'

'Awkward?'

'Yes – she's a bit of a flirt, I'm afraid.'

'Ah, yes,' Milo said. 'She was skinny-dipping in the pool before you got back.'

Alice's face fell. 'Oh my God!'

Milo laughed. 'I'm joking!' he said. 'It's only her sister who skinny-dips on a first date.'

Alice blushed.

They reached his moped outside the gate of the villa. 'You don't mind me coming here? I had to find you again.'

'How *did* you find me?' Alice asked.

'Kethos is a small island. I asked a few friends.' He smiled but his smile soon turned into a frown. 'You *are* glad I found you, aren't you?'

'Of *course* I am!' Alice said. 'I didn't know what to do. I couldn't get away to the villa yesterday. Stella insisted that I spent the day with her.'

'And I can see she can be very—' he paused, 'demanding.'

'Yes, she can.'

He nodded. 'And you are too good to her. I think she takes advantage of that.'

'I think you're right.'

They looked at each other for a moment and then Milo smiled and Stella was instantly banished from Alice's mind.

'Today, I want to show you *every*thing, Alice!' he said excitedly.

'But shouldn't you be at work?'

'Ah!' He waved a hand in the air as if dismissing the thought. 'My boss is away and someone is covering for me.'

'What if he comes back early?'

'I'll tell him I had to spend a day with a beautiful girl. I'm sure he'd understand,' Milo said with a wink. 'A beautiful day and a beautiful girl – what man could resist?'

Alice laughed and gazed up at the clear blue sky. 'Well, it's certainly a beautiful day. Don't you ever have clouds here?'

'Clouds?' Milo said. 'What are clouds?'

'In the sky,' Alice said, pointing. 'Huge, white or grey fluffy things that block out the sun—'

Milo laughed. 'I know what clouds are!' he said. 'And we do have them, of course, but not as often as you do in England.'

'We seem to have them all the time,' Alice said, thinking about the lead-grey sky she'd left behind and how much she was dreading returning.

'But not here and not today.'

'So, what are we going to do?' Alice asked as he handed her a helmet.

'The question is, what are we *not* going to do?'

She giggled and got on the back of the bike, placing her hands round his waist.

125

Chapter 15

My smile couldn't possibly get any bigger, Alice thought, as they tore around the island roads on Milo's moped. Sitting on the back of a moped with a handsome man on a glorious island was so *un*-Alice-like. Something like that was far more likely to happen to Stella. *But this is happening to me*, she said to herself, clinging on to Milo as they took a sharp bend round a mountain and then descended towards a sea the colour of bluebells.

'That's Kintos,' Milo shouted back a moment later and Alice spotted a tiny town, its coloured buildings all jostling together, seemingly tumbling towards the blue water. She was instantly in love. There was a tiny white church with a blue domed roof and the road they followed dipped and curved, passing houses with shutters wide open to drink in the sunshine.

Milo took the bike down into the centre of the town and parked it outside a little row of shops. They were more modest-looking than the ones in Kethos but Alice adored them.

'This is one of my favourite little towns,' Milo said. 'If you can't bear the bustle of Kethos Town then you come here. Not many tourists make it to this side of the island, which is its blessing and its curse.'

'Why is it a curse?' Alice asked.

'Well, it's quiet which is nice but the shops struggle to stay open.'

'I guess it's hard to make a living on an island.'

Milo nodded. 'So many people leave each year. It's a shame when you have to leave a home that you love just to make a living.'

'Well, let's make sure that I'm a very well-behaved tourist,' Alice said.

Milo watched as Alice proceeded to go from shop to shop, buying postcards and guidebooks. She even bought a little stone statue of Aphrodite. Alice had noticed that Aphrodite's image was everywhere – her beautiful face gracing a thousand postcards and picture frames.

Ever since she'd found out she was going to Kethos, she'd wanted to read all about Aphrodite and the legends that tied her to the island and now she bought as many different trinkets as she could find depicting the goddess of love, from a keyring to a pendant.

Milo laughed at her. 'You are Aphrodite-crazy!' he said. 'I'll have to take you to see her temple in the south of the island.'

'I'd love that,' Alice said.

There was one last shop in the little row which was selling exquisite rugs and blankets.

'All from the local sheep,' Milo said. 'It's the softest wool in the world.'

Alice smiled. She was sure it was just Milo's island pride speaking but, when she reached out and touched it, she realised he was right and she soon spotted a beautiful woollen blanket with a great red rose at its centre. Her fingers danced over its softness and she knew she had to have it.

'Let me buy it for you,' Milo said.

'Oh, I couldn't.'

'Please,' he said. 'It is my gift to you so you will always remember Kethos.'

She watched as he took the blanket to the shop assistant and it was neatly folded and wrapped and placed in a secure bag so its journey back to England would be as comfortable as possible.

'Thank you so much, Milo,' she said as he handed her the bag. 'I don't deserve such kindness.'

He shook his head. 'Of course you do and it is my way of thanking you for coming to my island.'

She leaned forward and kissed his cheek and then blushed at her forwardness. 'I'm sorry,' she said.

'Don't be sorry,' he whispered to her and then they left the shop together. 'The rose is the flower of Aphrodite, you know? Perhaps that was why you liked it.'

'The rose is a symbol of love in our country too,' she said and then felt her cheeks flood with colour again. He'd bought her something with the emblem of a rose on it. A blanket might not be as romantic a gesture as a bunch of roses but it would last forever and Alice would treasure it always.

'Now,' Milo said, clapping his hands together, 'I show you something very special. He's why a few of the tourists visit us here.'

'He?'

'Come with me,' he said, leading the way down to the far

side of the seafront, past a row of fishing boats. There was a taverna and Alice could see a little crowd of people and could hear the sound of laughter. What was going on? Perhaps it was a street performer. But no, it wasn't. It was a pelican.

'His name's Pelagios,' Milo said. 'It means *from the sea* and he's a bit of a celebrity around here.'

Alice had never met a pelican before and marvelled at its happy white squatness and its enormous yellow beak which she was quite sure could devour a dozen tourists. He strutted up and down the harbour as if he owned the place, his great bulk giving him the appearance of a portly gentleman.

One of the shops was selling fish and Pelagios was getting his fill of them, his flat upper mandible opening wide, allowing the throat pouch, which was baggy and flabby, to be filled with fish. He then seemed to pause before tipping his great head back whilst the food found its way down his throat.

'He knows where he's looked after,' Milo said. 'We often come here and feed him.'

'We?' Alice said.

'I mean, when I was growing up. My family,' he said.

'He's amazing!' Alice said. 'We don't have anything like him in Norfolk. Just a few ducks on the village pond.'

Pelagios seemed to know that he was being talked about and turned his round yellow eyes on Alice, staring at her as if trying to ascertain if she had anything to donate to the beak fund.

'Is he quite safe?' Alice asked as the big bird waddled towards her.

'He's very friendly,' Milo said and then his eyes widened

as the pelican walked right up to Alice and stretched his long neck up towards her before sitting down at her feet and then something bizarre happened. His great throat pouch started to vibrate.

'Oh!' Alice cried as she watched the strange scene before her. 'What's he doing?'

'I don't know,' Milo said. 'I've never seen anything like it in my life but I think he likes you!'

The locals were all laughing but Alice didn't dare move for fear of scaring the bird. A little old lady pointed at Alice and said something in Greek before cackling like a witch, her eyes streaming with tears.

'What did she say?' Alice asked Milo.

'She said Pelagios has chosen you as his mate.'

'Oh my God! What shall I do?' Alice was rigid now and quite unable to move.

Milo leaned forward and took her hand. 'Don't move too quickly,' he said.

Alice walked slowly away with him but the pelican got up and waddled after her, his throat pouch still vibrating alarmingly fast. 'He's following us,' Alice whispered in alarm.

'He's following *you!*' Milo said. 'You have an admirer!'

'It's not funny!' she said.

'Just keep moving,' Milo said.

Luckily for Alice, the pelican soon got distracted by a child who had bought a helping of fish and they made their escape.

'Are you okay?' Milo asked once they were at a safe distance from the amorous pelican.

'I think so!' Alice said, taking a deep breath.

'I think we need a drink,' Milo said with a laugh.

They were just walking along the old harbour wall when a dark-eyed man stepped out of a shop in front of them and grabbed hold of Alice's arm. He stared at her and then he started talking to her in Greek.

'I'm sorry but I'm English,' Alice said. 'I don't understand you.'

Milo – whose face had darkened with anger – stepped in and his tone of voice was unlike anything Alice had heard before.

'It's all right,' he said a moment later when the man walked away. 'He's got the message.'

'What did he say?'

'He wanted to know if you'd marry him.'

'*Marry* him?' Alice said in surprise. These Greek men certainly didn't waste any time. 'And what did you say to him?'

'I told him you were my sister and that you were married with six children.'

'Right,' Alice said, watching as the dark-eyed man turned back and gave her a pleading look, his hands open in a gesture which seemed to ask whether the husband and six children really mattered.

'What is it about you?' Milo asked once the dark-eyed man decided to give up.

'What do you mean?' Alice asked.

'I mean with the pelican and then that man?'

'I don't understand.'

'I mean, you seem to attract all this attention – *all* the time.'

'Oh, rubbish!' Alice said.

131

'No, it's not rubbish. I've been watching you. Wherever we go, the men just seem to want to look at you. *Be* with you.'

Alice shook her head. 'You're imagining things.'

'No, I'm not,' Milo said and his tone was more serious now.

'I'm not the kind of woman to attract attention like that. You've got it all wrong.'

Milo stopped for a moment and Alice turned back to look at him. 'There's something amazing about you,' he said.

'There isn't. There really isn't.' She took a deep breath. 'Look,' she said, 'I feel uncomfortable when you talk like this. Do you mind if we change the subject?'

Milo looked at her and then nodded. 'Come on,' he said, placing a protective arm around her shoulder. 'Let's get something to eat. I know the perfect place.'

He led them to a little taverna where they ate a mountain of fresh salad followed by *spanakopitta* which was spinach, feta cheese, spring onion and dill sandwiched between filo pastry and baked in the oven. It was the loveliest thing Alice had ever eaten.

After lunch, they got back on the moped and Milo drove up into the mountains to the south of the island, following a little road that gradually narrowed into almost nothing at all. The landscape was rocky and barren and the drop at the side of the road was precipitous.

Milo stopped the bike when the road ran out and Alice got off, taking her helmet off and luxuriating in the feel of the cool mountain air against her face.

'This way,' Milo said, leading her down a dusty track. There was a sudden dip and then the landscape opened out to reveal the ruins of an old temple. There were a few rickety columns, a crumbling wall and some kind of altar but it was the view that was really startling because you could see the whole of the island.

'You can see the whole heart!' Alice said, tracing the island's outline with her finger.

'We can't compete with the Parthenon but it's pretty amazing,' Milo said.

'What is this place?'

'It's the temple of Aphrodite,' he said. 'It's over two thousand years old.'

'What a shame it's not used any more,' Alice said, trailing her fingers across one of the fluted columns.

'Who says it isn't used anymore?'

'But it's all in ruins,' she said.

'The islanders still come here to worship Aphrodite,' Milo said in a voice which was low and reverential.

'They do?'

'Oh, yes,' he said. 'It's a sacred place.' He took her hand in his and led her towards the altar. 'They say that if you make love here, you will be bound together for all eternity.'

Alice's heart started racing and she felt as if she was being heated up by a great internal furnace. 'They really say that?'

Milo nodded and took a step towards her so that their bodies met. 'Bound together forever.'

Alice closed her eyes and, when she felt Milo's lips upon hers, she didn't protest but kissed him right back and she was quite sure that the spirit of Aphrodite was smiling down over them.

Chapter 16

The lights were on in the villa by the time Alice got back.

'Hello!' she called as she closed the door behind her.

'You've been gone for *hours!*' Stella said, emerging from the living room.

'I did say I was going out.'

'I bring you on this holiday and I hardly see you!' Stella cried.

'But you never seem to enjoy my company when we are together,' Alice pointed out as kindly as she could.

'That's not the point. I'd rather have *your* company than be totally bored out of my head.'

Alice winced, knowing that that wasn't a compliment.

'Anyway,' Stella continued, 'it's not fair that you're running around with some man and I'm stuck here on my own. Just what do you know about this man, anyway? He could be anybody.'

'He isn't just anybody. He's Milo Galani and he's lived on Kethos all his life.'

'And that's *all* you know?'

'At the moment, that's all I need to know,' Alice said, taking off her shoes and putting her carrier bag down on the floor.

'What's that?' Stella asked.

'Just a blanket.'

'Did he buy it for you?'

'It was a gift, yes.'

'God, Alice, you're so naïve. He's just some cheap holiday lothario. How do you know he doesn't charm every single tourist who crosses his path?'

'Does it matter if he does?' Alice said.

'Don't *you* think it does?'

'Look,' Alice said with a sigh, 'I hardly ever get to have fun – you know that – you're always pointing it out to me. But Milo is a really sweet guy and I know this can't go any further than a holiday romance so can't you just let me enjoy it whilst it lasts?'

She left Stella standing in the hallway, charging up the stairs to the privacy of her bedroom and closing the door behind her. That hadn't been true, had it? The bit about not going any further than a holiday romance. Alice knew in her heart of hearts that she didn't want it to end. It was so much more than a holiday romance to her and she couldn't bear the thought of going back to her old life in England at the end of the week.

Leaning against the door, she closed her eyes and thought of Milo. They'd made love at the temple of Aphrodite and it had been wonderful. Milo had been both tender and passionate with her and they'd slept in a warm embrace together afterwards.

But, as much as Alice hated to admit it, Stella did have a point. Just how much did she know about Milo? What if he was just some guy who seduced every tourist who came his way? She hadn't let it worry her until now but today had got pretty intense between them with the looks they'd exchanged and the moments they'd shared. She was really beginning to develop feelings for him. But just who was he?

As soon as Milo had dropped Alice off, he reached inside his jacket pocket for his phone and discovered that it had gone flat. He cursed. He wanted to let Hanna know that he was running late but that he was on his way for Tiana. Hanna was pretty easygoing and Tiana always loved being there and he was sure it would be okay but, all the same, he hated being late. He'd just have to make up as much time as he could on the way there.

He knew he should have charged his phone up before he left home but he'd been so anxious to find out if Alice was all right that he hadn't had the time. He smiled as he thought about their day together. He'd been so relieved to have found her and she'd seemed happy to see him too, hadn't she? He hadn't been imagining it this time, he felt that for certain. And then, at the temple…

He gave a long, low whistle. He mustn't think about such things when he was on his moped – it was far too dangerous. Yet, he couldn't get the image of Alice out of his mind. Her deep blue eyes, the softness of her skin and the way the breeze had caught her hair. She had been so beautiful and yet she was always denying the fact that she was. Did she not see it herself? When she smiled, the whole world seemed to light up. He wasn't the only one to notice it either, he thought, as he remembered the outspoken dark-eyed man in Kintos.

'And the pelican,' he said, laughing to himself at the memory. No, Alice was the most beautiful woman he'd ever seen because she made him feel the sort of happiness he had only ever imagined was possible.

When he arrived at Hanna's, a young woman answered the door.

'Is Hanna there?' he asked, surprised to see a stranger in the house.

The young woman shook her head. 'Are you Milo?'

'Yes,' Milo said, immediately on alert.

'Hanna is sick. She's in bed. I'm looking after her.'

'And Tiana? Where's Tiana?' He was trying to keep his voice under control.

'My husband took her home.'

'What? *When?*'

The woman shrugged and Milo wanted to shake her by the shoulders at her casualness. 'Two hours ago? Maybe three. I don't know. We tried to ring you but there was no answer.'

'My phone was flat,' he said. 'Look, I've got to get home. Give Hanna my love, okay? Tell her I'll call tomorrow, won't you?'

Milo leapt onto his moped and drove at almost twice the speed he normally did, taking the corners way too fast, but he had to get home as quickly as possible. Tiana had been left alone, he thought. She'd been taken home by a strange man and left in the house on her own.

Common sense told him that she would be all right. She was a sensible, mature girl, but what if something had gone wrong? She was still a child, after all, and accidents happened.

What if she'd tried to cook something and had burnt herself? What if she'd gone swimming alone and had drowned? Or what if she'd fallen over and knocked herself out? The image of Tiana in a thousand different positions of danger assaulted Milo's mind as he rode home and, even though he was going much faster than usual, time seemed to be slowing down and the journey seemed never-ending.

Finally, he was home but there was something else to worry about because there, outside their house, was his brother's car.

He cursed to himself.

'Tiana?' he cried as he ran into the house but he was immediately stopped by the bulk of his brother, Georgio, who filled the doorframe of the kitchen and glared at Milo.

'So, you're back at last.'

'Where's Tiana?' Milo cried.

'In her bedroom with Sonya,' Georgio said, his face dark and thunderous.

'Is she okay?'

'Yes, no thanks to you.'

Milo raked a hand through his hair. Of all the times for his brother to show up.

'My phone went flat and Hanna fell ill and somebody brought Tiana home before I got a chance to find out,' Milo explained, knowing it was going to do him no good at all.

'Hanna's an old woman,' his brother said with a glare. 'She shouldn't be looking after a young girl.'

'Hanna is a perfectly capable woman who's raised more children than anyone else on Kethos.'

'Well, she shouldn't be looking after them now,' Georgio said.

'Milo!' Tiana's voice suddenly screamed and she ran into the kitchen to hug her brother. 'Hanna got sick and this man brought me home in his old van that made a funny chugging noise every time we went round a corner.'

Milo's eyes widened in horror at the expression on his brother's face. It was like pouring petrol onto an already roaring fire.

'Imagine what we thought, finding her here on her own,' Georgio said. 'Anything could have happened to her!'

'I was okay, Milo. I didn't break anything,' Tiana said just as Sonya appeared at the door.

'Milo,' Sonya said and he knew that that was the beginning and the ending of the niceties. 'We were so worried. We got here and Tiana was all on her own!'

'I know,' he said. 'It's never happened before but my mobile went flat and Hanna–'

'It's unforgiveable,' Sonya said, moving towards Tiana and wrapping her arms around the child's shoulders. Tiana squirmed in an attempt to get away but the grip was vicelike. 'I can't believe how irresponsible you are. Just imagine if something had happened to her.'

'Nothing happened to her!' Milo said.

'Absolutely *nothing* happened to me,' Tiana echoed.

'This can't go on,' Georgio said. 'This is *exactly* the sort of thing we've been worried about, isn't it, Sonya?'

Sonya nodded.

'Tiana,' Milo said, 'why don't you go through to your bedroom and make sure it's nice and tidy?'

For once, Tiana didn't argue. It was as good an excuse as any to get away from Sonya and she took it without hesitation.

'This is just bad timing,' Milo said, as soon as Tiana was out of earshot. He knew how lame he sounded but it was the only excuse he had.

'Bad *timing*?' Georgio snapped. 'It's just *bad*.'

Milo tried not to grind his teeth in anger. His brother had always had the ability to make him feel about six years old. 'Why couldn't you turn up at any other time when we're both sat in the kitchen having dinner together – a dinner made from fresh ingredients – put together by us? Or turn up when I'm helping her with her homework or cleaning a cut when she's fallen out of a tree.'

'What?' Sonya all but screamed.

Milo winced. Maybe it hadn't been such a great idea to mention that. 'My point is, I'm here for her. I'm here for her when she's stuck on her homework or if somebody at school has upset her and she's crying. I'm here for her when she's got a temperature or a tummy bug or is too tired to walk to bed and needs to be carried. I'm here for her when she wants to go into town for girly things or if she's outgrown a pair of shoes.'

'But you weren't here for her today,' his brother said.

Milo took a deep breath. That's all that counted in his brother's eyes, wasn't it?

'Look, this is not the time to talk about it,' Milo said.

'Then when is?' his brother asked.

'I don't know what you expect me to say to that,' Milo said.

'We *need* to talk about this, Milo. We can't keep putting it off.'

140

Milo shook his head. 'It can wait – if there really is anything to talk about at all.'

'*If?*' his brother hissed. 'This can't go on. Just look at the life you lead!'

'What do you mean?'

'Out till late with God only knows who.'

'It's not late and tonight was a bit out of the ordinary, anyway.'

'A young man like you shouldn't be raising a girl. It's just not right,' Georgio went on.

'She's my sister – why isn't it right? I can't think of anything *more* right.'

'Because you're not settled. What kind of a life can you hope to give her? Your lifestyle, your job, a different woman every week—'

'That's not true!' Milo shouted, his voice fuelled by anger.

'I just think you should reconsider things,' Georgio said. 'I think we all made a mistake when we left Tiana here with you. Everything got so confusing after Mama died and we all thought it was best that she stayed here – in the home that she knew – but she should have been with us – right from the beginning. I think we can all see that now. For a start, Sonya and I have two salaries coming in. We can provide a stable environment for the girl.'

'But we agreed, Georgio – she's happiest here. She doesn't need two salaries – she *needs* to be here.'

'Well, we don't see that any more,' Georgio went on. 'Sonya and I have been talking.'

'Talking?' Milo said, his voice laced with sarcasm.

'*More* than talking,' Sonya interjected.

Georgio nodded. 'Nobody's saying you haven't done a great job with Tiana. We all know that you're far more responsible than many your age.'

Milo gave an affronted laugh.

'But it's time, Milo. We all know it.'

'Do we?' he said.

'Yes,' Georgio said. 'It's time to put Tiana first.'

Chapter 17

The next morning, Tiana's little head was barely visible above her duvet when Milo went into her bedroom to wake her up. He drew back the blush-pink curtains and light streamed into the room, bouncing off the oval mirror and lighting up the pop stars in the posters on the walls whose names Milo could never remember.

'Tiana?' he called softly. 'Wake up! It's time to get up for breakfast.' There was a light groan followed by a sob and Milo was by her side in an instant. 'Sweetheart? Are you okay?' He pushed her dark hair away from her face and felt her forehead. It was certainly warm but was it something to be concerned with? 'Don't you feel well?'

This time, a little squeak left her. 'Tummy hurts.'

'Okay,' he said. 'You rest there, my love.' He drew the curtains, plunging the room back into darkness. She must have caught the bug that Hanna had, he thought, which meant he wouldn't be able to go to work that day.

Leaving the bedroom, he made a call to his colleague, Lander, to let him know that he wouldn't be in and then something occurred to him.

Alice!

She was going to meet him in the gardens and now he

wasn't going to be there. Could he trust Lander to say that he was unable to make it in to work but *not* to reveal the reason why?

He rang Lander back and did his best to explain but his colleague merely laughed at the subterfuge.

'You'll be found out!' he said and Milo knew that he was probably right.

There had been rain in the night and the gardens at the Villa Argenti were scented with a thousand perfumes from the plants, flowers and the earth itself. Everything looked newly washed and fresh, replenished from the life-giving rain. Alice had read that Kethos didn't get much rain and she expected that Milo welcomed every single drop of it to keep his garden beautiful and lush. Of course, there was an irrigation system in place and the millionaire owner had probably fixed it so that his grass was never anything other than emerald, but nothing could compare with the sweetness of rain.

Alice inhaled deeply as she walked down the main path. At first, she didn't worry about the fact that she couldn't find Milo. She just thought he'd be pottering around somewhere in the depths of the grounds and had every belief that their paths would cross sooner or later. Indeed, the excitement of turning each corner and emerging from behind each tree in the knowledge that she might then see him heightened her senses and added to the anticipation of seeing him again.

What would they say to each other? Maybe they wouldn't say anything at all. Maybe he would greet her with a kiss. Alice tried to imagine it and felt quite weak doing so but she was quickly awakened from her delicious daydream by the sight of a man approaching her. He looked barely out of his teens and he was looking intently at Alice.

'Hello?' she volunteered.

'Are you Aleeeece?' the man said.

'Yes,' she said.

'I have to say that – er – Milo isn't here.'

'Oh,' Alice said.

'He say sorry.'

'Okay,' Alice said. 'Will he be here tomorrow?'

'I do not know,' the man said.

'I see.' She bit her lip. She would have to come back again tomorrow. That was the only thing she could do but what a waste of a beautiful day. They had so few of them left now. 'He's all right, isn't he?' she asked the man.

'All right?'

'Yes – he isn't ill, is he?'

The man shrugged which Alice thought was a strange response but perhaps his English just wasn't that good.

'You are a very beautiful woman,' the young man suddenly said. 'Your eyes – your hair—'

Alice shook her head. It was happening again. 'I have to go,' she said, and she made a hasty retreat to the exit.

'You're back early,' Stella said from behind her sunglasses. Alice sat on the edge of the lounger next to her but didn't answer. 'He stood you up, didn't he?'

'He wasn't there,' Alice said and her voice sounded horribly woebegone.

145

'He stood you up,' Stella repeated matter-of-factly.

'He couldn't get in to work. It isn't the same thing.'

'So what was his excuse?' Stella asked, putting her magazine down and placing her hands on her hips which looked funny on somebody sprawled out on a sun lounger.

'He didn't leave an excuse,' Alice said.

'He's married,' Stella said and Alice visibly flinched at the word. Stella saw and smiled. 'He's married *and* he's got six children.'

Alice blinked in astonishment. Wasn't that *exactly* what Milo had told the dark-eyed man in Kintos about her as a joke – that she was married with six children? Maybe he'd been thinking about his own situation.

'You do talk some rubbish,' Alice said, standing up.

'Oh, really?' Stella said, lowering her glasses and squinting at Alice. 'So where is he, then? Why didn't he leave a proper message for you? Why didn't he call here?'

Alice had already wondered that. He'd called round before. Couldn't he have found time to do so again? What was so important that he couldn't have let her know what was going on? He knew that she'd be going home soon.

'The day after tomorrow,' she said to herself.

'What?' Stella asked.

'Nothing,' Alice said, walking back into the villa. She closed the French doors behind her and slumped down on one of the sofas. She felt deflated and defeated. What was happening with Milo? His colleague had been vague and uneasy when she'd asked him if Milo was ill. *Was* he ill? Was it serious? Alice wanted to know. And, if he wasn't ill, what was going on?

She had to find out and, if Milo had been able to find out where she was staying by just asking a few questions, surely she could find him by doing the same?

Tiana had been sick twice and had then slept for the rest of the morning and right into the afternoon. Milo had contacted Dr Papadis who lived at the bottom of the hill. He was retired but was always happy to help anybody out if he could. He'd taken Tiana's temperature and pulse rate and listened to her heart and had said that there was no cause for alarm.

'She is young and strong and it is only a tummy bug. It's going around at the moment.'

Milo had sighed in relief, thankful that it was nothing more serious.

'Lots of fluids, lots of sleep and let her rest for a couple of days until it is out of her system.'

That was the rub, Milo thought. He'd have to take more time off work. It was a good job his boss was away and Lander could cover for him, but what was he going to do about Alice?

Milo couldn't help thinking that his brother and Sonya should have shown up at that moment. A sick child in bed for two or three days might have put them off quickly enough but he couldn't help acknowledging that he could use some help – just someone to babysit for a couple of hours whilst he went to see Alice. But that would be admitting to Georgio and Sonya that he couldn't cope on his own with Tiana and he'd be leaving himself wide open for them to step in, and he wasn't about to do that.

But what on earth must Alice be thinking about him? This was the worst possible scenario – him unable to see her the day after they'd made love. What if she was thinking he had used her and didn't really care about her at all but was quite able to brush her off with a simple excuse about not being able to see her again? His guts churned in dismay at the thought but what could he do? He couldn't leave Tiana even for a moment and, the truth was, he didn't want to. She came first even if he was falling in love with this woman from England.

This, he thought, was what his life was going to be like for the next few years. Tiana was still only ten years old and his responsibility was to her. He really shouldn't be thinking about his own life – especially not something as self-indulgent as a love life – that much was clear now.

Later that afternoon, after wearing the old table top in the kitchen thin with the drumming of his fingers, he tiptoed back into Tiana's room.

'Are you feeling any better?' he asked, stroking her hair and realising that her head was still hot. 'Do you want anything to eat?'

She shook her head and buried it further into the pillow.

'Give me a call if you need me,' he said. 'Okay?'

He returned to the kitchen which was fast feeling like a prison. How could he get in touch with Alice?

Forget her, a little voice said. *She's leaving anyway. Nothing's going to come of it.*

But, as much as he knew that was true, he wanted to see her again. He didn't want things to end like this with so much left unsaid. He wanted to say goodbye. He wanted to *kiss* her goodbye.

'Milo?' Tiana's little voice broke into his thoughts and he was back in her bedroom in an instant.

'Yes, my sweetheart?' he said, sitting on the edge of her bed and squeezing the tiny shoulder that was protruding from the bedclothes.

'I got scared. I didn't know where you were.'

'I'm right here, sweetheart,' Milo said. 'I'm right here and I'm not going anywhere.'

Chapter 18

Alice didn't want to leave the villa for the rest of the day because she sincerely believed that Milo would call and explain everything and she didn't want to miss him when he arrived. Of course, that meant spending the rest of the day with Stella, but the villa was big enough for the two of them and Alice was determined to remain positive.

Something must have happened to him, she kept thinking over and over again. Maybe there'd been some emergency at home like the washing machine had exploded or his moped had broken down. There might be any number of explanations for him not to be able to leave her a message and explain things properly.

'If only I could think of one really good one,' she said to herself.

As the day wore on, she thought again of her idea to try and find Milo. If he wasn't going to come to her, why shouldn't she try to find him? Maybe he'd done something simple like twisted his ankle or broken his wrist and couldn't ride his moped either to work or to see her. Perhaps he was sitting on the island somewhere, hoping and praying that she'd make an effort to find him.

With this thought whirling through her brain, she left the

villa, shouting a quick goodbye to Stella. She decided it was probably best that she didn't ask about Milo at the Villa Argenti for fear of them being put on stalker alert, and Milo's colleague didn't seem to know much anyway and there had been that slight problem of him coming on to her. What was it with the men on Kethos she wondered? She'd never had this effect on men back home in England.

Putting thoughts of flirtatious Greek men out of her head, she walked into town. She'd got to the harbour before she'd worked out what she was going to do but fifty-five minutes later, a little bus dropped her off at the town of Kintos.

Pelagios was there, waddling along the harbour front and Alice ducked her head for fear of being spotted by him. Now was not the time for an amorous encounter with a pelican.

Ignoring the lure of the pretty shops, she went into the little taverna where she had shared a meal with Milo and walked boldly up to the counter. The man who had served them immediately recognized her and a huge smile bisected his face.

'Ah!' he said. 'The beautiful English girl!'

Alice bit her lip. She was alone and no longer had the protection of Milo when it came to overly-romantic men, but what choice did she have if she wanted to find him?

'Hello,' she said politely. 'I was here yesterday.'

'Yes, yes!' he said nodding enthusiastically. 'And you came back today! This is good news indeed. It means you like me, yes?'

'No!' Alice said quickly. A little too quickly, perhaps, judging by the look of dismay on his face. 'I mean, I came here hoping you could help me. I was with a young man – remember?'

151

'Oh,' he said. '*Him!* I remember. But I do not think he was right for you. He was – too young. *Much* too young! You need an older man. A man with – how you say – *experience!*'

Alice shook her head vehemently. 'But I need to find him. It's important. His name's Milo Galani and I don't know where he lives. I was hoping you might be able to help.'

'You want to know where he lives?'

Alice nodded. 'Please help me. I'll do anything.' It was the wrong thing to say because the man's face immediately lit up and he crossed to Alice's side of the counter in record time and grabbed her hands in his, kissing them fervently.

'Anything?' he said, his breath heavy and ragged and the colouring of his face rising alarmingly.

'Please let go of me!' Alice cried, trying to tug her hands away from him but his grip was too strong. 'I said – let *go!*' Before he could even think to respond to her protest, Alice's foot shot out and kicked him in the shin. It wasn't a terribly hard kick but it was enough to startle him into submission, giving Alice time to flee the taverna and bolt into a little shop further along the harbour.

Her heart was racing wildly and there were tears in her eyes. This was not turning out the way she'd imagined. All she wanted to do was find Milo but how could she do that when nobody would even listen to her?

'Hello?' a voice suddenly called from behind her. Alice turned around and came face to face with a woman in her thirties with long dark hair and a kind smile. 'You are English?' she asked.

'Yes,' Alice said. 'And you speak English?'

'Not so good,' the woman said with a little smile.

'But better than my Greek,' Alice replied. 'Can you help me?'

The woman nodded. 'I try.'

Alice told the woman about Milo – how they'd met and how she needed to find him but didn't know where he lived. The woman listened quietly, nodding occasionally and then, when Alice stopped, she shook her index finger excitedly.

'You need to speak to Alexandros,' she said.

'Who's he?'

'The postman. If your Milo lives near here, Alexandros will know.'

'Of *course!* I should have thought of that!' Alice said excitedly. 'Thank you so much.' She leaned forward and hugged the young woman who giggled like a child.

Leaving the shop and following the directions the woman had given her, Alice soon found the little cafe which Alexandros regularly patronised and, sure enough, there he was, sitting in a pool of sunshine with a glass of something tall and cool in his right hand. He looked ancient. At least ninety, Alice thought, although that couldn't be right if he was still working. Maybe his job had exposed him to every hour of sunshine on Kethos and his skin was paying the price for it.

She suddenly felt nervous as she rooted around in her handbag for a pen and a piece of paper. She'd been warned that Alexandros didn't speak any English but he nodded when she showed him her piece of paper with Milo's name on it and watched as he took her pen from her and proceeded to doodle a little map on the back of it, chattering away in Greek and motioning with his hands.

Finally, he gave her the piece of paper and Alice thanked him. She was just walking away when he called out to her, motioning to his drink and nodding towards her with a great fat smile on his ancient face. Alice shook her head as politely as she could and fled the scene.

The little bus that left the town of Kintos fifteen minutes later was even smaller and rattlier than the other two buses she'd experienced on the island but she didn't mind. *As long as it takes me to Milo*, she told herself, looking out of the window and then down at the doodle that Alexandros had made for her and recognising the bend in the road and the little church that he had drawn. Hers was the next stop just outside a small village at the bottom of a hill.

When Alice got off the bus, she was immediately aware of the silence. Kethos Town and Kintos had been full of cheering noise but this place was different. This, she felt, was the real Kethos – the Kethos that Milo adored – and she could see why. Few tourists would make it to this part of the island. There were no shops here, no monuments and no tavernas. There were barely any locals either, judging by the size of the village, but the place held a magical aura with its tiny white houses and uninterrupted view of the sea.

Looking down at her map once more, she followed the road up the hill, passing a small herd of goats, their little bells tinkling merrily. The house, according to the postman, was just around the next bend. He'd marked it with a large cross as if treasure might be buried there and Alice certainly hoped that he was right.

A nervous hand flew to her hair which she did her best to flatten, fearing that it had gone flyaway in the warm breeze. Before leaving the villa, she had changed into the violet dress that she'd bought in the little boutique in Kethos Town and, for once in her life, she didn't feel overdressed. She felt as if she was wearing exactly the right thing.

Turning the corner, she saw the tiny white home that the postman had indicated was there and saw Milo almost immediately but some instinct told her not to call out. He had his back to her and she looked lovingly at the dark curls of his hair.

She watched for a moment. He was carrying a large basket which he put on the ground and she smiled as she saw him take out two stripey shirts, placing them on the washing line. But her expression changed a moment later when he picked up a tiny dress and pegged it onto the line.

It was the dress of a little girl.

Chapter 19

Alice walked away as quickly as she could, disappearing around the bend in the road before Milo had a chance to spot her. There were so many thoughts skydiving in her head but the one that wouldn't let go was perhaps the silliest.

I've been skinny-dipping with a married man!

She stopped for a moment and closed her eyes in horror. She wasn't the sort of woman to do such a thing and it filled her with dismay that Milo had put her in that position. What sort of a man would do that? But she knew what sort – the good-looking, charming sort of man who knew he could get any woman he wanted under any circumstances and she had gone and fallen for him.

Or maybe he wasn't married at all, she thought. That was a definite possibility but one thing was certain – he was a family man. She hadn't bothered to stay and see if he had the washing of six children to hang out but any number of children meant that he had lied to her. He had hidden the truth in order to get his own way and that was unforgivable.

She walked on towards the village but didn't stop to wait for the bus. It wasn't due for another hour and she was so mad that she couldn't bear to wait for it and so began the long walk back to Kintos.

The road was quiet and her bare legs were soon covered in a fine layer of dust but she didn't notice. She kept wondering if she should have confronted Milo. Maybe she should have heard his explanation but what was there to hear? That he was sorry? Would he be? Or would he turn on her and ask her what her problem was – saying that she had got exactly what she'd wanted? Somehow, she couldn't believe that Milo would do that but she really didn't know what to believe any more. Here she was thinking that he was one person – a sweet-natured man who had such a very great appetite for life – but she really didn't know him at all, did she? And he'd been hiding this whole other life from her all the time.

For a moment, she tried to think back to the conversations they'd had. He'd been a little vague about his family, it had to be said, but she hadn't thought anything of it. Just because she'd volunteered so much information about herself, it didn't follow that he'd want to divulge anything about his own life but, now, she wished she'd probed a little bit more. She felt like such a fool and, what was even worse, was that it meant that Stella had been right. Alice had been naïve and Milo had taken complete advantage of that.

By the time she got back to the villa, she had cried all the tears that she was going to allow herself to cry and she was determined to put it all behind her. What did it matter anyway? What had she thought was going to happen at the end of the week? Whatever had passed between them was going to have to wrap itself up in some shape or form before she got on the plane to go home. That was the nature of holiday romances, wasn't it? She was just going to have to accept it and the sooner the better.

Stella was in the living room when Alice walked in and immediately pounced upon her.

'Where did you go? Did you find him? Was I right?'

Alice had been thinking about what she was going to tell her all the way back. If she said she hadn't found him, Stella would be speculating all evening and, if she said that she had then she'd never hear the end of it about Stella being right. She took a deep breath.

'You were right,' she said, deciding to get it over and done with and let her sister have her moment of glory.

'I told you!' Stella said, a great smug grin on her face. 'I just knew it – the minute I saw him.'

'No, you didn't,' Alice said but she really didn't have the energy to argue.

'I can always tell a married man when I see one. I've dated enough, remember?'

'I remember,' Alice said.

'So, what did you say to him? I hope you gave him a piece of your mind!'

'I don't want to talk about it,' Alice said, knowing her sister would have wanted tales of slapped faces and punched noses at the very least.

'Oh,' Stella said, disappointment etching her face. 'Well, you can't say you weren't warned, can you? It was your own fault.'

My own fault for falling in love, Alice thought to herself. That was harsh. She shook her head. Anyway, she hadn't been in love. It was ludicrous to think that was possible in such a short space of time. Love took time. It wasn't something you could just create with a smile and a naked swim in the sea. It took friendship and trust and she'd had neither of those things with Milo, she could see that now.

'I'm going to have a shower,' she told Stella and she walked up the stairs to her bedroom.

'I told you, didn't I?' the taunting voice of Stella followed her until she shut her bedroom door.

The next morning, Milo was stirring a pan of porridge in the kitchen when Tiana walked in, thin and fragile in her nightgown. She'd been sick in the night but had then slept right through.

'Hey!' he said. 'You okay?'

She nodded and sat down at the breakfast table. He poured her a glass of mineral water and noticed that she was still pale but that her eyes looked a little brighter.

'Here,' he said a minute later, spooning some porridge into her favourite pink and blue bowl and swirling some honey onto it, 'eat this. It'll warm you up and put cherries in your cheeks.'

She smiled. 'Are you going to see your new friend today? The English lady?'

'No,' Milo said. 'I'm staying here with you.'

Tiana took a dainty mouthful of porridge, decided that it tasted very good and dug her spoon deeper for a bigger portion. 'But she's leaving today, isn't she?'

Milo nodded. 'Yes.'

'And this is the last chance you'll get to see her?'

'It is.'

Suddenly, Tiana dropped her spoon to the table with a clatter and there were tears in her eyes. 'I've ruined it for you. I've ruined your time with her by getting sick!'

'No!' Milo said, taking her hands and squeezing them in his.

'But I have!' she said and a fat tear dropped onto the wooden table.

'Look,' Milo said, pulling out a chair and sitting down next to her, 'I don't think it would have worked out anyway.'

'Because of me,' Tiana whispered.

'No, not because of you,' Milo said.

'Then why?'

Milo sighed. He didn't want to lie to Tiana but he didn't want to tell her the truth either. She was right when she'd said it wouldn't work out because of her but he wasn't going to admit that.

'Just because—' he paused, wondering what he was going to say, 'she's English. She has to go home.'

'But she could make *this* her home!' Tiana said.

Milo smiled. 'Sweetheart, we hardly know each other.'

'But you like her, don't you?'

Milo closed his eyes. He'd been doing his utmost to put Alice out of his mind for the sake of his little sister and here she was putting her right back there again.

'I like her, yes!' he said at last.

'Then you *have* to see her,' Tiana said.

Milo shook his head. 'But I'm not leaving you.'

'But I feel better!' she said. '*Much* better!'

'I don't care. I'm still not leaving you.'

'But it's all right. I've been on my own before and I was fine,' she said.

'But that was a mistake. That shouldn't have happened and it's not going to happen again,' he said.

Tiana leaned across the table and took her brother's hands in hers. Milo stifled a laugh because the action mirrored his of a moment ago perfectly and he was touched by it. 'You've got to see her – *please!*'

He frowned. He felt as if he was being tested – as if Georgio and Sonya had planted a secret camera in the house and were recording his every move, seeing if he would fall into this trap of leaving Tiana on her own.

'Tiana – I *can't.*'

'You *have* to!' she begged him. '*Please!*'

He took a deep breath. What was he doing? If Georgio and Sonya turned up now they'd have an absolute field day, yet he so wanted to see Alice again and explain things. *Really* explain things. He shouldn't have tried to hide his life from her but he wasn't going to leave Tiana – not for anyone.

'We have to let her go, Tiana,' he said at last. 'It just isn't–'

'I can go with you!' Tiana suddenly burst out.

'What?'

'I can go with you so you don't have to leave me here on my own!'

'Tiana – you're as fragile as a butterfly right now.'

'But I only have to sit on the bike and hold on to you and I've done that *hundreds* of times.'

Milo felt his heartbeat accelerate at the idea. He could take Tiana with him and explain everything to Alice. She'd have to understand then, wouldn't she, and it would mean he would have Tiana with him and wouldn't have to leave her alone in the house. This could really work.

'Get dressed,' he said.

There was a mad flurry of activity as the two of them prepared to leave the house. Milo grabbed hold of Tiana's shoulders a moment later and examined her.

'Put your coat on,' he told her.

'But it's too warm!' she protested.

'*Coat!*' he said, and she ran back to her room to find it. 'And don't run!' he yelled after her.

Two minutes later, they were both on the moped and heading down the hill.

'Go faster, Milo!' Tiana shouted from behind him.

He shook his head. As much as he wanted to speed along as fast as the little bike could, he wasn't taking any chances today.

'Are you okay?' he called back to her. 'Not feeling sick?'

She squeezed him in response and he carried on, passing through the little villages that lined the road until they reached the outskirts of Kethos Town.

Suddenly, he felt nervous. Was he doing the right thing? He'd been blinded by the certainty that telling Alice the truth was the best way forward but what if she had other ideas? What if it was the very last thing she wanted to know about him? What if she ran a mile?

He groaned. Of course she was going to run a mile. She

was going to run approximately fifteen hundred of them, wasn't she? So what difference would it make anyway?

He turned into the road that led up the hill away from Kethos Town and soon the villa was in sight. He pulled up alongside it. The gate was closed but that was nothing unusual. They both hopped off the bike and Milo led the way, opening the gate and marching round the side of the villa, hoping and praying that Alice would be sitting out by the pool but she wasn't. He peered into the French doors but there was nobody around.

'Have they gone?' Tiana asked, pressing her nose up against the glass and shading her eyes so she could see inside.

Milo turned to look at her. 'They must have gone for the first ferry. I think we're too late.'

'What time does the ferry go?' Tiana asked. They stared at one another for a moment and then they both raced back to the moped. This time, Milo sped down the hill into Kethos Town, hoping that Tiana could cope with the speed. What time did the ferry go? It was half past the hour, wasn't it? He glanced at his watch. It was nine twenty-six. They weren't going to make it, were they?

Reaching town, he cursed as they met a delivery van that was blocking the one-way system. Milo tooted but the driver just gesticulated to him and refused to budge.

'Hold on!' he told Tiana, doing a mad three-point turn and revving back up the hill, dodging an oncoming bike whose rider swore loudly at him. Tiana giggled and clung on tighter.

With a few nifty manoeuvres, Milo negotiated his way through the traffic-laden streets towards the harbour, hoping that he was in time and that the little ferry wouldn't have left yet but, as they got their first glimpse of the harbour, he saw that they were too late. The little ferry – perhaps for once in its life – had left bang on time and was already leaving a beautiful white wake behind it as it headed across the sea towards the mainland.

Milo felt the heavy weight of Tiana's head against his back and he knew that there would be tears in her eyes but what surprised him most of all were the tears that were filling his own.

Chapter 20

Alice dared to look down at the tiny island once they were airborne. It was a little cloudy and she remembered her conversation with Milo about how there were never any clouds over Kethos. *But there are today*, she thought, gazing out of the window past Stella's shoulder and noting how the wispy whiteness of them blocked part of the island's famous heart shape.

A broken heart, she thought.

She leaned back in her seat and closed her eyes, blocking out the last view of the island. She didn't want to see it any more. Like Milo, it was part of her past but, even though she'd told herself that a hundred times since seeing him the day before, she had still looked out for him as they'd left the villa, wondering if he would suddenly turn up on his little moped with an amazingly simple excuse for everything and, as she'd boarded the ferry, her eyes had dared to scan the streets of Kethos Town.

Stella had noticed and had shaken her head. 'You're still pining after him, aren't you? Well, he's not coming. He's probably making baby number seven with his wife right now.'

Her sister certainly knew how to twist the knife, Alice thought.

The journey home was unbearable. There was a crying baby on board the plane but even that wasn't making as much noise as Stella who found something to moan about at least every ten minutes. Alice kept her eyes resolutely shut and pretended she was asleep.

When she finally got home to her little cottage, she locked the door behind her and slumped into her favourite armchair by the empty fireplace, relishing the first moments of silence that she'd had to herself all day and cursing herself for having ever gone to Greece in the first place. She'd been foolish to have thought that a holiday with Stella would be anything other than torturous. She should have said no. She would have been better off taking a week off work and sitting in her favourite chair reading a big pile of novels.

As she pottered around the kitchen trying to find something to eat, her mind floated back to Kethos and she couldn't help wondering what Milo was doing. He was two hours ahead of her so he would probably have had dinner by now. Perhaps he was putting some of his many children to bed.

'I'm not going to think about him,' she said to herself. He probably wasn't thinking about her, was he? Not with six or seven children to see to.

After eating a rather dull pasta supper, Alice showered and went to bed. The unpacking could wait; all she wanted to do now was sleep and forget.

When she awoke the next morning, a coldness swept over her as she realised where she was. Home. She was no longer on the little Greek island with the promise of a day of sunshine and fun before her. She was on the outskirts of Norwich with a day of work ahead of her. Life was back to normal.

She got out of bed and began the usual ritual of getting ready to go to work, her body carrying her through the motions with little need for consultation with her brain. Reaching into her wardrobe, her hands automatically went for a white blouse, a dark skirt and a cardigan in a shade that purported to be 'dove' but was just a bog-standard grey. This was the true her, wasn't it? She couldn't wear turquoise or violet to the office. It just wasn't her. That other Alice had been nothing more than a dream but she had awoken now and had accepted a life that was far less colourful.

She'd just shut the front door when a familiar figure walked up the path. It was Wilfred the postman and he was looking flustered.

'Are you okay?' she said. 'You've gone quite pink!' She reached out a hand to touch his arm and he leapt in the air.

'Alice!' he said, breathing out her name in an alarming manner, his voice seeming to have lowered by at least an octave.

'Wilfred?'

'You're *wonderful*,' he said, his eyes scarily huge in his face as his postal bag dropped to the ground.

She frowned. What on earth had got into him this morning? 'Wilfred – you're scaring me! Do you want to sit down?'

'No,' he said. 'I feel I could *fly* when I'm with you, Alice! Why would I want to sit down?'

'I really think you should go home. You don't sound normal,' Alice said, genuinely concerned.

'That's right! I'm not normal because I've realised something for the first time in my life!'

'What?'

'That I'm in love!' he said, his pink face now practically glowing. 'And it's with you, Alice! *You!*'

'I've got to get to work,' Alice said quickly, perturbed by the strange behaviour of her normally dour postman.

'Don't leave me!' Wilfred said, grabbing hold of Alice's arm as she walked away. 'You can't leave me like this!'

'Wilfred – let *go* of me!' Alice tugged and her arm was free. 'Go home,' she told him. '*Please* go home!'

She shook her head as she walked away. What on earth had got into him? She had never seen him like that before. She glanced back quickly to make sure he wasn't following her but luckily he wasn't. He'd picked up his bag once again and was off on his round as if nothing out of the ordinary had happened.

Alice made her way to the bus stop. Bruce was standing there, half-hidden behind his newspaper as usual. He turned around to give Alice his usual nod but then something strange happened and he did a double take so fast that Alice felt sure his neck would snap.

'Hello, Alice!' he said.

She started. She hadn't been sure if he'd even known her name before because this was the first time he'd used it.

'God, you look great,' he said, shaking his head from side to side as if he didn't quite believe the image standing before him.

'Do I?' Alice asked.

'You look amazing. *Amazing!* What? I've never told you that before?' he asked.

'No, Bruce – you haven't.'

'Haven't I?' His eyebrows shot into his hairline and he looked genuinely appalled by this declaration. 'Well, you'll have to forgive me. You will, won't you?'

'Bruce – this is all very—'

'Alice! You must forgive me!' He dropped his newspaper to the ground and took hold of both of her hands in his, wringing them tightly. 'I couldn't live with myself if I thought I'd done you wrong.'

'But you haven't!' Alice assured him, eager to put a stop to all the nonsense.

He shook his head. 'I fear I must have done if I've never told you how wonderful and special you are to me.'

'What?'

'You must *know* that, mustn't you? I mean, a woman like you can't go through life without knowing the effect she has.'

'Bruce – I don't know what you're talking about.'

He took a step towards her and she instinctively backed away.

'Alice,' he said, his voice raspy and laced with intent.

Luckily, the bus arrived at that precise moment and Alice leapt onto it and sat next to an elderly woman, leaving no room for Bruce to pursue her further. Fifteen minutes later, she hopped off and lost herself in the crowds in the centre of Norwich, hurrying to work before she could be accosted by any more mad men.

What had got into Wilfred and Bruce that morning? Wilfred usually did nothing but moan about his aching joints and the woes of the world and Bruce never even noticed her so what was so different about this morning?

Reaching the office, Alice made a hasty retreat to the ladies' where she stood gazing at her reflection in the mirror above the sink. What was going on? She'd never got so much male attention in her life before but why now? It was more than the fact that she'd got a bit of a tan and a few highlights in her hair from the Greek sunshine, wasn't it?

Of course it is, a little voice said. *It's the wish.*

She shook her head. The idea was ludicrous. Besides, she didn't believe in wishes. She'd only made it because she'd been on holiday and it had been a bit of fun. It was nothing more than that. But what did you do if you didn't believe in wishes but they came true anyway? Alice really wasn't the kind of person to believe in such whimsy and yet she had placed her hand on the statue of Aphrodite and made that wish.

She thought back to the holiday and remembered the boy on the bicycle, the dark-haired man in Kintos, the babbling gentleman outside the villa and the waiter at the taverna. Even the pelican had been amorous.

'What did I *say?*' she asked her reflection. 'What were the words?'

She thought back to the moment she'd been standing in the garden, her hand touching Aphrodite's dress.

'I wanted men to notice me,' she said to herself at last. But the pelican wasn't a man, was it? Alice shook her head. Maybe Aphrodite had a sense of humour. The Greek gods were well-known for being mischievous, weren't they?

Alice left the sanctuary of the ladies' and made her way to her desk. Whichever way you looked at it, Aphrodite was just a statue – an inanimate object. She wasn't a goddess who

170

could grant wishes. She'd never even existed. She was a myth, a legend, a storybook heroine. Alice was just getting carried away. There was probably some perfectly logical explanation for the odd behaviour of Wilfred and Bruce. Maybe they'd had one too many the night before. Maybe their water had been contaminated. Or maybe it was just the fact that it was spring and they were exercising their masculinity.

Alice switched her computer on and prepared herself for the boredom that lay ahead. Actually, she was quite looking forward to a morning of routine jobs after the extraordinary behaviour of Wilfred and Bruce but, by lunchtime, She realised that there was something seriously wrong. Her inbox was jam-packed with emails and they weren't the normal kind of emails either. For a start, there were an alarming number from her boss.

The first one seemed normal enough:

Alice, I must talk to you.

It sounded a little ominous, perhaps, but it was in Larry's usual curt style.

The second one was a little more concerning:

I really must speak with you at your earliest convenience. It's very important.

What could be so important, she wondered? Was there a sudden vacancy they needed to advertise for? Had some vital piece of legislation been decided upon whilst she'd been away?

The third message followed hard upon the heels of the second one:

Alice – see me in interview room number one <u>now</u>.

She looked up from her desk. What was it with all the

171

emails? Larry usually just ordered her around from the comfort of his desk. She swallowed hard, left her desk and walked towards interview room number one.

The door was ajar and she stepped inside and there, standing by the window with his back to her, was Larry.

'Shut the door, Alice,' he said. She did as she was told. 'And sit down.'

'Goodness, I feel like I'm about to be fired,' she said as she sat down in the chair that was usually reserved for interviewees. 'You're not going to fire me, are you?' she joked but then saw the expression on his face. He looked deadly serious. 'Oh, dear! You are, aren't you?'

'*Fire* you?' he said. 'Are you kidding? I'm not going to fire you!'

Alice sighed in relief. 'You looked so serious. I thought I was in trouble!'

'It's nothing like that,' he said.

'What is it, then?' Alice asked, completely confused now. She watched as Larry paced the room for a moment, loosening his tie and smoothing a hand over his bald head. Finally, he came to a stop and placed his hands on the table between them, his shoulders slumped forward.

'I'm leaving my wife, Alice,' he said.

At first, Alice didn't know what to say. Even though she had been working alongside Larry for the last three years, they had rarely spoken about their private lives so this sudden declaration was quite shocking.

'Oh,' she said after a moment's silence. 'I'm sorry to hear that.' She really was too. She'd chatted with Monica Baxter at

172

a few office parties and she'd seemed like a sweet soul and they'd been married for absolutely ages. In fact, Alice was pretty sure that their twentieth anniversary was coming up. Hadn't Larry mentioned it just last month? Yes, she felt sure he had. He'd booked some fancy restaurant where you had to reserve a seat at least six months in advance. So what had happened?

'I must admit that it's come as a bit of a shock,' he continued.

Alice nodded, hoping that he wasn't going to confess that Monica had been having an affair or something. She really wouldn't know how to respond to something like that. She'd never talked to Larry before about anything more important than the photocopying.

She waited for him to say something else, wondering how long he would keep her. He obviously needed to talk to somebody and she couldn't help feeling sorry for him.

All of a sudden, he cleared his throat and sat down in the chair opposite her.

'What is it?' she dared to ask, seeing a strange look cross his face. Now she came to think of it, he did look rather flushed. He wasn't about to have a heart attack, was he?

'Alice,' he said. 'I'm leaving my wife.'

'Yes, you said.'

He frowned. 'You don't understand. I'm leaving my wife for you.'

For a moment, the words hung in the air between them and Alice wondered if she had heard him right.

'Pardon?' she asked.

173

'I'm leaving my wife for *you*,' he repeated.

'I don't understand what you mean,' Alice said with a nervous little smile.

'I mean, I'm in love with you, Alice, and I can't understand how I haven't noticed it before.' His forehead was ridged and furrowed as if he was in some sort of pain and his hands were reaching out towards her across the table like a pair of predators.

Alice automatically leapt up out of her chair. 'I can't listen to this,' she said, making a run for the door.

'No!' Larry yelled, springing up from his chair with the speed of a man half his age. He grabbed Alice's arm and spun her around. She tried to wriggle free but his grip was too firm.

'Larry!' she shouted. 'You're hurting me!'

He let go but placed a hand firmly on the door so that she couldn't escape. 'Listen to me, Alice. You mean the world to me and I have to be with you.'

'For goodness' sake – you're a married man!'

'Yes, but I'm married to the wrong woman.'

Alice shook her head. This couldn't be happening – it was just too surreal. 'You really need to think about what you're saying,' she told him as she looked desperately around the room for some hidden exit that she hadn't noticed before.

A strange sound left Larry – part groan, part howl. 'What have you done to me?'

'I haven't done anything!' Alice said, hopelessly.

'I didn't feel like this when I left home this morning. You must have *done* something, Alice!'

'What do you think I could possibly have done?'

He clutched his head like a bad actor. 'I've got to get out of here.' He opened the door and charged out into the corridor.

'Larry, where are you going?' Alice called, following him as fast as she could.

'I don't know,' he said, mopping his brow with an oversized handkerchief. 'Home.'

'You won't do anything stupid, will you?'

'You mean like leave my wife?' he cried, causing a few heads to pop up from behind their computers in the open-plan office.

Alice watched as he grabbed his briefcase from under his desk. 'We'll talk about this tomorrow,' he said, stopping briefly and giving her a strange woebegone look before leaving the department.

Alice stood dumbstruck. This was crazy. Larry Baxter had barely acknowledged her existence over the last few years and yet here he was professing his undying love for her and telling her that he was going to leave his wife.

She returned to her desk and sat down, her hands shaking visibly in her lap. It was the wish, wasn't it? First Wilfred, then Bruce and now Larry. It was too much to believe that it was a coincidence. She could see that now.

It was then that something else occurred to her.

'Milo.'

She'd thought she'd met the man of her dreams and that they'd genuinely fallen in love but it had only been the result of the wish, hadn't it? Sadness swelled her heart as she realised that, even if there hadn't been the obstacle of him being

175

married with an enormous family, he'd never really been in love with her anyway, had he?

Alice closed her eyes and sighed. Milo was in the past now and she had quite enough to deal with in the present.

'Oh, God!' she whispered. 'What am I going to do?'

Chapter 21

Alice spent a sleepless night tossing and turning in bed, her head full of the images that had assaulted her throughout the day: Wilfred's pink face, Bruce's haunting gaze and Larry's grabbing hands. They couldn't all be in love with her, could they? The idea was ludicrous. And then there'd been that strange incident as she'd walked past the playing fields on her way home from the village shop that evening. The local rugby team had been out practising and one of them had looked up and wolf-whistled at her. Alice had never been whistled at in her life and hadn't been able to keep a smile from her face at the compliment whether it was politically correct or not. But then something strange had happened as, one by one, the other team members had stopped what they were doing and turned to look at her.

'Hey!' one of them had shouted. 'Stop!'

'It's Alice,' another one had said. She wasn't sure who he was or how he knew her name but, as soon as the word had left his mouth, the whole field started chanting *Alice, Alice, Alice* until the air was quite full.

Alice had begun to run which had been a mistake because the rugby team had begun to run too and, if it hadn't been for the clumsy guy who had fallen over, and the two men who had started a fight, Alice would probably have been in the centre of a rugby scrum right now.

She shook her head as she remembered fleeing from the scene with her carrier bag of potatoes. Never before had she witnessed anything as bizarre.

As she lay in the dark of her bedroom, the sound of a fox calling from across the fields, she tried desperately to come up with a logical explanation for the events of the day but her mind always circled back to the same thing – the wish. The wish to be noticed by men – *really* noticed.

It was then that something occurred to her. If this was all real then surely she couldn't be the only one to have made a wish on the statue. Were there other people around the world who had made wishes that had come true?

She swung her legs out of bed and switched on the lamp, pulling on her dressing gown and running through to the spare bedroom where the computer was. She switched it on and waited for the screen to come to life. She wasn't really sure what she was looking for or if she would find any answers at all but surely she couldn't be the only one who had fallen under the strange spell of the Aphrodite statue.

Alice entered two things into the search engine: *Aphrodite* and *Villa Argenti* and, almost straightaway, discovered a forum that had been set up. She scrolled down the pages, reading the stories.

'I wished for true love and met my husband a week later. We've been married for five years now and have twin girls!'

Another one read:

'I asked the statue to help me win back my girlfriend and it worked! We're getting married next year.'

There were so many. There were wishes for holiday romances, wishes for marriage proposals and wishes just to be noticed by someone, and each of the wishes had come true. But was it all to do with wishes or was it only coincidence? The sceptic in Alice told her that only the positive outcomes had been documented here and that there were probably hundreds or thousands of people whose wishes hadn't been granted. How was she to know?

'And does it really matter anyway?' she said to herself.

The more she thought about it, the more she couldn't help wondering if she was completely mad for wanting to rid herself of all this male attention and for not taking full advantage of the situation she found herself in.

As she switched the computer off and saw her reflection in the dark screen, she smiled to herself. If she was going to be the centre of all this attention, shouldn't she just go along with it and enjoy it whilst it lasted? Having Larry Baxter trap you in an interview room might not be a dream scenario, and a hairy postman declaring his undying love to you might be a situation best avoided, but the experience with the handsome rugby team had been rather good fun and what would it be like if she suddenly caught the attention of somebody she really liked? What would happen the next time Ben Alexander walked into her department?

Alice returned to bed and couldn't help smiling at the thought of being able to seduce a handsome man. It was as if the spirit of Aphrodite was working its magic upon her.

* * *

When Alice walked into her department the next day, she caught Larry's eyes and saw his face flood with colour and he promptly made a big fuss about moving his chair to the other side of the desk so that he'd have his back to her, which suited Alice perfectly. She didn't want to be the constant recipient of his lustful looks all day. So, she was able to get on with things, only once having to ask his advice on something, which he managed to give without turning around.

It was just before one o'clock when Ben Alexander walked into the department. Alice was about to take her lunch break which consisted of a flat, homemade sandwich eaten on a lonely bench in the local park, so she was in no hurry whatsoever.

'Hello, Ben,' she said as he came level with her table. He was wearing a navy shirt which brought out the blue of his eyes and the dark red of his hair. 'Is there something I can help you with?'

At first, he didn't seem to notice her. There was nothing unusual in that, of course, and Alice tried not to take it personally but then he turned round and looked at her – *really* looked at her.

'Have you done something to your hair, Anna?' he asked, his head cocked to one side as he studied her.

'No,' she said, stroking it self-consciously. 'And my name's Alice,' she said, feeling confident enough to tell him that now.

'Pardon?'

'My name's Alice – not Anna,' she said with a little smile as if she was the one with the apology to offer.

'Really?' he said.

'I think so. At least it's been Alice for the last twenty-odd years.'

Ben's face seemed to fall. 'Why didn't you tell me before?'

She shrugged. 'It's not important,' she said, straightening the files that were sitting on her desk.

'Not important? But it's the *most* important thing in the world!' he said, moving towards her and instantly setting her pulse racing.

'It is?' she said.

'Yes!' he said earnestly, staring so deep into her eyes that she felt quite dizzy. 'Listen,' he said, 'I was just heading out for some lunch. Perhaps you'd like to join me?'

Alice's eyes doubled in size. 'Me?'

'Of *course* you!' Ben said with a little laugh.

Alice smiled and pushed the dusty folders to the back of her desk, grabbed her handbag and nodded before Ben had a chance to change his mind.

It was the strangest feeling in the world leaving the office with Ben Alexander. Alice swore that both the receptionists did double takes as the two of them swiped their security cards one after the other and shared a compartment in the revolving door, and Sara Fitzgerald from the finance department, who'd once been caught in a compromising position with Ben behind a Swiss Cheese plant at the office Christmas party, looked particularly cross when she saw them walking down the street together.

So, this was what it felt like to be one of the beautiful people, Alice thought, as they walked through the crowded streets of Norwich together, although she guessed that it was Ben people were noticing and not her. It really was very amusing to see the looks the women were giving him – little nods and whispers to one another as they saw him.

But he's with me, Alice thought to herself with a big smile.

'Come on,' he said, 'I want to show you my favourite haunt.'

They walked into the centre of town until they reached the colourful canopied market where Alice loved to lose herself whenever she needed to top up her kitchen supplies. She adored the bright displays of fruit and flowers and could never resist a quick peep at the book stalls too but, today, they marched right past and turned right down a tiny alley.

Wheeler's was a small establishment that sold very expensive health food and the tiniest cups of coffee Alice had ever seen, but it was a cut above your average eatery and had wonderful views across the deckchair-like canopies of the market. More importantly, she was there with Ben and he was paying her more attention than he'd ever put her way over the long years she'd been working under the same roof as him.

After ordering lunch, they chose a table by the window and sat down. Alice bit her lip and then smiled at him.

'Wow!' he said. 'I do love the way you do that.'

She giggled. If that was the reaction a smile got then what

would happen if she started to flirt with him for real she wondered? 'You're staring at me!' she said.

'I can't help it,' he said, tilting his head to one side. 'Smile again.'

'You're making me feel self-conscious,' she said.

'Well, you should be – conscious of how beautiful you are.' That made Alice smile and Ben laughed. 'There it is!' he said. 'Men would pay good money for that smile. They'd sail ships across oceans to see it!'

Alice rolled her eyes in mock annoyance but she was really lapping up every minute of praise that he was lavishing upon her.

'I bet you tell all the girls that,' she said, knowing full well that he'd dated half of the building society whilst the other half were just biding their time.

He shook his head. 'No,' he said, 'because they're nothing compared to you. *Nothing!*'

Alice laughed again. She knew these were dreadful clichés tumbling out of his mouth but there was such conviction in the way he said them that it was hard not to believe him and she did so want to. How many years had she spent gazing at him as he walked into her department, wondering what it would be like if he turned to look at her one day and smile? Now, here he was paying her all the attention she'd ever wanted and she couldn't believe it.

'There's something quite—' Ben paused, a serious expression on his face, 'quite radiant about you. It's as if you've swallowed a rainbow or something.'

Alice buried her head in her hands. 'Don't say such things!' she said.

'Why not?' he asked, crestfallen.

She looked up and saw how earnest he looked. 'It just sounds so fake,' she said.

'But I'm being honest, Alice. I just want you to know how special you are.'

'But I'm not.'

'You *are!*' he said, grabbing her hands across the table so that they were hovering precariously over her bowl of tomato and basil soup. 'I don't know what it is about you,' he continued, 'but you're different from everyone else.'

Alice swallowed hard. She didn't want to say that she was probably the only one woman in Norwich having had a wish granted from the goddess of love. 'Let's talk about something else,' she said.

'I can't think of a single subject other than you when you're sitting so close to me.'

'Try, Ben,' she said.

He took a deep breath and let go of her hands. 'Okay, then,' he said. 'What do you want to talk about?'

'Anything,' she said. 'I don't know a thing about you other than your job, of course.' That wasn't strictly true, Alice admitted to herself. She'd once looked in his file and knew that he'd studied Maths and Statistics at St John's College in Oxford and that he was a Cancer born on the cusp with Gemini which might account for his flirtatious nature.

'What do you want to know?' he asked, taking a bite out of his wholemeal roll.

'Anything you want to tell me.'

He took a sip of his coffee. 'I was born in London and

moved to Norfolk when I was eight. I've got a younger brother called James. He works as a teacher in a school in Ely. He's got three children and I adore them.' He grinned and Alice's heart warmed at the sight of it. 'I'd love to have kids,' he said. 'Hey! Maybe we can have some!'

'Ben!' Alice exclaimed.

'Yeah! I've always wanted a large family. Like *The Waltons*, you know?'

She laughed at his enthusiasm. 'I think it's a bit early to talk about children.'

'Don't you want children?' he asked.

'Yes,' Alice said, 'only not before we've ordered coffee.'

He smiled. 'Fair enough,' he said.

'Tell me about work,' she asked. 'Do you like it? You always seem happy at the office. Is it what you've always wanted to do?'

'Is it ever what we really want to do?' he said and he looked a little jaded. 'I mean, I can't remember thinking at school that I wanted to work in a building society. It's not the stuff of daydreams, is it?'

'No,' Alice said. 'It isn't.'

'I mean, don't get me wrong – it isn't as bad as some jobs. I know I bring in a pretty decent salary and there are plenty of perks and everything. I could be a lot worse off but—' he paused and his blue eyes looked wistful.

'What?'

'I just get restless sometimes,' he said.

Alice nodded in agreement.

'And I have to get away.'

Alice remembered seeing the postcards Ben had sent his department over the years from different corners of the globe from India to Fiji, New Zealand to Brazil.

'But I always end up coming back, don't I?' he said, popping a cherry tomato in his mouth. 'I know! We should run away together,' he suddenly said, his face lighting up with boyish enthusiasm. 'Just take off and never come back. Wouldn't that be brilliant? We could buy one of those old Volkswagen camper vans and drive and drive until the road runs out. What do you think?'

'What do I think?' Alice said, trying to look serious for a moment as she thought of taking off with Ben and spending whole days and nights with him, camping out under the stars and talking over baby names. 'I think you're completely mad – that's what I think.'

'Yeah!' he said. 'Mad about *you*.'

Alice blushed. She could have sat there all day listening to Ben but she caught sight of the clock above the till and realised that they were horribly late.

'We've got to go,' she said. 'Larry will kill me.'

'Not if I tell him you were with me doing some very important work.' They stood up and Ben took her hand.

This isn't real, Alice kept telling herself – the looks, the declarations and the hand-holding – they weren't *real*. But, as they walked through the centre of Norwich, passing Jarrold's on their way back to the office, Alice couldn't help but pretend that it was and it felt wonderful.

Chapter 22

It was strange, Milo thought. One week had gone by since Alice had left Kethos and the whole island seemed empty without her. How could one person make such a difference to your day-to-day existence when you hadn't even known they were alive two weeks before? It didn't make any sense to Milo and yet here he was feeling as if the gods were punishing him for having fallen in love. Maybe it was Aphrodite's fault. Maybe Alice had wished that he'd fall in love with her but then it would be unrequited. Perhaps Alice was some twisted soul who'd had her heart broken just before coming to Greece and had decided to wreak revenge on him.

He'd only seen Alice at the gardens twice but they weren't the same without her. Every corner he turned, he expected to see her. He could imagine her standing there under the dappled shade of a tree or sitting by the edge of one of the pools, trailing her long fingers in the cool water, her sweet smile playing about her face.

Every time he passed the statue of Aphrodite, he would glare at it.

'You're torturing me, aren't you? You are a cruel woman, Aphrodite,' he told her. His torture wouldn't end with him

187

leaving the villa gardens either. It would follow him home and torment him there too.

What does she think about you? a little voice would taunt. *You abandoned her without so much as a goodbye – that's what you did in her eyes. She hates you. She despises the beautiful Greek ground you walk on.*

'She's probably forgotten all about me,' he'd say to console himself but he hadn't forgotten about her, had he? He felt that he never would either.

If only I'd had a chance to explain, he said to himself. That didn't mean to say that Alice would have understood, though, did it? She might have slapped him in the face and told him he was a despicable liar and it would have served him right too but he couldn't help thinking that she would have forgiven him. It wasn't in her nature to hold grudges, was it? She was kind and understanding.

Or was she? How was he really to know? They'd had so little time together that it was totally possible that the sweet, kind girl had all been an act. She might have been playing some game with him and he might have just been a holiday fling. So why was he getting so worked up about her? He had to put her out of his mind because he'd probably never see her again. It was true that Kethos had its fair share of what Milo called 'Repeat Offenders' – holiday-makers who would come back year after year – but he doubted if Alice would return. If she'd been playing games with him then she wasn't likely to come back and, if she hadn't been – if she'd sincerely had feelings for him – she wouldn't return because he'd screwed things up good and proper.

Put it behind you, he told himself. *You have a life to lead – a good life – and you were perfectly happy before this girl from England arrived.* But he couldn't help but acknowledge the fact that everything seemed so drab and colourless now that she'd gone.

It had been a strange week, Alice thought. Ever since she'd arrived home from Greece, she'd felt like a different person – as if she'd slipped into the skin of somebody else completely. It was the wish, wasn't it? All the male attention she was receiving was having a strange effect on her. At first, it had been baffling and a little frightening but she had quickly learned to enjoy it and let it take her along for the ride. It had given her a strange kind of confidence that she had never known before. She was no longer Alice the Gooseberry, watching other people falling in love and enjoying the pleasures of life. She was a main player now and she was loving it.

What did it matter if it was all because of some wish and it wasn't real? She really didn't want to think about what would happen if the wish suddenly fizzled out and she went back to being plain old Alice whom men ignored, because she was having too much fun in the here and now.

Things with Ben were going so well. Since lunch at Wheeler's, they'd been out twice: once to the cinema to see a rather dreadful art house film called *The Thirteenth Rejection* about a struggling writer who commits suicide, and whose book then goes on to become a huge bestseller.

'I thought it was going to be inspiring,' Ben had said as they'd left the cinema and they'd both had to laugh about it.

The second date had been to a private view at a posh gallery in Tombland where Alice had almost got crushed to death and had had two different kinds of wine spilt down her dress.

'I'm so sorry!' Ben had said, ushering her out into the street. 'But you liked the paintings, right?'

Alice had stood there for a moment not quite knowing what to say. 'I'm not sure,' she said. 'I couldn't quite make out what they were paintings *of*.'

Ben nodded thoughtfully. 'Good point,' he said and the two of them had giggled all the way to the nearest pub.

He'd kissed her for the first time that night. He'd dropped her off at home and had walked her to her door and, under a sky packed full of stars, he'd bent forward and his lips had brushed hers.

'You're amazing,' he'd said.

As she'd closed the door behind him and listened to his car pulling away, she felt as if she was floating somewhere above the earthbound Alice. Life was suddenly very rosy. She even looked forward to going in to work, knowing that Ben would find the least excuse to come down to the department to see her.

But it's not real, the voice kept telling her. *It won't last.*

Alice shook her head in denial and did her best to put the little voice out of her mind.

With all the excitement of dating Ben, Alice had overlooked the fact that spring had arrived in her little corner of Norfolk and, leaving her house one day, she took a moment to enjoy it. There were primroses and daffodils everywhere and bright celandines glowed like gold along the banks. The air was lighter and sweeter and, although there were still weeks of frosty nights ahead, there was a real feeling that the bad weather was a distant memory.

So, Alice wasn't that surprised to see Wilfred the postman wearing shorts that morning but she made the mistake of acknowledging the fact.

'You're looking very spring-like, Wilfred,' she said innocently enough.

'Alice! I'm so pleased you noticed,' he gushed.

It was hard *not* to notice his great white knobbly knees when they were heading right towards you, Alice thought, but she didn't share that particular thought with him.

'It's a lovely day, isn't it?' she said, thinking it best to direct the conversation away from his knees.

'Every day's a lovely day when you're close by,' Wilfred said and his mailbag hit the ground with a thud. Alice gulped. 'Alice!' he said and, once again, his voice seemed to deepen so that it sounded as if it was coming up from somewhere south of his belly button. 'I have to tell you something.'

'Do you?' Alice said with a little whimper. 'Only I have to catch my bus.'

'But that won't be here for at least five minutes,' he said, 'and what I have to say can't wait a moment longer. Not a single moment!'

'Oh, dear,' Alice said, almost involuntarily.

'Although, I could fill all the hours of every day until I die telling you how much I adore you, but five minutes will have to do.'

For one dreadful moment, Alice thought he was going to go down on one knee right there in the middle of the lane but he merely grabbed her hand and started to kiss it.

'Wilfred!' she cried. 'Please stop!'

'I can't,' he said, slobbering on her hand some more. 'I have to show you how I feel.'

'Well, I wish you wouldn't. Somebody will see!'

'Let them see!' Wilfred said. 'I want the whole world to know how I feel about you!'

'Even Mrs Myhill?' Alice said as she saw a stern figure walking towards them with remarkable speed for a woman in her eighties.

'What are you now doin', Wilfred Cringle?' she asked, her Norfolk accent strong and her glare penetrating.

'I was just telling Alice how wonderful she is,' he explained, letting Alice's hand drop.

'Well, I don't know about that but I *do* know that you're late with my post,' she said, stabbing him in the shoulder with an angry finger.

'Oh, I am sorry, Mrs Myhill,' Wilfred said, seeming to recover himself. Alice seized the opportunity to escape round the corner out of sight and hurried along to the bus stop, silently praying that it was running on time and hadn't got stuck behind a combine harvester like the day before.

She'd almost forgotten about Bruce because he had been away for a couple of days but her heart sank when she saw him there and, as soon as he saw her, he looked totally thunderstruck as if he'd never seen her before in his life. Alice took a deep breath and prepared for the onslaught.

'How do you do it, Alice?' he asked, his face soft with adoration.

'I'm not doing anything, Bruce,' she said, knowing that no amount of deflection was going to stop him.

He laughed. 'And you're so witty too!'

'Really, I'm not,' Alice said as stone-faced as she could.

This time, Bruce bent double with laughter. 'Oh, Alice!' he said, mopping his eyes with an old-fashioned handkerchief. 'You are the limit! Nobody makes me laugh as much as you do!'

Alice frowned and Bruce laughed even more, pointing to her face whilst his own turned crimson with mirth. What was going on? Was this about being noticed by men, she wondered? Was it not all about looks, then? Perhaps she should have been more careful with her choice of words when she'd made the wish or maybe it was that wicked Aphrodite having a laugh again by making other people laugh at her.

The bus arrived just as Alice felt sure Bruce was about to rupture his spleen with so much hilarity and Alice sat next to a teenage girl and sighed with relief when Bruce had to move on down the aisle to the back.

What a way to start a morning, she thought, although she was getting rather used to it. If it wasn't for Ben, though, she really felt as if she would go mad but the thought of meeting him at lunchtime got her through the daily toil as well as coping with the deluge of unwanted male attention.

Larry Baxter was still skilfully avoiding all eye contact with Alice which had been most unnerving for the interviewees they'd been seeing over the last couple of days and she couldn't help wondering what they must think about their strange behaviour. It had probably put them off working there and Alice couldn't blame them. Larry was twitchy and kept fiddling with the cuffs of his jacket until one pinged off and rolled across the carpet. He'd then leapt up to retrieve it, caught Alice's eyes and started jabbering away. Alice had tried to calm him down, reaching out and touching his arm but that had been a mistake and he'd pulled away and fled from the room before she could stop him. The interviewee who'd had the misfortune of witnessing this bizarre scene hadn't got back to them when they'd later offered her the job.

Perhaps the most frustrating thing about the whole business was that Alice couldn't even confide in Ben about it all. She so desperately wanted to tell him about Larry's weird behaviour and the embarrassing moments with Wilfred and Bruce but she realised that Ben was a part of this charade too and she couldn't even begin to explain things to him without jeopardising their relationship.

That lunchtime, with the sun shining and the sky as blue as forget-me-nots, they walked to the Castle Museum where they found a bench. They'd bought freshly-made sandwiches, sugary jammy doughnuts and fruit smoothies – which were an attempt to counteract the effect of the doughnuts.

'This is nice,' Alice said as they polished off the doughnuts. She couldn't help thinking that, just a few weeks ago, she would have sat on a bench very like this one, watching all the happy couples parading by whilst she sat on her own.

'Has Larry talked any more about the position opening up in New Business?'

Alice shook her head. Larry hadn't talked about anything much at all to her. In fact, it was beginning to be a bit of a worry. They really couldn't go on like that. Alice had even been thinking about a transfer but she realised that the problem would just duplicate itself somewhere else unless she went to an all-female department.

'He's a funny bloke,' Ben said. 'I don't know how you put up with him.'

Alice looked surprised. She hadn't expected Ben to come out with such a thing. 'He's all right,' she said.

'But are you really happy working with him? I mean, he's so pompous and you're so lovely. You could do anything, Alice.' He looked at her and his eyes were deep and sincere.

'Well, I do often wonder if there's another life out there waiting to be led.'

'Like I do' Ben said excitedly.

Alice smiled. 'I guess.'

'We should do something about it,' he said and fear flooded through Alice again. How long could she keep this up with Ben? She should tell him the truth. She should tell him now.

'Ben, listen – there's something I need to—'

'I hope you're free tonight,' he interrupted, leaning in close to her.

'Ben, I want to—'

'*Are* you free? Or have you got a dozen other men queuing around the block for you? I bet you have.'

'No, I don't,' Alice said and she couldn't help but smile.

'So you're free?'

'Well, I'll have to check my diary,' she teased and then

wished she hadn't because Ben's face fell. That was the trouble with being attractive to men – you had a responsibility not to let people down. 'I was joking!' she added quickly.

He smiled with relief. 'Then I'll pick you up at seven thirty.' He got up from the bench and extended a hand to help her up.

You should tell him. Get it over and done with, the little voice said. But, as she placed her hand in his and received a smile for her pains, she thought she might just put the big confession off for a little longer.

Chapter 23

Alice looked at the row of pretty dresses in her wardrobe. Since Ben had asked her out, she'd bought a few more colourful pieces and now couldn't decide what to wear. He hadn't said anything about their date that night so that left Alice in the dark as to what to go for, so she decided to wear the plum-coloured velvet dress with the scoop neckline and the long sleeves.

Once the dress was on, she popped her feet into a pair of new shoes with the most modest of heels and then went into the bathroom to do something about her face. Staring at herself in the mirror, she wondered how far the wish would carry her. Would Ben notice if she decided to be plain old Alice and go sans make-up or if she deliberately left her hair a mess? It would be fun to find out but Alice was too self-conscious and she wanted to look her very best for Ben.

Just as her lipstick was halfway to her mouth, the doorbell went and Alice froze in a panic. Ben was awfully early, wasn't he? She quickly applied a coat of Summer Rose and tied her hair back. She'd have to beg at least five more minutes if she was going to look anywhere near presentable.

But it wasn't Ben at the door. It was Stella. Her face was stony and glum as she pushed into the hallway without so much as a hello. Alice hadn't seen her sister since they'd got back from Kethos and she knew that an unannounced visit meant trouble.

'Is everything okay?' Alice asked.

Stella shrugged as she flopped down onto Alice's sofa, pulling a cushion onto her lap.

'I'm fed up,' she said.

Alice sat down beside her. 'What's up?'

'Everything,' she said.

'Oh, dear.'

Stella nodded. 'Miles broke up with me.'

'Miles? Who's Miles?'

Stella turned and glared at Alice. 'My boyfriend,' she said.

'Since we came back from Kethos?'

'Well, of course since we came back from Kethos!' She groaned and she really did look sad.

'What happened?' Alice asked, genuinely concerned now.

'He said—' Stella paused.

'What? What did he say?'

'He said he didn't want to see me again because I was too young.'

'Too young? Well, how old was he?' Alice asked.

'Twenty-six,' Stella said.

'But that's not much older than you.'

'I know!' Stella said in exasperation.

'It doesn't make any sense. Are you sure that was his reason?'

Stella's gaze hit the floor and Alice immediately knew that she was hiding something.

'What is it?' Alice asked.

Stella's face had turned quite pale and Alice was beginning to get worried. What on earth had this Miles person said to her sister?

'He said,' she began at last, 'he said that I was *childish*. Isn't that awful?'

Alice bit her lip until she could trust herself to speak. 'Well—'

'How could he say such a thing?'

'I really don't know,' Alice said, supportively.

'I mean, I'm not childish, am I?' she asked, turning her big blue eyes onto Alice and searching for an answer that would make her feel better.

'Well, you can be a little—' Alice paused, choosing her words carefully. She didn't want Ben arriving in the middle of a full-blown argument. 'A little demanding, I'd say.'

Stella shifted on the sofa. 'That's rubbish. I'm not demanding at all.'

'Well, you have to admit that you like things your way,' Alice said gently.

'Of course I do. Doesn't everybody?'

'But you don't always go about it the right way,' Alice said.

'What do you mean?'

Alice glanced at the clock. The time was ticking away and she'd have to make a move before long. 'Do you want a cup of tea?' she asked kindly.

Stella nodded. 'And have you got something to eat? I haven't got a thing at home.'

'You can take a look but you'll have to prepare it yourself,' Alice said as they walked through to the kitchen and switched the kettle on.

'I think I'm going to extend my kitchen,' Stella announced casually, thoughts of Miles's cruel words obviously forgotten.

'What?'

'It's way too small, don't you think?'

Alice frowned. 'Why would Dad pay for that when he doesn't even live there any more?'

'Because it's the right thing to do for the house,' Stella said. 'Just think about it. The house will be worth more if we extend. Nobody wants a pokey old kitchen. It's *far* too small. You're lucky you don't have to put up with it yourself.'

'Are you kidding me? Just look at this place,' Alice said, gazing around the tiniest of rooms. 'It's about the width of a rolling pin and not much longer either.'

'Yes, but it's not so important for you, is it? I mean, this is just rented.'

'I don't think Dad can afford it, Stella.'

'He's got the money.'

'How do you know that?'

'And I think it'll definitely be worth it. It's an investment,' she said with a little nod.

'But all his money's tied up in the house and what little he has left over is for nursing fees,' Alice pointed out. 'You'll have to come up with the money yourself if you want to do any work on the house.'

Stella gave a scoffing sort of a laugh. 'I haven't got the money!' she said.

'What happened to that interview you were going to?' Alice asked, suddenly remembering that Stella had said something about it whilst they were in Kethos.

Stella pouted as she went about poking through Alice's kitchen cupboards in search of something to eat. 'It was awful and I didn't get the job. They asked me all kinds of silly questions.'

'They usually do in interviews.' Alice glanced at the cooker clock. 'Stella, I'm afraid I've got to get moving.'

'You're going out?' Stella said with a frown.

'Yes. I do go out occasionally, you know,' Alice said.

'No, I didn't know,' Stella said. 'You're not going to wear your hair like that, are you?'

'Why not?'

'Because you don't suit it up. Not like me,' Stella said, posing in front of the glass in the back door, a handful of blonde hair in her hands. 'Can't you stay? I really need somebody to talk to.'

'I'm sorry, Stella, but I've really got to get going.'

Her sister's eyes suddenly doubled in size like a cartoon character's and filled with tears. 'Everything's going wrong and I can't even talk to my sister about it.'

'Of course you can, only not tonight.'

'You're so mean.'

'You can stay and have your tea here but I'm going out,' Alice told her.

'Can't I come with you?'

'Certainly not. I'm going on a date.' It was then that the doorbell went. 'Oh, heavens!' Alice said as she realised that she hadn't finished getting ready.

'I'll get it,' Stella said.

'No need,' Alice said, nimbly pushing past Stella before she managed to answer the door to Ben.

'Hello,' he said, his eyes bright as the hallway light caught him. 'Are you ready?'

'Hi!' the bright voice of Stella cried as she pushed Alice out of the way.

'Hello,' Ben said in surprise.

'I'm Stella,' Stella said with her huskiest voice as she extended a hand. Ben shook it and Alice couldn't help but notice how long she managed to hold onto it for.

Ben smiled but then his gaze returned to Alice. 'Shall we get going, then?'

Alice nodded. 'Just give me a moment,' she said and they all walked into the hallway together. Alice rushed back up the stairs to finish getting ready. She didn't want to leave Stella with Ben longer than was absolutely necessary and returned in record time. Only they weren't in the hallway where she'd left them. They were in the sitting room and Stella was perched on the sofa, her long legs crossed and her face animated with interest in whatever it was Ben was talking about.

'So that's kind of how the department's run,' Ben was saying. Stella nodded her head as if it was something she really cared about. 'Ah,' he said as Alice walked into the room. 'You look amazing.'

Alice stroked the front of her dress self-consciously and fiddled with her hair and she couldn't help noticing that Stella was giving her a look as if to say, what on earth did you do to ensnare this one?

* * *

Ben had booked the best table in a restaurant that Alice had only ever dreamed of eating at. He guided her to the table with his hand resting in the small of her back and then he pulled out her chair like a true gentleman.

'You look beautiful tonight,' he whispered in her ear before sitting down opposite her.

'So do you,' she said and then smiled. 'Handsome, I mean. You look handsome.'

The waiter arrived and handed them the menus and Alice's eyes almost popped out of her head at the prices but Ben seemed perfectly calm. That's what came of being a manager, she thought, remembering seeing his salary increase at the end of last month.

They took their time ordering, talking about the events of the day and swapping sweet nothings across the table.

'Here's to us,' Ben said, opening the champagne bottle and filling their glasses after they'd finished their starter and had moved on to their main course. Alice was just thinking that she had never been treated so well in her life when she realised that she had. Milo had treated her like a queen, hadn't he? And he hadn't relied on fancy restaurants and expensive champagne either. He had cooked for her himself and taken her to secret places that nobody else knew about.

But he also lied to you, a little voice said. *He lied to you, used you and conveniently forgot about you.*

She shook her head. Why was she thinking of Milo now? Hadn't he been filed away in the back of her mind in a compartment named 'Things to Forget'? She was with Ben now and she was happy. She was *quite* sure she was.

'You know, I still can't get over how I've never noticed you before,' Ben said.

Alice smiled at him. 'It's easy to overlook somebody like me,' she said.

Ben shook his head. 'All this time we've wasted,' he said, 'but we can make up for all that now, can't we?'

Alice nodded happily. 'Yes,' she said, knowing full well how many years she had wasted being plain and, even if this new Alice was a freak and a fraud and even if it wasn't going to last forever, she was going to make the very most of it right now with Ben.

They were just mulling over the desserts when a tall blonde waltzed over to their table and, without so much as hello, bent down and placed a scarlet lipstick smudge right across Ben's cheek.

'Lynne!' Ben exclaimed.

'Long time, no see, darling,' the woman said.

Alice watched in horror as the woman pulled a chair from another table and sat herself down next to Ben.

'Er – let me introduce you,' Ben said hurriedly. 'Alice – this is Lynne. Lynne – Alice.'

Lynne gave a sickly sort of smile to Alice and then her gaze snapped back to Ben.

'It *has* been a long time, hasn't it?' Ben said.

Lynne laughed. 'I'm just trying to remember exactly when it was. I can't make my mind up. Was it that awful conference in Leeds where we stayed in that nasty little hotel or that weekend in Monaco where we stole those gorgeous hand towels? Do you remember? They were all embroidered in gold.'

Ben's face had reddened and Alice couldn't help wondering if it was because of the reference to staying in hotels with this woman or because of the stolen towel incident.

'Ben and I go back years, don't we, Ben?' Lynne said, giving Alice the once-over and obviously not liking what she saw.

'We certainly do, we certainly do!' Ben said, swallowing hard.

'You know, I've often wondered what happened to you,' she continued, laying a perfectly manicured hand on his. Ben pulled his hand away and the woman visibly flinched.

'Well,' he said at last, 'it was lovely seeing you again.'

Lynne glared at him as if daring him to brush her off but he maintained his stance and she soon scraped her chair out from behind her.

'Goodbye, Ben,' she said. 'And good luck to you,' she said, turning her icy stare on Alice. 'Whatever your name is.'

'It's Alice,' Alice said without missing a beat. They watched as Lynne stalked across the restaurant.

'Sorry about that,' Ben said when he was quite sure she was out of earshot.

'Goodness,' Alice said. 'She was quite – *predatory*.'

'Yes,' Ben said. 'She could be quite scary once she got those talons into you,' he said, taking a good draught of wine.

'Does that happen a lot?'

'What?' Ben said, the colour from his face finally settling back to something approaching normality.

'I mean, I guess you have a lot of ex-girlfriends.'

'I've had one or two,' he said. 'Everybody has a past.'

'Not as colourful as yours, though,' Alice said, berating herself for her irked tone. Why had the incident with Lynne got to her so much? This was how it was going to be with Ben, wasn't it? He was a good-looking man – way out of Alice's league – and he attracted a type of girl that would always look down on Alice.

'What do you mean by that?' Ben said with a frown.

Alice sighed. What *did* she mean, she wondered? 'I mean, you're so handsome.'

He laughed. 'And you're beautiful.'

'No, I'm not,' Alice said quickly.

Ben shook his head. 'You're always selling yourself short, Alice.'

'But I'm not beautiful,' she said.

'And I'm sure you've had just as many boyfriends as I've had girlfriends,' he added.

Alice felt her heartbeat accelerate as she thought of the woeful lineup of old boyfriends like Michael who'd still lived with his mother and had had to be home by nine o'clock each evening or Rick who'd forgotten to pick Alice up for their date one evening because he'd got back together with his ex.

'Listen,' Ben said at last, his hand reaching across the table to take hers, 'let's not talk about the past. It's the present I'm interested in.' He gave a warm smile and Alice's insecurities were banished. For the moment.

They ordered voluptuous desserts with swirls of chocolate, drank sweet tea and drove home. Alice did her best not to think about Lynne, she really did, but her beautiful, haughty face kept staring out at her from her mind's eye and Alice couldn't help but wonder how many other ex-girlfriends of Ben's would give her the once-over and make her feel as if she had no place by his side.

'You're very quiet,' Ben said as he pulled up outside her cottage and switched the engine off.

'Just thinking,' she said.

'What about?' he asked, leaning in closer to her.

'Us.'

'Us is a very good thing to think about,' he said and she couldn't help but smile. He was very good at making her smile.

'Do you want to come in?' she asked nervously.

Ben took her hand in his and brought it up to his mouth and kissed it. 'I'd love to,' he said, 'but I think we should wait.'

'What do you want to wait for?' Alice said, half-panicked in case Ben was seeing her for who she really was.

'This is special, Alice,' he said, 'and I don't want to rush things.'

Alice swallowed hard. It was the last thing she'd expected him to say and his sweetness made her feel so guilty.

'Okay,' she said at last, and closed her eyes as he kissed her.

'Good night,' he said a moment later as she got out of the car. She watched as he disappeared into the night and a terrible sadness settled in her heart. Why couldn't all this be happening because of who she was – who she *really* was? Why couldn't Ben have noticed her weeks ago before the wish had been made?

As she turned to go inside, she was aware of a ghostly

presence next door. It was her neighbour, old Mr Montague. He was standing in his front garden behind the wooden gate and the air was filled with smoke from his cigar. He did look a funny sight standing in the moonlight in his saggy pyjamas. Alice didn't often see him but she knew that his wife had thought he'd given up smoking years ago and didn't know about him sloping off to the garden every night for a quick one. He'd once confided in Alice that he told his wife he was on slug patrol.

'Are you all right, Mr Montague?' she said.

He nodded and then his eyes lit up. 'Alice! Is that you?' He shuffled forward in his furry slippers and almost crashed into the little wooden gate.

'Yes, Mr Montague.'

'You're out late. Got yourself a fancy man?'

She smiled at the old-fashioned term. 'I'm not sure,' she said honestly.

'You be sure to choose carefully, now. A girl like you deserves somebody who will love and cherish her for who she really is.'

Alice blinked hard in the moonlight as Mr Montague's words struck home. 'But how can I be sure of that?' she asked. 'How can I be certain that a man loves me for who I truly am?'

Mr Montague beckoned her forward with a bony finger and Alice dared to approach the gate. 'Come closer,' he said.

Warily, Alice took another step forward. 'What is it?' she asked, feeling Mr Montague's hot breath on her cold cheek.

'Oh, Alice!' he whispered and, before she could get away, he had her shoulders clutched in his bony hands and was kissing her cheek with an alarming sucking sound.

'Mr Montague! Please let me go!'

'Alice! My Alice!' he cried into the night air. 'You're my one true love! How did I never see it before?'

'Because there is nothing to see. I haven't changed and neither have you. You're a married man and this is madness! Madness!' She shook his hands away from her and tore up her garden path, jamming her key in the lock as quickly as she could.

She was shaking so much that she could barely put the safety chain on the door. This had got to stop. She couldn't go through this any more. Her life was falling apart and for the first time she realised that the old life hadn't been so bad after all. She might not have got quite so much male attention but at least everybody had been honest. At least she didn't have to put up with this mad charade of passion.

She walked through to the kitchen and made herself a cup of camomile tea to try and calm her nerves, taking it through to the living room and sitting down on the sofa. For a moment, she thought she could hear a radio but then realised that the sound was coming from outside.

Alice stood up and moved to the window, listening for a moment, trying to work out what it was. It sounded like some sort of animal in pain but then she realised it wasn't an animal. It was old Mr Montague.

'He's singing!' she said, gasping in horror as she caught sight of the old man at her garden gate still wearing nothing but his saggy pyjamas. What made matters even worse was he was down on one knee, an ancient guitar in his arms which he wasn't really playing, just holding for support.

Alice's hand flew to her mouth as she watched him, trying to make out the words he was singing. He kept saying her name over and over again, that much was clear, but there didn't seem to be any sort of rhythm or tune. He was just making it up as he went along and the result was the most awful noise Alice had ever heard. She had to stop him.

Opening the window, she leaned out. 'Mr Montague – it's the middle of the night! What are you doing?'

'I – I – I,' he stuttered, 'I'm serenading you.'

'I think you should go to bed.'

He nodded enthusiastically. 'Yes! Oh, yes!'

'Your *own* bed, Mr Montague,' Alice said.

There then came a strange cry from Mr Montague's house and the burly figure of his wife came crashing through the undergrowth. '*What* is going on, Ernest Montague?'

'I – I – I'm serenading Alice,' he said as if it was the most natural thing to be doing in the middle of the night.

'You stupid old fool!' his wife bellowed. 'Nobody wants to hear you croaking into the night like a hoarse frog! Least of all Alice. Now get inside, you big oaf!'

Alice watched as Mrs Montague cuffed her husband around the head and dragged him back into the house. She sighed in relief, shutting the window and drawing the curtains sharply; then, taking a deep breath, she walked through to the bathroom where she stared at herself in the mirror above the sink.

'You're not up to this,' she told herself. 'It's all going to go horribly wrong if you don't end it now.'

But she didn't want to end it. She had real feelings for Ben and she was beginning to believe that he liked her for the woman she truly was and wasn't just momentarily dazzled by her because of the wish she'd made.

She stared at her reflection for a moment, knowing what she had to do. She had to tell him the truth, didn't she? Ben was a decent man and, if she had any real feelings for him at all, she would be honest with him.

Getting into bed later that night, she nodded to herself in the darkness. I'm going to do this, she thought. I'm going to tell him the truth.

Chapter 24

There was a letter on Milo's doormat when he got home with Tiana one evening. A real white envelope without a cellophane window and with a handwritten address. It would have been a nice change from the usual bills and junk mail if only Milo hadn't known who it was from. Georgio.

He waited until Tiana had skipped along the corridor to her bedroom before he opened it, glaring at the oversized handwriting which seemed to be shouting down at him.

Milo, it began abruptly. *You never answer your phone. You refuse to discuss things with us when we visit and you make all sorts of excuses whenever we meet. You leave me no choice but to write to you.*

Sonya and I have been talking...

Milo groaned. So they'd been talking again, had they?

...and we really think that Tiana would be better off with us here on the mainland. We've been worried about her for some time.

'Oh, have you?' Milo said. 'Like the time she twisted her ankle skipping? Or the time I rushed her to the dentist with a roaring toothache?'

We think that it would be better for her if she was here with Sonya now that she is working from home. Sonya would be here for her constantly – a better choice than an unreliable babysitter.

Milo scoffed at the reference to his beloved and loyal Hanna.

Tiana is growing up fast, the letter went on, causing Milo to physically flinch. His brother's tone seemed to suggest that Milo wasn't aware of this fact but he was all too aware of it. Each and every day.

And we think it is selfish of you to keep her in a place that is doing her no favours. Just think of the school for a start.

Milo thought of the tiny school in the next village where the one classroom was half-empty because of the lack of children. He and his brothers had gone there and, he hoped, his own children would go there too. It was constantly threatened with closure but it had somehow struggled through to the twenty-first century and the small classroom size meant individual attention from the teacher. Tiana wouldn't get that in a big school on the mainland, would she?

The letter went on.

She needs a better class of education and she needs to meet more children of her own age. It just isn't good enough, Milo—

'What's that?' Tiana asked, surprising Milo, having sneaked into the room. She placed a tiny hand on the letter but Milo quickly whipped it out of her way.

'Nothing,' he said in a manner that was far too hasty for Tiana to believe him. 'It's just a silly letter begging for money.'

'Will you give them any?'

'No,' he said, scrunching the letter up into the tiniest, tightest ball imaginable, 'not a single penny.' He opened the bin and threw the letter inside and then tipped the remains of some soggy cereal from a breakfast bowl on top of it so there'd be no chance of Tiana reaching inside and discovering what it really said.

'Come on, Tiana,' he said.

'But I've got to do my homework.'

'Later – we're going for a walk first.'

She looked at him as if he'd gone soft in the head but then did as she was told.

They left the house together a couple of minutes later. The air was soft and warm and the ground was dry and firm and already beginning to crack, leaving lizard-like patterns across the land.

Milo did his best thinking when he was outside and he really needed to think hard now. Since his brother's last visit, he'd tried to put the issue out of his mind but he'd known that it would rear its ugly head again at some point and would have to be faced. He felt truly sad that Georgio and Sonya weren't able to have children of their own – it must be the most heartbreaking of situations to face when one wanted a child so desperately – but that didn't give them the right to force Milo's hand and take Tiana away from him.

They followed the little track from their house towards an olive grove. It belonged to a farmer but he didn't mind the locals walking amongst his trees. In fact, local legend had it that half of the population for miles around had been conceived in this very grove, which made Milo anxious on summer evenings when Tiana would declare that she was going to play there.

Milo loved the ancient olive trees with their thick, gnarled trunks and sinuous shapes and he had to admit to bringing two or three girlfriends there himself over the years. But now wasn't a time to think about romantic trysts amongst the trees.

'Tiana,' he said at last as they reached a dip in the path, 'I want you to be absolutely honest with me.' They sat down in the grass. The earth was still warm after a full day of sunshine upon it.

Tiana looked at him. 'Am I in trouble?'

'No,' he said. 'Why do you ask?'

She shook her head.

'Tiana?'

She pouted. 'It wasn't my fault.'

'What wasn't your fault?'

'That Costas fell over.'

'I'm sure it wasn't,' Milo said, wondering what on earth she'd done.

'I only pushed him a *little* bit,' Tiana confessed.

Milo frowned. He hadn't been expecting this. 'Why did you push Costas?' he asked, thinking of the rotund little boy who, if truth be told, was a horrible bully.

'Because he said I looked like a donkey,' Tiana said, her eyes round and watery.

'You look nothing like a donkey!' Milo said with a laugh.

'Well, that's what I said!' Tiana said, quickly blinking her tears away.

'And that's when you pushed him over?'

Tiana nodded. 'He's such a roly-poly, he wouldn't have felt anything when he fell.'

Milo grinned. He was glad that his little sister could hold her own. He gazed out across the olive grove for a moment, his vision blurring with the silver-green of the trees.

'Listen,' he said after a moment, 'I know we've talked a little about this before but I need to hear you say it again.'

'Say what again?'

'That you're happy.'

'At school?' Tiana asked.

'At school. At home. Here on Kethos.'

She nodded. 'Of course I am. I tell you *all* the time!'

Milo laughed and picked up her little hand and kissed it. 'I know,' he said. 'I just like to hear you say it.'

'You're funny,' she said.

'It's just that I want to be sure – absolutely sure – that this is the right place for you because there are choices, you know.'

'I know,' she said.

He nodded. 'And I won't mind if you decide to go somewhere else.'

'With Georgio?'

'Yes,' he said.

'You really wouldn't mind?'

'No,' Milo lied. 'I wouldn't mind if that was what you wanted.'

'You mean, you wouldn't miss me?'

His dark eyes widened. 'Of course I'd miss you!'

'Are you trying to get rid of me?'

'No!' he said, aghast at the sad look on her face. 'It's just that some people might think it unfair that I keep you here.'

'You mean that's what Georgio thinks?'

'Yes.'

'He wants me to live with him, doesn't he?'

'Yes, he does,' Milo said. 'Because he's your brother too and he misses you.'

'But I don't know him,' Tiana said and Milo's heart sang with love at her honesty. Georgio was more like an uncle to Tiana because he'd left home years before she'd been born but perhaps that was the card he was playing – he was older and wiser. Mind you, Milo was old enough to be her uncle too only their relationship was totally different because he'd been around when Tiana had been born. He'd seen her take her first steps and heard her speak her first word. He'd been there for all the firsts, hadn't he? Whilst Georgio dropped by twice a year for her birthday and for Christmas.

'If you went to live with Georgio and his wife, life would be very different but it might not be a bad idea for you,' Milo said, each word squeezed out of him most unwillingly. But he couldn't put himself first here. He needed to think of Tiana. She would be a teenager before he knew it and then what would happen? Was he sure he'd be able to handle her then? And would she be happy being marooned on an island? He had to think about her. He couldn't put himself into this equation – it wouldn't be right or fair.

'But I like it here,' she said, plucking at the short grass.

'But that's only because it's all you know,' Milo said. 'You could get to know another place just as well as here.'

'Then why don't you move?'

Milo flinched. She had an uncanny ability to strike at the very heart of things. 'Because this is my home,' he said.

'And it's my home too.'

He nodded at her sage statement. There was no arguing

with that and he was so relieved to hear it. It was what he'd hoped for, of course, but he had to give his brother a chance because that was only fair, wasn't it?

'Good,' he said, squeezing her hand.

'Can we go now?' she asked. 'My bottom's gone numb.'

Milo laughed. 'Mine too,' he said and they both stood up, brushing each other's bottoms down.

They walked back through the olive grove together. The sun was beginning to set and the sky was streaked with peach and tangerine. A light wind brought the scent of the sea to them. Milo saw the gentle expression on Tiana's face and knew that she loved it all as much as he did and that she'd never be able to live anywhere else and for that he was eternally grateful because he knew there was nothing that Georgio could do about that.

Chapter 25

It was the morning of the day of the truth. That's what Alice had decided. She had to tell Ben everything that had happened to her since she'd made the wish on the statue of Aphrodite. It was the only way she could live with herself. But the trouble was, Ben was nowhere to be found. She tried his extension number over and over again but it was always picked up by somebody else.

'He's in a meeting,' she was told.

All morning? Alice looked at the clock. It was after eleven. She had to calm down and wait until her lunch break.

Larry was his usual weird self, avoiding all eye contact with Alice as he shuffled around the office, and grunting blunt responses to her whenever she tried to talk to him. How long could this go on for, she wondered?

Finally, lunch time arrived and, not being able to wait a moment longer, Alice left her desk and walked up the stairs to the finance department. As soon as she walked through the door, she knew something was wrong.

'Oh, he's left already,' Tamara Philips said when Alice asked where Ben was and she gave a sly sort of a smile that sent chills down Alice's spine.

Alice left the office, wondering where Ben had gone and

why he hadn't called in on her on his way downstairs. She tried his mobile but it went to the answering service and she didn't want to leave a message so she went along to their favourite sandwich shop and then on to the gardens at the Castle Museum.

That's where she found him and he obviously wasn't waiting for her.

'Ben?' She mouthed his name but, luckily, no sound came out because he wasn't alone and Alice instantly recognised the woman he was with. It was Lynne and they were sitting on what Alice had come to think of as their bench. She froze for a moment, not knowing what to do. Should she confront him and start accusing him or give him the benefit of the doubt and act as if nothing out of the ordinary were happening? Or should she just slink away and ignore it?

But she didn't get a chance to make her mind up because Ben looked up and saw her standing there with her salad sandwich in one hand and her raspberry smoothie in the other.

'Alice!' he cried but she'd already turned and, picking up her pace, she headed towards the city centre, hoping to lose herself amongst the lunchtime shoppers, but she wasn't quick enough and Ben had soon caught up with her. 'Alice – please stop!'

'Don't even bother, Ben,' she said, relieved that Lynne hadn't accompanied him. 'This whole thing is wrong!'

'What are you talking about?' Ben asked, wide-eyed.

'I'm not meant to be with you, Ben,' Alice said simply. 'We never should have happened.'

'Look, is this because of Lynne? Because nothing's going on between us, I swear! She rang me up asking to see me. What could I say?'

'You could have said *no*,' Alice told him.

'It sounded important.'

'Oh, really? So what was it then?'

He looked cagey for a moment.

'What was it, Ben?'

'She wants to get back together. She said we never should have broken up.'

Alice took a deep breath and then sighed it out slowly. 'Well, maybe you *should* get back together.'

'What?' Ben cried, his voice high and panicky. 'How can you say that?'

'Because I think it's probably the right thing to do,' she said. 'We're not meant to be together.'

'Why do you keep saying that, Alice? I don't understand you sometimes.' He took a step forward and reached out to take her hand but she was still holding her sandwich. 'Come and have your lunch.'

'What – with you and Lynne?'

'No, not with Lynne – just me.'

Alice looked at him. It would be so easy to stop things now, she thought – to walk away and forget about her and Ben. It had all been a huge mistake and the sooner it was all over, the better.

'*Please*, Alice,' he said, his blue eyes full of warmth, and something inside Alice just melted. She couldn't make the break – not yet – and so she allowed Ben's arm to slip around her waist and lead her to a bench that wasn't occupied by an ex-girlfriend.

Milo and Tiana were in the kitchen when the earthquake happened. At first, there was nothing more than a distant rumble that could easily have been mistaken for thunder but then the cups and plates on the kitchen table started to judder and Tiana looked up from where she was doing her homework, her dark eyes full of fear.

'Get under the table!' Milo yelled from the other side of the room and Tiana slid off her chair and flung herself to the safety of the ground underneath the hard wood. It was a move she'd rehearsed before because, although earthquakes weren't common in Kethos, they were possible.

As the rumbling continued, Milo dived under the table and held Tiana against him and felt her fingers curl around his arms.

'It'll be all right. It'll soon be over,' he said, kissing the top of her head and holding her close. He could feel her shaking or perhaps it was just part of the quake, he wasn't sure. Perhaps he was shaking too.

He watched as the whole room shook by an unseen force. It would be easy to imagine that the ancient gods had awoken and were displeased. Many of the older residents believed in such things.

'You must not anger the gods,' they would say, gazing mysteriously into the sky or pointing into the mountains. Milo didn't believe in it all, of course. He believed in tectonic plates and the irrepressible force of nature. Still, whatever caused them, it was of no comfort when it was your own house that was being pushed, pulled and pummelled to within an inch of its life.

A white plate smashed to the floor. It was followed by the old china teapot which had been their mother's pride and joy. *Crash!* The work of a careless and thoughtless second by Mother Nature. Milo only hoped that would be the only damage and that their little home would survive intact. His salary as head gardener wouldn't stretch to structural repairs on the old place.

It was at times like this when your mind descended towards darkness. What if this was the end, Milo thought? What if his time was up? Would he have truly lived the life he had wanted to? Would his existence have counted for something?

A kaleidoscope of images spiralled through his mind: the little home which he loved, his beautiful sister whom he adored, and the island that he held so close to his heart. Yes, he had lived a good life but it was much too soon to think about it all being over. Besides, he had only just started and there was so much more to do.

What about his plans to have his own garden to open to the public one day? A garden that was truly his own where he could grow exactly what he wanted where he wanted, taking cuttings and collecting seed and selling his own plants to the public. And what about the wife and children he'd always envisaged? That wasn't to be just an idle daydream, was it?

And Alice. Where was she? Would she hear the news about their little island and would she find out about his death if this was to be the end? Would she wonder what his last hours were like and have any regrets that she didn't try to get in touch with him again? Would she even come out to Kethos to try to search for his remains amongst the ruins?

He shook his head. He was becoming hysterical. He needed to stop thinking that the ground was going to crack open and swallow him at any moment and just calm down. He kissed Tiana's head again and squeezed her.

'It's all right,' he said. 'There's no need to panic.'

'I'm not panicking,' she replied as another plate hit the tiled floor and smashed, and he couldn't help but smile knowing that it was his little sister who was the calming influence here.

He'd lost all track of time whilst they were cowering under the table. How long had it been since the first rumble? Five minutes? Twenty minutes? He cocked his head and listened. The world seemed to be settling. It seemed to be straightening up again.

'Has it stopped?' Tiana asked in a small voice a moment later.

'Don't move,' Milo said, getting out from underneath the table. His limbs had seized up and he stretched as he looked around the kitchen at the broken cups and plates and then ventured into the hallway and opened the front door. Everything looked perfectly normal. His moped had fallen over and a couple of buckets had been tipped onto their sides but the earth was still intact. A little stone wall at the end of their driveway had cracked but was still standing. They'd got away lightly.

Tiana joined him.

'I told you to stay where you were!' Milo said.

'But it's over now, isn't it?'

'There might be aftershocks,' he said.

'Mama's teapot is broken,' Tiana said.

'Yes, but at least our bones aren't,' Milo said.

'I think I'd rather have broken bones than a broken teapot,' Tiana said and Milo hugged her to him.

'We still have her casserole dish, don't we? It's safe in the cupboard.' Tiana nodded. They kept it in a snug wooden box filled with straw because it was so precious.

'And there's orange juice all over my homework.'

'I think your teacher will understand,' Milo said.

They both walked back indoors together, marvelling at the wonky pictures on the walls and the broken crockery everywhere.

'Mind where you step!' Milo said, guiding Tiana over a large broken bowl which had smashed onto the kitchen floor. It was going to take hours to tidy up.

Tiana ran through to her bedroom.

'Careful!' Milo shouted after her, following her down the hallway. He stood in the doorway of her bedroom and saw her sitting on the edge of her bed, a broken photo frame in her hand. 'You shouldn't have picked that up!' Milo said, taking it from her.

'It's cracked,' she said, tears in her eyes.

'Just the glass,' he said. 'We can fix it.' He looked at the photo. It was the only one they had of Tiana with their mama. Tiana was just a few weeks old and their mama was cradling her in her arms, a huge smile on her face as she looked at the camera with her large sloe-dark eyes.

'She's so beautiful,' Tiana said.

Milo nodded and sat down on the bed next to her. 'We'll get a new frame for it.'

They were silent for a moment, each lost in their own thoughts as they looked at the photograph.

'Why did she die?' Tiana asked at last.

'She got sick,' Milo said. 'You were so small at the time. You don't remember. But Mama got very sick and there was nothing the doctors could do.'

'What was wrong with her?'

Milo took a deep breath. 'She had a tumour,' he said. 'It's a bad growth that you can't get rid of.'

'And it killed her?'

Milo nodded.

'So she's with Papa?'

He nodded again. 'Yes. She's with Papa.'

'He got sick too, didn't he?' Tiana said.

'Papa was very old,' Milo said. 'But he loved you so much. Mama did too.'

'You're not going to die, are you?' Tiana suddenly asked.

'I'm not planning to,' he said with a little smile.

'I'm not either,' she said resolutely, her eyes wide.

'Good,' he said. 'Then we've got each other. The two fierce survivors of the great Kethos earthquake. We can survive anything now.'

Tiana smiled up at him. 'Yes,' she said. 'We're indes—' she paused, looking for the right word.

'Indestructible?' Milo said.

She nodded. 'Yes!'

'And we're indescribable,' he said.

'No, we're not!'

'And we're indigestible,' he said with a grin.

'Milo!' she giggled and punched him in the ribs.

'Ouch!' he yelled. 'And we're—' he paused.

'What?' she asked.

'We're in this together!'

'Yes!' she said. 'That one is true!'

Chapter 26

It was only when Milo arrived at the Villa Argenti the next day that he saw the full extent of the damage of the earthquake. His side of the island had got away lightly in comparison and he looked around his beloved garden in despair.

The Goddess Garden had taken the brunt of the quake and one of Artemis's hounds had cracked in two and Athena had lost an arm but actually looked better for it, Milo couldn't help thinking. More traditional, he thought. She'd probably pass for an ancient work of art now and scholars would come from all over the world to gaze upon her and write sonnets.

But it was his beautiful Aphrodite that almost caused him to shed a tear. She lay smashed in at least a dozen different pieces, her lovely face gazing up at the sky uncomprehendingly.

'What should we do with her?' Lander asked him as they looked at the broken beauty who no longer towered above them but had been brought down to earth.

'We'll have to take her to that guy who did the repair on Hera last summer after that idiot tourist carved his initials into her bottom. Mr Carlson will be furious. Aphrodite is his favourite. He'll want her mended or a new one made,' Milo said.

'I don't think they'll be able to fix her,' Lander said, running his finger along the crack around her pretty neck.

'We have to try,' Milo said.

'I don't know much about statues,' Lander said, 'but she looks pretty dead to me.'

Milo shook his head. 'We can't allow her to be dead. We have to try and save her. She's too important to the tourists to let her go,' he said, not daring to add that she was just as important to him.

'And what about the garden?' Lander asked, looking around. The damage to the plants was nothing compared to his master's beloved statues but it still had to be cleared up. Terracotta pots had cracked, a wall had come down and the greenhouse had lost most of its windows.

'Look,' Milo said, 'it's Friday afternoon. There's not a lot we can do now, is there?'

'I guess not,' Lander said.

'Let's just tidy up as best as we can and think about how we're going to sort the rest of it out before his highness returns next week.'

Friday afternoons were usually a time to wind down in the office. They were a time to sort out any bits of paperwork before the weekend exodus, to tidy away, to file and move on. So, it came as rather a surprise when Larry Baxter's wife turned up.

Monica Baxter was a tiny woman with a big attitude. She looked as if she spent half her life in a beauty salon and the other half in London's Bond Street and, today, she didn't look pleased. Larry was in an interview with someone and Alice was just about to offer Monica a cup of tea whilst she waited for him but it wasn't a cup of tea she wanted. It was Alice.

'I trusted you, Alice Archer!' she all but screamed.

Alice flinched as the little woman hovered menacingly over her desk. 'I beg your pardon?'

'I thought you were different.'

'Mrs Baxter – what are you talking about?'

'What am I talking about?' Her scarlet-painted mouth quivered in a frightening manner. 'I'm talking about *you* trying to seduce my husband – *that's* what I'm talking about!'

The whole of the open-plan office fell silent and Alice blushed to her very soul. 'I think we should talk about this somewhere else,' Alice said.

'I bet you do, you double-crossing floozy!'

Alice leapt up from her chair and did her best to guide Mrs Baxter through to a vacant interview room and closed the door behind them. 'Please sit down.'

'Don't you tell me what to do!' Mrs Baxter said. She looked quite wild now and Alice wondered if it was a good idea to be trapped in a room with her.

'I don't know what Larry's been telling you,' Alice ventured, 'but–'

'He's not told me a single thing!' Mrs Baxter said. 'He just talks about you in his sleep – every single night.'

'Oh, God!' Alice said and she watched as Mrs Baxter sank into one of the interview chairs as if all the air had been

230

knocked out of her and there was nothing Alice could do but sink into the chair opposite her.

'I just can't understand it,' Mrs Baxter went on, a look of complete astonishment on her face. 'I mean, you're so *plain*. I didn't think I needed to worry.'

'But you *don't* need to worry,' Alice assured her. 'Nothing's happened, I promise you. It's all just some misunderstanding. I'm not seeing your husband. He doesn't even look at me in the office if you want to know the absolute truth. I'm seeing Ben Alexander.'

'Ben Alexander? From the finance department?' Monica Baxter looked perplexed. 'Well, excuse me for saying so but you're just not his type.'

As much as it pained her, Alice had to agree with her. 'Listen,' she said, 'something strange has been going on but I can't really say any more than that.'

'What are you talking about?' Mrs Baxter said.

'I mean, this thing with Larry. All you need to know is that nothing's happening. I *promise* you,' Alice said, wringing her hands together like a bad actress.

'And why should I believe you?'

'Because you *know* me!' Alice said. 'We've talked at a dozen office parties. You know the sort of person I am.'

'I *thought* I did!' Mrs Baxter said, her scarlet mouth narrowed into a thin, mean line.

'But you *do* know me and you know I couldn't go behind your back like that.' Alice looked at Mrs Baxter beseechingly and saw that she was beginning to calm down. 'And Larry – well –' Alice paused, wondering how she could

231

phrase this without insulting the poor woman, 'he just isn't my type.'

Mrs Baxter stared at her for a moment, her lips twitching nervously and then a tiny smile shone through and a little giggle emerged. 'He isn't your type!' she said and she made a strange snorting sound.

'No,' Alice confirmed. 'He isn't.'

Mrs Baxter snorted again. 'He isn't my type either!' she said.

'Mrs Baxter?'

'Oh, God!' she suddenly exclaimed. 'You must think I'm such a fool.'

'No!' Alice said. 'Not at all.'

'How could my Larry ever hope to attract a young woman like you even when you are so plain-looking when he's so – so – well, he's not exactly George Clooney, is he?' She seemed to be half-laughing and half-choking and Alice became alarmed.

'Mrs Baxter – let me get you some water!' she said, getting to her feet.

'I'm fine!' she said, catching her breath, her hand clasped dramatically to her chest. 'Oh, dear! I don't know what came over me. You've got to forgive me, Alice.'

'There's nothing to forgive,' she assured her.

'How could I ever have thought that Larry and you—' she shook her head.

'You have absolutely nothing to worry about,' Alice told her. 'There's nothing going on.'

Slowly, Mrs Baxter got up from her chair and made her way out of the interview room.

'Are you sure I can't get you a cup of tea or something?' Alice asked.

Mrs Baxter shook her head and then stopped abruptly. 'You mustn't say anything to Larry about this. You won't, will you?'

'Of course I won't,' Alice said, but she could already see that half the office was buzzing with gossip and she was sure it wouldn't take long before word reached him about his wife's terrifying outburst.

Alice watched in relief as Mrs Baxter headed down the stairs and then she returned to her desk. It was only five minutes later when Ben entered the office.

'Hey!' he said as he approached her desk. 'What on earth's been going on? The whole building is talking. Somebody told me Monica Baxter came in and picked a fight with you!'

Alice rolled her eyes. News sure travelled fast in a building society but how on earth was she going to explain it all to Ben? She took a deep breath, knowing that now was the time. She had to tell him everything and she couldn't put it off any longer.

'There's something you should know,' she said quietly.

'Oh, God! You're not having an affair with Larry, are you?' Ben's face crumpled in disgust.

'Keep your voice down!' Alice said, flapping a panicked hand at him. 'Of course I'm not having an affair with Larry.'

'Well, tell me what's going on!'

'That's what I'm trying to do!' Alice said, leaving her desk and ushering Ben into one of the interview rooms, closing the door behind them. Alice couldn't help feeling a sense of déjà vu and wondered if she was destined to spend the whole day explaining her way out of awkward situations.

'So what the hell is going on?' Ben leant against the table at the far side of the room and crossed his arms in front of his chest. It was a serious, no-nonsense pose that struck fear into the heart of Alice and she swallowed hard.

'Just give me a minute,' she said, wondering where on earth she was going to start. At the beginning, of course, she told herself, trying to maintain some sense of control but the words that first tumbled out of her mouth were startlingly *un*controlled.

'I made a wish and it's come true,' she said.

Ben frowned. 'What are you talking about?'

Alice took a deep breath and tried to slow her thoughts down. 'You know when I went to Kethos?'

'That Greek island?'

She nodded. 'Well, there was this statue in a garden – a statue of Aphrodite, the goddess of love.'

'I know who Aphrodite is,' he said.

Alice nodded. 'Of course,' she said. 'Well, she's meant to make wishes come true. If you wish for love.'

'So?'

'So I made a wish. I wished that men would notice me – *really* notice me.' Alice paused, waiting desperately for Ben's response.

'I don't understand,' he said at last. 'What's some silly wish got to do with anything?'

'*Everything!*' Alice said in exasperation. 'You never would have looked at me if I hadn't made that silly wish.'

'What?' Ben said, his eyes full of surprise.

'Face it, Ben – you never noticed me before and I've been under your nose for years.'

'But that doesn't mean anything,' he said. 'My mum and dad worked together for years before Dad finally asked Mum out. People come together at the right time – that's what I think.'

Alice shook her head. 'This is different.'

'How's it different?'

'I've been—' she paused.

'What?'

'I've been getting a lot of attention lately.'

Ben's eyebrows drew close together and his face suddenly looked dark. 'This *is* about Larry, isn't it?'

'It's not just Larry. It's – well – lots of men.'

'Alice!' he said, his voice abnormally high.

'Not like that!' she said. 'It's all really superficial.'

He shook his head. 'Let me get this clear because I'm really struggling here. You're saying I've fallen in love with you because of some silly wish you've made on an inanimate lump of stone? That I've had no choice in the matter? Is that what you're saying?'

'That's exactly what I'm saying. I'm sorry, Ben.'

There was a pause where they just stared at each other for a long time. Ben was the one to break it.

'Alice – I don't understand,' he said. 'This just seems insane.'

'No, Ben! It's all true. At least I think it is. I can't explain it really but everything's gone mad since I came back from Kethos.'

He stared at her, his bright eyes narrowed and uncomprehending. 'I thought this was all too good to be true,' he said at last. 'I thought you were perfect.'

'But I'm not,' Alice said. 'I'm far from perfect. I'm plain and dull and—'

'And you're mad, aren't you? You're one of these crazy, neurotic women who can't accept it when a man falls in love with her. You've got to question it and pick it apart until nothing's left.'

'*Please*, Ben – I'm not. Really I'm not. I wouldn't make something like this up. I couldn't even begin to.'

'You don't believe I really have feelings for you, do you?' he said.

Alice looked at him and the pained expression on his face tore at her heart. 'I daren't believe it. I can't allow myself to.'

'Well, if that's the way you feel, I think we should probably end it,' he said, his gaze holding hers for a moment.

Alice nodded. 'I do too,' she said slowly.

Then he did something totally unexpected – he walked across the room and took her face in his hands and kissed her. It was a sweet, tender kiss and Alice felt tears welling up in her eyes. What was she doing? Why was she pushing him away like this? She must be mad.

'Goodbye, Alice,' he said. It seemed a strange thing to say because she knew she would see him every day for the rest of their working lives together but she knew what he meant. They'd never be together like this again.

She closed her eyes as he left the room. She'd never felt such a heavy weight of sadness before but she knew that this was the right thing to do and, as she opened her eyes and watched him walk away, she couldn't help feeling a little bit relieved.

Chapter 27

Being irresistible to men wasn't all it was cracked up to be, Alice couldn't help thinking when she got home that night. Things were getting out of hand. She'd thought she could control everything but it was becoming obvious now that she couldn't.

She thought of the wounded expression on Ben's face as she'd told him she thought they should break up. How was she going to face him the next time he came into the department? And how was she going to stop Larry from talking about her in his sleep? Wilfred the postman and Bus-Stop-Bruce were still professing their undying love for her too and old Mr Montague had been waiting by his garden gate to serenade her when she'd got home from work.

'I've got to stop this,' she told herself. 'There's *got* to be an answer.'

Dropping her handbag on the floor and kicking off her shoes, she went through to the spare bedroom and found the copy of the book, *Know Your Gods,* but there was nothing in there about wishes going wrong so she turned her computer on, searching for the forum she'd found where other people had detailed their experiences about making a wish on the statue of Aphrodite. Surely there were some negative experiences amongst them? Not everyone could have had a happy ending, could they?

Sure enough, Alice soon found what she wanted.

Two years ago, I made a wish on the statue of Aphrodite in the gardens at the Villa Argenti. I wanted to become a man magnet. It was such a stupid thing to wish for but I've always been unlucky in love. Men just don't look at me and I wanted to change that.

It was a total nightmare.

Alice shook her head. Here was somebody who was experiencing exactly what she was going through but what had happened to her? Had the nightmare stopped? Or was this poor woman still being plagued by too much male attention? Alice had to find out.

'Kerry Colter-Webb,' she read the name at the top of the entry. There couldn't be too many women with that name, she thought, immediately logging into Facebook. Sure enough, there was just one and, on her page, it listed 'Greek Goddesses' amongst her interests. Even better than that, her home town was listed as Bury St Edmunds which wasn't that far from Alice. This had to be the woman, Alice thought, as she prepared to send her a message, telling her how she, too, had made a wish on the statue of Aphrodite – a wish to be noticed by men – and how her life had been a nightmare ever since.

It was only an hour later when the reply landed in Alice's inbox.

Dear Alice, it read, *we must talk. Give me a call on the number below and we can arrange to meet.*

Kerry.

* * *

239

It was Saturday morning and Alice had arrived way too early in Bury St Edmunds in her anxiety to be on time and had been forced to pace the cathedral grounds. Everywhere she looked, she was reminded of Aphrodite and the dreadful mistake she'd made because the gardens were full of rose bushes. Aphrodite's flower, she thought, cringing at the thought that the plants were mocking her.

She looked at her watch. She was still early so she walked into a little art gallery and looked at some Suffolk landscapes in oil that she couldn't afford to buy. There was one with what looked like a temple in the distance. A Greek temple in the middle of Constable country? Alice peered closer and saw that it wasn't a Greek temple at all but part of a ruined church. She moved away from the painting, her heart beating as she thought of the temple on Kethos – the place where she and Milo had made love. She hadn't thought about it for a good few weeks now. She'd managed to block Milo out when she'd been seeing Ben but, suddenly, all her memories of Kethos came back to her and she couldn't shake them away.

'They say that if you make love here, you will be bound together for all eternity.'

Milo's voice drifted back into her mind. She took a deep breath. *Bound together for all eternity*, she mused. Eternity had obviously become a lot shorter in the modern world, she couldn't help thinking.

Leaving the gallery and heading towards the café where she was going to meet Kerry, Alice couldn't help wondering what the next hour was going to reveal. Would Kerry confirm that her suspicions about the statue were right? Or would she simply be mad – as Ben had accused her of being. His words still stung her and she wished with all her heart that she could make him believe her but, as she took a seat in the corner of the café by the window, she knew that it was well and truly over between them and she had to put him out of her mind.

She ordered a hot chocolate as she waited and, just as she was checking her watch for the fifth time in as many minutes, the door of the café opened and a woman walked in. She caught Alice's eye and they seemed to recognise that they were there to meet each other.

Kerry Colter-Webb was about forty-five. Her hair was short and dark, threaded through with strands of grey. She wasn't beautiful. She was of average height, had a plain face and looked as if she constantly struggled with diets. Alice could totally understand why she'd made her wish. They were two of a kind, weren't they?

She smiled at Alice as she pulled out a chair opposite her and sat down. 'Right,' she said without any preamble, 'tell me *exactly* what's happened.'

Alice took a deep breath and started at the beginning, working her way through the many different disasters that had befallen her since making her wish. When she stopped, she looked at Kerry and saw her simply nod her head and, in that moment, she felt as if a great weight had been lifted from her. This woman understood her, didn't she? She didn't think Alice was mad because she knew she was telling the truth.

Kerry then told her story. Like Alice, she'd been on holiday to Kethos and had stumbled upon the statue of Aphrodite quite by accident.

'It was summer and the villa gardens were buzzing with people and there seemed to be a bit of a queue by this one statue so I hung around for a while to see what was happening and people were making wishes,' she said, smiling at the memory as if she could see the scene before her once again. 'Hand after hand was reaching out to touch the goddess and I wanted a go too. It's silly really because I've never believed in that sort of thing before. Coins in fountains, fortunes in cookies – it's all complete nonsense, isn't it? But I really felt drawn to the statue and my hand was reaching out and I was making a wish before I knew it.' She looked wistful for a moment but then her coffee arrived and the romantic haze lifted.

'I don't believe in wishes either,' Alice said.

'Strange, isn't it?' Kerry said. 'I denied it for so long too. I thought I must have got a nice tan or something and that's why I was suddenly turning heads.'

'I thought that too!' Alice said.

'But it became a nightmare pretty quickly. At first, I thought it was brilliant. It was like an incredible superpower. I really felt like a goddess!' She grinned and she looked like a teenage girl for a moment – one that's been told she's beautiful for the first time in her life.

'So what happened?' Alice asked, stirring her hot chocolate absentmindedly as Kerry continued.

'The same that's been happening to you, I imagine. Men – *all* of them – started noticing me for the first time in my life. The things that were happening, the compliments I was getting—' she paused and then shook her head. 'I had to keep telling myself that it wasn't real although I so wanted to believe in it all.'

Alice nodded. 'Yes!' she said in complete sympathy.

Kerry gave a little laugh. 'There was this man who lived in the flat above mine. I'd had a secret crush on him for months but he never took any notice of me. I could have taken my rubbish out stark naked and he still wouldn't have batted an eyelid but, as soon as I got home from Kethos, he started making a move on me. He sent me flowers and chocolates. He even bought me this gold heart pendant. It was really something,' she said.

'So, what happened?'

'Oh, I sold it. You get a good price for gold these days.'

'No,' Alice said, 'I mean, what happened with the man?'

'We went out on a few dates,' she said, 'and I soon realised that he was just an ordinary bloke. That's the thing about this wish – you might have it come true but it's not a cure-all. This guy I'd been fantasising about was a bit boring, truth be told, and his flat was a total mess. You know, I found a sock in his kitchen sink?'

Alice grinned.

'Anyway, I let things go on far longer than I really should have,' Kerry said, moving on from the sock in the sink incident. 'It was fun, you know? I liked being the centre of attention for a while. Who doesn't? And I had a feeling it wasn't going to last forever but I had no idea it would be me who'd want to put a stop to it but it just became unbearable. I mean, how many men do you really need falling in love with you on a daily basis? It gets a bit monotonous after a while.'

'So, what did you do to stop it?' Alice asked.

'I went back to Kethos,' Kerry said, 'and I went straight back to the villa. The statue was still there, of course, but I wasn't sure what to do.'

'Was there a gardener there?' Alice suddenly blurted unexpectedly.

'Where?'

'At the villa.'

Kerry shrugged. 'I can't remember. Why?'

'Oh, no reason,' Alice said, secretly glad that Kerry wasn't going to confess to a wild affair with Milo before she reversed the wish. 'Go on.'

'Well,' Kerry said, looking into the middle distance as if seeing the statue once again, 'I placed my hand on the statue and I asked her to stop the wish. I told her I didn't want to be a man magnet any more and that she could have her wish back and give it to some other poor soul.'

'And it worked?'

'It seemed to. The rest of my time on Kethos was pretty quiet. I seemed to be back to my usual dull and unremarkable self.'

Alice smiled in sympathy.

'And you've not had any repercussions?'

'See what you think,' Kerry said, clearing her throat and beckoning the young man over who had taken their order. 'What's the soup of the day?' she asked, batting her eyelashes and beaming him a smile.

'Mushroom,' he said with a straight face.

'Thank you,' Kerry said and watched as he returned to the counter. 'See? Nothing. Absolutely nothing! And you know what? It's *such* a relief!'

Alice nodded. 'Did you enjoy it, though? The wish, I mean.'

Kerry looked deep in thought for a moment and then a little smile danced across her face and she nodded. 'You'd be a fool not to make the most of it, wouldn't you? And I certainly did that but the joy doesn't last forever. I guess it's like suddenly winning the lottery or something. At first, you can't believe your luck and you splurge out, buying yourself all the things you could never afford before but then the novelty wears off and you're left with that hollow feeling. You know what I mean?'

Alice nodded. She knew.

'But you *have* to undo it, Alice,' Kerry said. 'You can't let it ruin your life and it will if you go on like this.'

The café door opened and a middle-aged couple walked in. They took a seat at the table next to Alice and Kerry and it wasn't long before the man clapped eyes on Alice.

'Hello, gorgeous!' he said, giving her a lascivious wink.

His wife turned around and glared at Alice. Kerry was glaring at her too.

'Okay,' Alice said at last. 'I'll do it. I'll go back to Kethos.'

245

Chapter 28

It had been a dirty, dusty day at the Villa Argenti and Milo had cut himself twice on shards of broken terracotta from the pots that had been smashed by the earthquake. They had spent most of the day chucking old pots into the wheelbarrow. They'd be recycled as crocks to place in the bottom of other pots when planting so that was some solace at least. Nothing was ever wasted in a garden – not by Milo, anyway. Mr Carlson would have had a team of workers come in and sweep everything up to take to a landfill site if he'd been around but Milo knew that even the most unpromising bits of rubbish could be turned into something useful in a garden.

The statue of Aphrodite was another issue altogether. She couldn't be recycled. Milo was convinced she couldn't even be fixed.

'She'll have to be replaced,' he told Lander.

'Mr Carlson won't like that,' Lander said.

'I know,' Milo said. 'We'll have to get a replica.'

'What about the tourists?'

'They won't know the difference,' Milo said. 'Aphrodite is Aphrodite to them.'

But she wasn't to him. This Aphrodite was special. His

employer knew it and he knew it. They'd never find a replica that was good enough.

They got to work moving the pieces of broken statue. It felt strange. Milo almost felt like a surgeon as he carried the bits of body over to the wheelbarrow. It was hard and heavy work but they had soon moved the statue to the entrance gate.

'What's going to happen now?' Lander asked.

'The repair guy will pick her up,' Milo said. 'I gave him a call.'

'What about Athena? And Artemis's hound?'

'He might be able to repair those on site,' Milo said. 'He's going to take a look when he picks up Aphrodite.'

Lander nodded and the two of them went their separate ways as they did their best to tidy up the rest of the garden. They'd had to close it to visitors until it was safe again and Milo missed their idle chatter.

For a moment, he thought about the time he'd first seen Alice in the garden and how they'd chatted so easily to one another, sitting together on the white bench under the fig tree as if they were old friends. How sad he felt that he wouldn't see her again – that bright smile and those kind eyes. He couldn't help wondering whom she was smiling at now and if they knew how lucky they were.

He blinked hard, trying to dispel the image of Alice from his mind. He had work to do and he couldn't be standing around daydreaming about a woman he was never going to see again.

* * *

That evening after work, Milo stopped by a little shop on the edge of town and picked up a bag of Tiana's favourite sweets. She'd been having nightmares since the earthquake which seemed odd as she'd been so calm throughout the quake itself. It just went to show you that you could never second-guess how somebody was feeling just from their outward appearance, he thought, especially a little girl.

He hadn't spoken to Hanna since before the earthquake and hoped that her home had survived without too much damage. As he rode up the track to her house, he saw, with relief, that it was fine.

The island had been lucky. This time. Geologists were always warning them that 'the big one' was on its way but what were they expected to do? Milo didn't want to leave Kethos and it would take more than the threat of an earthquake to get him off the island. Besides, it wasn't much safer on the mainland. If the earth was going to throw a tantrum then the islanders would just have to get on with it as best as they could. They were a tough lot and had learnt to live with the quirks of Mother Nature.

Getting off his bike, he walked towards the front door which – as usual – was open, the smell of a fine dinner wafting out into the air.

'Hanna!' he called, entering the kitchen.

'Milo?' she said, surprise in her voice as she appeared in the doorway.

'I'm not late, am I?' he asked.

She shook her head. 'I wasn't expecting you at all.'

'What do you mean?'

'Your brother – he took Tiana,' she said and, as soon as the words were out of her mouth, Milo's heart plummeted. 'Didn't he tell you? He said he'd told you.' Her voice was high and anxious now.

'No, he didn't tell me,' Milo said, raking a hand through his hair and leaving it sticking out at the side of his head so that he looked as if he'd been electrocuted.

'Oh, Milo!' Hanna's hands flew to her face. She knew that the brothers were always fighting about who should take care of Tiana but nothing like this had ever happened before. 'He told me he'd spoken to you and that everything was fine.'

'He lied,' Milo said through gritted teeth. 'Why didn't you stop him?'

'But I didn't know! And he's her brother,' Hanna said. 'How could I stop him?'

Milo took a deep breath. He had to calm down. He was upsetting Hanna and it wasn't her fault. His face was anguished and he did a funny sort of dance right there in the kitchen as if he didn't know what to do or which way to go. The last ferry had left the island and there was no way of getting to the mainland tonight unless he took a little boat out himself and he'd never been one for seafaring.

'I've got to go,' he said at last, leaving the house.

'Milo – I'm so sorry!'

'I'll sort it out,' he called to her as he marched towards his bike, swearing under his breath.

It was a reckless Milo that rode home that evening – a Milo that wouldn't have ridden like that if Tiana had been with him. But she wasn't with him. She'd been taken from him.

He blinked hot tears from his eyes. He was not normally the sort to cry but his anger and fear had got a hold of him. He just wanted Tiana back but what could he do? Georgio had no right to come and take her without saying anything. It wasn't fair on him and it certainly wasn't fair on Tiana.

Had he even bothered to collect any of her things before dragging her off to the mainland? He doubted it, but just in case he had stopped by their house, Milo increased his speed. Maybe they were still there. Maybe Tiana had somehow managed to run away, causing Georgio to miss the last ferry. Maybe…

The front wheel of the bike suddenly skidded and a cloud of dust blinded him as he struggled to keep control. He lost control and the bike hurtled towards the rocky precipice at the side of the road.

Chapter 29

Alice was searching for the cheapest flight to Athens on her computer at home when the phone rang. It was her father's nursing home.

'Alice? I think you should come quickly,' Sam told her. 'It's your father. He's asking for you.'

Sam was there to greet Alice when she arrived half an hour later.

'How is he?' she asked as she walked into reception.

'Not good,' Sam said. 'He had an uneasy night. He was calling out for you.'

Tears pricked Alice's eyes. 'Can I see him?'

'Of course. He's in his room.'

Alice took the stairs up to the first floor and ran down the corridor that led to her father's room. She knocked lightly on the door and then went in. Her father was sitting up in bed, a blank expression on his face.

'Dad?' Alice was beside him in a moment, sitting on the bed and taking his huge hands in her tiny ones. 'Are you okay?'

He didn't answer but kept staring straight ahead. Finally, he spoke.

'Where are they, Stella?'

'Dad – it's not Stella. It's *Alice*.' She squeezed his hands.

'Where are they?' he persisted.

'Where's what?'

'The papers. The papers I signed.'

'I don't have any papers, Dad. I'm Alice.' She frowned. What on earth was he talking about?

'I shouldn't have signed them,' he said. 'What have you done with them? I need to talk to Alice.'

'Daddy – it *is* Alice. Look at me!' But, even as she cupped his face in her hands, he didn't seem to be focusing on anything.

It was then that Sam appeared at the door. 'Everything okay?' he said. 'I heard raised voices.'

'He keeps talking about some papers,' Alice said. 'He seems to think that he's signed something. Do you know anything about it?'

Sam shook his head. 'No, but I've heard him talk about it before. He's been having these episodes when he doesn't make any sense at all,' Sam said as he stepped into the room and shut the door behind him. 'And it's hard to tell what's real and what isn't.'

'What do you mean?'

'Well, some patients have been known to create whole worlds which simply don't exist other than in their mind. Like dear Mrs Plendign on the ground floor. She has whole conversations with her daughter, Rose, but she never had any children. Then there's Mr Folger who talks about his brother all the time but he died over fifty years ago. To hear him, though, you'd think he was still around.' Sam scratched his chin. 'It's sometimes impossible to know what residents are

252

talking about. Maybe your father's confused about something that happened years ago.'

Alice looked at her father's pale face and picked his hands up again. She sat there with him for another hour until he fell asleep and she thought it best if she left.

The residents of the home were watching *Some Like It Hot* in the lounge. It was film night – one of her father's favourite nights of the week – and he was missing it. Mind you, half of the people in the lounge had nodded off too.

Sam stood up from where he'd been kneeling beside Mr Keely. The old man had a habit of kicking his shoes off and then getting up and tripping over them but Sam had double knotted the laces this time.

'Everything okay?' he asked as he approached Alice.

'He's asleep,' she told him.

'I'll keep an eye on him.'

'Thank you,' Alice said, turning to go.

'Alice?'

She stopped as Sam caught up with her, the breathy sound of Marilyn Monroe singing *I Wanna be Loved by You* reaching her. 'Yes?'

His eyes took on a wistful look and Alice swallowed. 'It might not be appropriate for me to tell you this but I can't stop thinking about you. You're the most wonderful—'

'You're right, Sam,' she interrupted quickly. 'It isn't appropriate.' And, without delay, she made a beeline for the door, realising that she had to get home and book that flight to Athens right away.

* * *

Something was throbbing with pain but Milo couldn't tell what exactly. He tried to move and winced. Everything seemed to hurt and he cursed to himself as he realised what had happened.

He lifted his head and instantly regretted it. He was still wearing his helmet but it felt like a cannonball on his head as he looked around and saw that he'd landed on a rocky ledge about twenty feet below the road. Where was his bike? He tried to sit up and cried out. He felt like a gigantic bruise. He only hoped he hadn't broken anything. He was still miles from home and it was beginning to get dark.

Taking his helmet off and turning round, he peered over the ledge to where the land tumbled away towards the sea. There was nothing but rock and scrub but Milo soon spotted something else. His moped – his beautiful moped.

He swore to himself. He could see that it was totally beyond repair – its silver body broken and dying on the mountainside because of his carelessness. He sank back down for a moment and closed his eyes. Could the day get any worse? At least he'd been spared the fall, he thought. He could so easily have gone tumbling down the mountain too and could, at this very moment, be dying right alongside his moped.

'Be thankful for that,' he told himself as he got up with a groan and dusted himself down. His jeans were ripped and his jacket was torn but nothing appeared to be broken. He had to get off this ledge but his head was pounding and he couldn't think straight so he stood for a few moments, listening to the distant hush of the sea far below then, reaching up to grasp the branch of an ancient tree, and hoping it would take his weight, he levered himself up from the ledge and scrambled over the rocks to the road above.

From there, it was a long, slow and painful walk to the nearest village where he managed to convince somebody that he wasn't a complete madman and that he really needed a lift home.

As soon as he got back, he slumped onto the sofa in the living room and rang his brother's number but, of course, there was no reply. Georgio wasn't likely to answer the phone, was he?

The house was so quiet without his little sister and he sat staring at the empty yellow armchair that she loved so much and in which she wasn't sitting. It was full of her dolls that she always refused to put away and he was glad of their silent company tonight. It was as if a little bit of Tiana was present in their glassy eyes.

He felt so hollow inside – as if a huge chunk had been cut out of him and he realised that it had been. Tiana was a part of him and he couldn't bear to be without her.

Chapter 30

Alice still had a key to the family home but had never used it because she knew it would upset Stella who thought of the old place as her own home now. But, as the bus dropped her at the end of the road, she knew the time had come to have a good look around.

Out of politeness, she rang the doorbell and breathed a sigh of relief when there was no answer. It felt funny to enter the house without Stella there and, for a moment, she could almost imagine that the clock had spun backwards and that she was coming home from school.

How long ago it had been when Alice had last felt the warmth of a family. It had all started to unravel as far back as when Alice had been twelve. That's when their mother had died from cancer and Stella had started to sink into her selfish ways. Their father hadn't known how to cope with her and so had indulged her every whim and Stella had grown up thoroughly spoilt. And Alice? What had become of that twelve-year-old girl? She looked in the hallway mirror and her pale face stared back at her. She'd battled on, hadn't she? Passing all her exams and then taking a job she didn't like and moving to a place she couldn't really afford. Then there'd been the trauma of moving her father into the home three years ago.

Life had thrown more than its share of hardship her way but she'd never given up.

'And I'm not giving up now,' she said to herself as she walked down the hallway into the kitchen. She looked around in horror at the empty takeaway trays on the draining board and the pizza box which had been dropped on the floor. Was that the reason Stella wanted a kitchen extension, Alice wondered – so she would have room to make even more mess?

She looked around, deliberating where she was going to start. Where would her sister keep important papers? In the dresser? That would be pretty organised for her but it was a good place to start so she opened the two large drawers but could see there was nothing in there but takeaway menus and taxicab cards and a brand new mobile phone that didn't look as if it had ever been used. Alice closed the drawer.

She walked through to the front room and tried the side cupboard but that only had their mother's beloved collection of crystal glasses which their father had always forbidden them to use. At least Stella was respecting that particular wish.

She looked around the room, noticing a brand new laptop in cherry red sitting on the coffee table and an expensive-looking cashmere jumper flung carelessly across a chair. Alice stroked the soft grape-coloured fabric and hoped that Stella had found it in a charity shop but knew that she'd probably bought it full price from a boutique on one of her trips into London.

She moved through to the hallway and climbed the stairs to the bedrooms. Stella's was easy to spot. It looked like a clothes shop explosion. There were jumpers, jackets and dresses strewn across the bed as well as the carpet. No surface was left bare. There were heaps of tangled jewellery – gold and silver chains unashamedly knotted together and brooches clambering over bangles. A whole city of glass perfume bottles jostled for space on the dressing table and glittering photo frames punctuated the gaps. Alice peered closely and saw that each perfect frame contained an image of Stella.

She opened the top drawer but soon discovered that it was full of underwear – expensive lacy underwear. The next drawer was filled with more jumpers – each so soft to the touch that Alice surmised that they must have been cashmere like the one downstairs. She frowned. How on earth was Stella paying for all these things when she refused to get a job? It was a question which Alice wasn't sure she wanted answering.

She opened the third and final drawer. It was a jumble of tights and stockings and it was clear that there wasn't anything paper-related to be found there.

As she stood back up to full height, something caught her eye. There was a little bedside table on which sat a pile of fashion magazines and Alice noticed a cardboard folder underneath. She crossed the room and picked it up, opening it to see what was housed inside and then she groaned.

She'd found what she thought she was looking for. It was a will. Not the kind of will drawn up by an expensive solicitor but one of those you can print from the internet and Alice was pretty sure that it wouldn't stand up in court.

She recognised her father's shaky signature at the bottom. So this is what he'd been so worried about. What exactly had he thought he'd signed away? Alice studied the document. Stella hadn't even bothered detailing anything – she'd obviously just been intent on getting their father's signature on it but Alice could well imagine what she was thinking of and she didn't believe that her own name would appear anywhere on the document.

It was then that she heard the front door open. Her sister was back. Quickly, she left the bedroom with the will in her hand and walked down the stairs, her heart thumping in her chest. She had no idea what she was going to say and wished that she was anywhere but there.

'ALICE!' Stella screamed as she saw her sister, her hand dramatically flying to her chest. 'You gave me such a shock!'

Alice stared at her for a moment, not sure where to begin.

'What are you doing here?' Stella continued.

'I'm trying to find out what *you're* doing!' Alice replied, her voice rising just a little.

'What do you mean?' she asked, dropping her car keys on the hall table. Alice held out the will and saw her sister turn pale. 'Have you been going through my things?'

'Of *course* I've been going through your things. How do you think I found this?'

'But this is my home!' she said. 'You've got no right to do that!'

'No, Stella – this is our father's home,' Alice said, following her into the living room. 'He's not dead yet!'

Stella had the good grace to look shamefaced for a moment. 'But—'

'He's written his will,' Alice told her. 'He wrote it years ago when he knew he was sliding into dementia.'

'But that's not fair!' Stella protested. 'That's before everything happened.'

'What are you talking about? Before what happened?'

Stella's eyes filled with tears but she didn't answer right away.

'Stella – what's going on?'

Stella sank onto the sofa but Alice remained standing. 'I'm in debt,' Stella said at last.

Alice blinked but didn't seem surprised. She sat down on the chair opposite her sister. 'How much do you owe?' she asked.

'I don't know,' Stella said.

'You *must* know! Is it a few hundred pounds? Or over a thousand? What?' Alice asked, exasperation in her voice.

'It's more than that.'

'*How* much more?'

Stella shrugged. 'I'm not sure. About eleven thousand pounds.'

Alice's eyes doubled in size.

'Don't look at me like that! You're always judging me.'

'I'm not always judging you,' Alice said, trying desperately to remain calm. 'I'm just trying to work out what's going on.'

'What do you mean?'

'God, Stella! I know you're not the world's greatest mathematician but you must know that if you spend more than you earn then you're going to end up in trouble. I mean, just look around you.' She pointed to the cherry-red laptop and the cashmere clothes. 'You haven't got a job. You've made no *effort* to get a job and yet you're spending money as if you've just won the lottery.'

'But I'm entitled to nice things,' she said.

'You're entitled to *nothing* – not unless you earn the money first,' Alice explained. 'I can't afford to go out and buy myself brand new clothes and I've got a full-time job!'

'But I like nice things.'

'I know you do,' Alice said. 'You've been spoiled. Dad used to spoil you all the time. He was wrong to do that but he knew how upset you were when Mum died and it was the only thing he knew how to do. He used to spoil Mum too – remember?'

Stella shook her head and Alice remembered just how young Stella had been when their mother had died.

'You look so much like her and I think Dad treated you a lot like Mum with all those gifts. I don't suppose it's your fault that you've grown so used to always having what you want but it has to stop. You're not a child any more. You've got to grow up and take care of yourself.'

Stella looked shaken for a moment.

Alice sat forward, directing her gaze at her sister. 'What did you think was going to happen? That you could get Dad to sign everything over to you? Did you really think he'd do that?'

'I don't know what I thought!' Stella cried. 'I just need the money.'

'And what would happen if you did get it? You'd have it all spent in no time and then be broke again. This can't go on, Stella!'

Stella looked down at the carpet and Alice couldn't tell if she was taking everything on board or if she was planning on replacing the ancient carpet with a new Axminster at the earliest opportunity.

'Do you know how worried Dad is about all this? He's going out of his mind,' Alice told her.

'He's already out of his mind,' Stella said.

'This isn't a joke, Stella. This is just the sort of thing that could tip him over the edge. He's weak and he needs to be kept calm.'

'Don't lecture me!'

'I'm not lecturing you.' Alice bit her lip and counted silently to ten. She needed to be calm. 'Just promise me you'll try and find work. Promise me you'll curb all this spending.' There was silence. 'Nobody is going to bail you out of this mess but you – can't you see that? Dad's not always going to be around to pick up the bills and I don't earn enough to look after myself half the time let alone a shopaholic sister. You've got to take care of this yourself, you see that, don't you?'

Stella nodded slowly and looked up at Alice. 'I'm sorry I'm always causing you so much trouble,' she said in a tiny voice. It was the first time that Stella had ever apologised for anything in her life.

Alice got up from the chair and sat down next to her sister on the sofa, hugging her to her and kissing her cheek. 'I'm afraid I don't have eleven thousand pounds knocking about but I'll help you where I can.'

'You will?'

'Of course I will.'

They sat like that for a moment longer and Alice couldn't help wondering what life would be like if the two of them were like this all the time. She almost felt close to her in that rare moment of calm but then Stella's mobile went and she sprang up to answer it.

'Oh, Andy!' she cried as if in relief. 'No, of *course* I haven't forgotten. Yes, I'll be there later. Give me an hour, okay? I've got to get changed. Just wait until you see the dress I've got! See you, honey!' She hung up.

'Are you going out?' Alice asked.

'Yes. To that new club.'

Alice's eyebrows shot up. 'You won't be spending any money there, will you?'

'Of course not!' Stella chimed. 'Andy will be getting all the drinks in, I expect. I'll only have to pay for a taxi home.'

Alice sighed. Had Stella been listening to her at all?

Alice's answerphone was blinking when she got home and she realised that her mobile phone had gone flat.

She pressed play.

'Alice? It's Sam. You need to come in right away.'

That was it. That was all the message there was and she knew exactly what it meant.

Chapter 31

Milo hated leaving the island but he had no choice. He'd called Lander at the villa to explain the situation and his colleague had said it was no trouble.

Boarding the first boat to the mainland in the morning, Milo stood at the rails and looked back at Kethos. The morning sunshine cast the water a deep peacock-blue and the white buildings of Kethos Town gleamed brightly. He wondered when he'd see his little island again and only hoped he'd have Tiana with him when he did.

He tried not to think of the worst that could happen – that Georgio wouldn't let him see her or that he'd got some sort of lawyer involved with papers drawn up or that he and Sonya had actually moved house to some town that Milo would never be able to find. They wouldn't do that, would they? Milo winced. Right now, he wouldn't put anything past that brother of his.

He paced the deck of the boat. His body was still sore after his moped accident and he realised that he'd probably done himself more damage than he'd first thought but he didn't have time for that now. A sprained ankle or wrist could wait; his sister couldn't.

As they approached the mainland, he tried to think how long ago it was since his last trip there. It was probably

Georgio's wedding which had taken place in a big modern hotel in Athens. The whole thing had been a big, brash affair with very little heart, it had seemed to Milo. If he ever got married, it would be in the little church near his home where he and his bride would be surrounded by the people he'd grown up with. Milo and his new wife would walk out of the tiny church to bright, wide sea views and the reception would be modest but satisfying – wholesome home-cooked food prepared on the island, not the fancy fare that had filled Georgio's reception.

He shook his head. Now was not the time to be thinking about mythical brides and weddings that might never happen. He had to focus on Tiana.

Milo wished that the boat would pick up some speed. Didn't they know that he was in a hurry? Georgio and Sonya had probably got Tiana signed up at some expensive school already and were trying to teach her how to speak without the gentle burr that was common to islanders. He felt his fingers curl up into an angry fist at the thought. He could well imagine Sonya pulling some godawful uniform onto his little girl and trying to flatten her unruly hair because she wouldn't want Tiana as she was – oh, no. She'd want to turn her into a neat little doll-child that wore perfect clothes, had perfect hair and didn't run around orchards climbing trees and falling out of them.

Finally, the boat docked and Milo sprinted off it and took a bus into the centre of Athens. From the station, he took a taxi and almost balked when told the price of his fare. He wasn't used to paying for such luxuries but he hadn't wanted to waste any time walking in the wrong direction whilst trying to find his brother's place.

Georgio and Sonya lived in an apartment in a block which towered over a narrow street and overlooked several other blocks just like it. Milo grimaced. There were no fields or orchards or views of the sea here.

Reaching the door of the flats, he realised he should have a plan. If he buzzed his brother's intercom, would he even let him in? Milo had a feeling he wouldn't. He had to get into the flats first.

He hung around for a bit, waiting for an opportunity and, after five minutes, an elderly lady came to the door, a shopping bag slung over her arm.

'Let me,' Milo said, holding the door open for her as she emerged.

'So kind,' she said, her bright eyes beaming up at him. She didn't turn around and question whether he should actually be allowed access to the flats and he walked quickly towards the stairs before she had the chance to realise that he wasn't a resident.

His brother's flat was on the seventh floor but Milo didn't trust lifts and certainly didn't want to risk being stuck in one when he'd come this far but his pace was a lot slower than he anticipated and he had to stop several times because of the throbbing pain in his right ankle.

Finally, he made it to the flat. Checking his battered watch face, he saw that it was half past ten. Would anybody be at home? He'd only thought of that now but surely they wouldn't have marched Tiana off to school already? Even they wouldn't be as cruel as to do that, would they? Surely they would allow her to settle in before forcing her into a new life.

He pressed his ear up against the door and listened. He could definitely hear voices and he felt his anger rise as he lifted his hand and knocked loudly on the door. He didn't have to wait long before Sonya greeted him.

'Milo!' she cried, her eyes wide.

'What? You think I wouldn't come as soon as I found out what you'd done?' He pushed past his sister-in-law and strode into the immaculate living room filled with furniture made from leather and glass. His brother was standing by the window on his phone but he hung up as soon as he saw Milo.

'Where's Tiana?' Georgio demanded.

For a moment, Milo was confused. 'What?'

'Where is she?'

'What do you mean?' Milo said, a look of fear crossing his face.

'She's not here, Milo,' his brother told him.

'Then where is she?'

'You think we're not trying to find out? We've been going out of our minds with worry!'

'*You've* been going out of your mind?' Milo said. 'You're not the one who's had her taken from him. *You're* the one who put her in danger, Georgio! You took her from her home and brought her to a place she has no business being.'

'But *this* should be her home too – here with us!'

'How can you say that? She hates the city and – right now – she's probably out there lost in the middle of it. God!' Milo's eyes were dark with fury. 'How could you do this? How could you be so selfish?'

267

'I'm doing what's right for her.'

'No, you're not – you're doing what's right for *you!* You just took her, damn you! As if you had a right to do that.'

'I have every right,' Georgio said.

'Goddam it!' Milo cursed. 'Have you ever had a conversation with her? *Have* you? And I mean something that goes beyond "How was your day at school?" because conversations with a kid are about more than that, you know?'

'Oh, and you know exactly how to behave around a kid, don't you?'

Milo bristled. 'I might not be the best father-figure to her. You might be older but she loves *me!*'

'Milo – *please!*' Sonya said.

'She's ten years old,' Milo continued, 'and you've taken her from everything she knows and loves. She doesn't want to be here. How many times do I have to tell you that? When are you going to understand that she's happy with me?'

'Stop, *please!*' Sonya begged, her eyes filling with tears. 'This isn't going to help Tiana. We've got to try and find her.'

Georgio had started pacing up and down the room. He looked pale and Milo's anger suddenly ebbed away as he realised that his brother was just as terrified as he was.

'Have you taken her anywhere since she arrived?' Milo asked, his voice calmer now.

'We haven't had time,' Sonya said, wiping her eyes with an immaculate handkerchief. 'We came straight home from the boat.'

'Which is her room?'

Sonya led Milo through to a bedroom at the back of the

flat. It was tiny and Milo could smell fresh paint on the walls and couldn't help noticing that they were pink just like her bedroom at home. The bed was covered in brand new soft toys and Milo felt himself softening just a little. They might not have gone about it the right way but it was obvious that they adored Tiana and were desperate to make a home for her here.

He cursed under his breath and turned around. 'Have you *no* idea where she might have gone?'

They both shook their heads.

'There's nowhere to go here,' Sonya said, her eyes filling with tears again. 'It's just streets.'

Milo nodded. He'd seen. There were no parks, no playgrounds, no open spaces that Tiana might feel tempted to visit. Anyway, this wasn't about running away to a park because she wanted to play. This was about her trying to get home.

'She's trying to get back to Kethos,' he said as the idea dawned on him.

'What?' Georgio said, the word exiting his mouth like a gunshot. 'That's crazy! Why would she do that? *How* would she do that?'

'Remember when we came over last year for the day?' Milo remembered the day he'd dragged himself away from Kethos so that they could exchange Christmas presents with Georgio and Sonya. He'd thought his last trip to the mainland had been for Georgio's wedding but it hadn't, had it? He'd almost forgotten about the rough boat ride over in December. Both he and Tiana had felt queasy but had she been paying enough attention to get herself home again on her own?

'You don't seriously believe she'd try to get back to Kethos, do you?' Sonya said.

Milo shrugged. 'I think we *have* to believe it. It's our only hope.'

Chapter 32

Alice couldn't help but smile when she saw her father's coffin. She'd been prepared, of course, because they'd talked about it many times in the past but the reality was, well, so much *brighter* than she'd imagined. How many other people would dare to have a green and yellow coffin, she wondered? He'd chosen the colours in honour of his support of Norwich City Football Club and there, amongst the brilliant yellow flowers and green foliage sat a stuffed toy canary.

Stella was mortified. 'I don't believe it! What was he thinking of?'

'The Canaries, I think,' Alice said, once again acknowledging how little Stella had known their father.

'I think it's terrible!'

'It's his funeral. He can do what he likes.'

'He always did,' Stella said.

Alice turned and glared at her. 'What's that supposed to mean?'

'Nothing,' Stella snapped.

Alice shook her head. She still couldn't believe he'd gone. The heart attack had been shockingly swift. He'd had one before and had been warned to take things easy.

'Easy?' he'd laughed. 'I'm stuck in a wheelchair for half the day and in bed for the other half. How much bloody easier can I take it?'

Alice smiled as she remembered and tears pricked her eyes as she realised that she'd never hear that wonderfully warm laugh again. He hadn't had many reasons to laugh over the last few years but his sense of humour had never left him.

Alice still couldn't believe that it was happening. After Sam's phone call, everything had seemed to happen in slow motion and yet it had all happened frighteningly fast. It didn't seem a moment since she'd been sitting on her father's bed with his hands held in hers and now they were at his funeral about to cremate him.

She closed her eyes as hot tears threatened to spill. He hadn't known who she was that last time she'd visited him and the memory pained her. If only they'd had more time together. If only he'd had some glimmer of recognition that day.

The funeral went as well as a funeral possibly could. Sam had taken a couple of hours off work to attend and Alice was glad of his company even though he kept giving her flirty little looks over the hymn books.

'He was a fine man,' he told her after the service had ended.

'Thank you,' she said.

'Alice,' he said.

'What?'

'There's something I really need to tell you.' His eyes widened and had that doe-like expression that Alice was now used to recognising.

'Not now, Sam,' she said, knowing that whatever Sam wanted to say had nothing to do with her father's funeral.

'But you don't know what I'm going to say,' he protested.

'I do,' she said, and hurried down the gravel path out of the churchyard. Now was not the time to hear another man's declaration of love.

After it was all over, there was a reception at the hotel near the care home and Alice was warmed to see so many residents there to pay their last respects to her father.

'Oh, look at him over there,' Stella said, nodding towards an elderly man who was standing by the window with a plate piled high with food from the buffet. 'He's still got his slippers on!'

'And you will too if you're lucky enough to reach his age.'

'Trust me,' Stella said, 'I will still be tottering around in my heels even when I'm ninety.'

Alice rolled her eyes as an image of an ancient Stella flirting her way around an old people's home whilst wearing heels assaulted her vision.

'I'm getting something to eat,' Stella said, leaving Alice's side. Alice couldn't eat. Her stomach felt as if it was somersaulting inside her but she did reach out for a glass of wine from a nearby tray. It was as she was finishing it off and contemplating a second glass that she saw the old woman sitting in a chair by the window. She hadn't noticed her before and wondered why. She was very striking with her smooth, shoulder-length silver hair and a blue and pink shawl embracing her body.

'Hello,' Alice said as she approached her and took a seat next to her. 'Thanks so much for coming today.'

'I'm afraid I didn't make the service,' the woman said. 'I have problems with my back, I'm afraid, and I can't sit up for long any more and I get awfully cold.'

'It was certainly cold in there,' Alice said, shivering at the memory of the icy church. 'Can I get you anything?'

'Oh, no thank you. I'm saving up for dinner.' She gave a little smile. 'At my age, food is one of the few things we have to look forward to.'

'How old are you? If you don't mind me asking.'

'I don't mind, my dear. I'm eighty-two.'

Alice smiled at her. 'You must have seen so many amazing things.'

'And been to an awful lot of funerals.' She pulled her shawl a little tighter around her shoulders. 'That's the downside of getting old. Amongst other things, of course. It's so sad to see all your friends go.'

Alice nodded.

'And your father was a very dear friend indeed,' she said, her pale eyes bright. 'He's going to be missed so much.'

Alice's eyes filled with tears.

'Oh, my dear, I didn't mean to make you sad.'

'No, you didn't. I'm happy. Really I am,' Alice said. 'It's just that everyone's so kind. They keep telling me the loveliest things about him today and it makes me realise how much he was loved.'

'He certainly was.'

Alice blinked her tears away and looked at the woman. 'You're Rosa, aren't you?'

The old lady smiled and nodded.

'I'm sorry we've not met before,' Alice said.

'That's all right. I know that your time with your father was always precious.'

'You mean there was never enough of it,' Alice said, sadness filling her eyes.

The old lady looked shocked. 'I didn't say that.'

'I know, but it's just that I feel I never had enough time with him,' she said with a sad smile.

'But that couldn't be helped. You're a working girl and I know how hard all you young girls work these days.'

Alice shook her head. 'But it's still a lousy excuse.'

'You spent every moment you could with your father. Everybody knew that. He was a very lucky man. I hardly ever get to see my family.'

'Don't you?'

She shook her head. 'My daughter lives in Lancashire and my son – well, he doesn't like care homes.'

'I'm sorry,' Alice said. 'That's awful.'

'That's life,' Rosa said.

There was a pause and they both looked out of the window on to the immaculate lawn. There was a little weak sunshine about and Alice spotted a statue hiding amongst the shrubbery. She cocked her head to one side. It looked like a classical figure. Could it possibly be Aphrodite or was her mind playing tricks on her?

'So, what are you going to do now?' Rosa asked, breaking into Alice's thoughts.

'What do you mean?'

'Well, your father said that you were only really living here because of him and, well, now that he's gone…' She looked up at Alice with questioning eyes.

'I don't understand,' Alice said.

'He told me that there was something about you – something hidden away that was waiting to get out. He said that you were suppressing it – that you were just going through the motions here but that something would take you away one day.'

'Really? He said that?'

The old lady nodded. 'Is there something? Something you want to do? I mean, I hope you don't mind me saying this but, with what your father is leaving you, you might very well be able to do it.'

'But I don't want to do anything,' Alice said, puzzled. 'I'm happy here.'

'Are you?' The old lady sounded surprised. 'But your father told me—' she paused.

'What?' Alice asked, desperate to know.

'He said that you would surprise everybody. He said that Stella might do the most outrageous things but you would be the one to do the most *amazing* thing.'

'How strange. He never said anything like that to me,' Alice said.

'But he must have been thinking it.' The old lady reached out and grabbed one of Alice's hands and she was surprised by its warmth. 'I hope you don't mind me saying all this to you,' she said. 'He loved talking about you. He was very proud of you, you know.'

Alice could feel the all-familiar tears once again. 'Thank you,' she said. 'Thank you so much for telling me all this.'

A young woman suddenly appeared at the side of Rosa and helped her out of her chair.

'Time to get you home, Mrs Reynolds.'

Rosa gave Alice a look of resignation and Alice said her goodbyes and watched as she linked arms with the young lady and was led away.

Alice turned and glanced around the room. She was looking for Stella but couldn't see her anywhere. She'd probably gone home, Alice thought, believing that she'd done her duty and that there was no point in hanging around any longer than was absolutely necessary.

Chapter 33

Georgio had alerted the police about the disappearance of Tiana but Milo wanted to do something more practical than hang around the flat waiting, on the chance that some overworked officer might ring them back with information. He wanted to get out there and pound the streets looking for her himself. He wanted to get back to the boat and see if she'd somehow managed to get there.

'Are you coming?' he asked his brother.

Georgio shook his head. 'I think we should all stay here in case she comes back.'

'She's *not* going to come back!' Milo shouted in frustration. 'She's trying to get away from here! *Here* is the *last* place you'll find her!'

'Oh, God, I can't bear it!' Sonya said, mopping her eyes. Her mascara had streaked down her face and, for the first time in his life, Milo saw her looking less than perfect. *Goodness*, he thought. She really did care about his little sister.

'I'm going out,' Milo announced. 'I can't stand around here doing nothing.'

'I'm coming with you,' Sonya said, getting up from the sofa.

Milo blinked in surprise. 'What?'

'What?' Georgio echoed.

'I need to *do* something!' Sonya cried.

'You need to sit down,' Georgio said.

'This is my fault,' Sonya said. 'I pressed you and pressed you until you agreed. I never once thought about Tiana. Milo's right – we put ourselves first.'

Georgio placed his huge hands on her shoulders. 'Don't think like that. We did what we thought was right.'

'But I must try and find her,' she said, making a move to find her handbag.

Milo looked pleadingly at Georgio and his brother read his mind. 'Sonya,' Georgio began, 'I don't think it's a good idea. Milo can cope perfectly well on his own.'

'But he's only one person,' Sonya said. 'We'll cover double the ground if I go as well.'

For a moment, Georgio looked helpless as his wife put a pair of stilettos on. She looked as if she was about to go out shopping rather than marching up and down the streets looking for a missing child.

'Darling,' Georgio said, 'you don't have to do this.'

'Yes!' she said, almost screaming the word. 'I *do* have to do this! Or *un*do it or—' she paused, and her beautiful mouth started to tremble.

Georgio stepped in and guided her back to the sofa. 'You're not in a state to go anywhere,' he told her gently, stroking her hair as she cried.

'But I've got to try.'

He shook his head. 'Milo will take care of things. I need you here with me.'

'You do?' she said.

'Of course I do,' he said, kissing the top of her head. 'And we need to stay here for Tiana. Both of us.'

Milo was relieved to get out of the apartment. Knowing that he was permanently broke, his brother had pressed some money into his hands just before he left.

'Let us know as soon as you find anything,' Georgio had said.

'Of course,' Milo had replied.

'Milo?' Georgio called as he'd headed for the stairs.

'Yes?'

'I'm sorry.'

Milo had nodded and had watched as his brother had returned to his flat and slowly closed the door.

He hailed a taxi outside the flat and spent ten minutes driving slowly up and down the neighbourhood streets, his eyes scanning every inch for Tiana but she was nowhere to be seen.

'Take me to the port,' he told the driver. '*Slowly.*'

He rolled his window down but he didn't hear the noises of the city. It was as if somebody had hit a mute button on the world and his vision focused on the streets, his head twitching from side to side as they drove to the port, trying to see down each and every street and alley they passed.

Would Tiana really have walked all this way on her own? He tried to get inside her mind. What would he do if he was in her position? He'd try to get home, that much was clear, but how? Would she have any money even if she could find her way back to the boat?

His mind whirred with worry at the different scenarios. She was a ten-year-old girl on her own in a large capital city. Part of him was hoping that she would go unnoticed and that she would be able to find her way back home by herself, quickly and quietly. The other part of him was hoping that some kindly person would notice her and help her but what if the wrong kind of person saw her first?

Milo closed his eyes as kidnappers, child molesters and murderers all jostled for space in his imagination.

'Tiana,' he said, whispering her name in despair as his eyes snapped open again for fear of missing her in the streets.

He wished with all his heart that Alice was there beside him, holding his hand and telling him that everything would be okay in that calm, quiet voice of hers. But she wasn't there; she was over a thousand miles away and certainly wasn't thinking about him and his problems.

When the taxi arrived at the port, he jumped out, flung some notes at the driver and ran down towards the boat for Kethos, stopping everyone he passed along the way.

'Have you seen a small girl? She's ten years old, long dark hair, about this high,' he said, gesturing with his hand. But everybody said no, shaking their heads and getting on with their own business. How could they be so callous, Milo wondered? Didn't they know this was Tiana who was missing? His dear, sweet, innocent sister whom he loved more than anything in the world. Didn't they care? Somebody *must* have seen her. How could a little girl – his special little girl – just disappear?

He dithered by the ticket office and then asked the man inside if he'd seen a little girl.

'I see many little girls. Many tourists. Everybody has a little girl with them.'

'But she would have been on her own,' Milo said but the man simply shook his head and Milo walked away.

To get on the boat or not to get on the boat – that was the question. Should he wait around the port, hoping he'd spot her, or get the next boat back to Kethos in case she'd already made her way back there? Could she have got there that quickly, he asked himself? She was a pretty determined young lady.

He got his mobile out of his pocket and rang Georgio.

'I'm getting the next boat back,' Milo told him. 'We can only hope that she made it on to one of the boats that's already gone.'

Georgio didn't try to stop him. In fact, he thought it best if Milo went home in case Tiana was trying to get back there.

Once on board, Milo couldn't relax. He paced up and down the deck, hobbling on his sore ankle and cursing every time he twisted it. He should sit down. He knew he was doing himself more harm than good and he wasn't making the time pass any faster by his strange hobbling march.

The sea was a dark, malevolent navy now and there were gunmetal-grey clouds hovering on the horizon. That's all they needed – Tiana desperately trying to get home in the middle of a raging storm.

The boat ride back to the island was the longest of Milo's life. He sincerely believed that he'd be able to swim faster with all the pent-up anxiety that was racing around him. When, at last, it docked, he pushed past the tourists and the locals, and he looked up and down the harbour, desperate to see his little sister there.

'Hey, Milo!' she'd call casually. 'What took you so long? I've been here *ages* and I was getting bored.'

But there was no sign of her and Milo's face fell with the weight of worry.

* * *

'He's selling the house?' Stella cried. 'He can't! It's my home!'

'It was *his* home,' Alice pointed out as diplomatically as she could. It was a few days after the funeral and the contents of their father's will had been revealed to the sisters. The family home was to be sold and, once bills had been settled, the proceeds were to be shared – equally – between Alice and Stella. There was also a small sum in a bank account and a few shares which didn't amount to much. The car had been left to Stella and her father's old watch had been left to Alice. The watch was probably worth more than the car was these days, Stella was quick to point out.

The possessions in the house were to be left to the discretion of the sisters and the beloved glasses that had belonged to their mother were to be shared between the two of them.

Stella didn't seem at all happy at any of the arrangements. 'But this hasn't been his home for the last few years. It's been *my* home.'

'But it has to be sold. There are bills to pay,' Alice told her. 'We have to get things sorted out.'

'And what am I meant to do?'

'Well, there's no rush,' Alice said. 'There's no telling how long it will take to sell the house and it's better if you stay. People prefer to see a home lived in although you'll have to have a good sort out and tidy up.' She cast her eye over the pile of clothes that had been dumped on a chair in the living room.

Stella looked shocked. 'And after? What happens then?'

Alice sighed. She was becoming exasperated. 'You'll just have to find somewhere else. You'll have plenty of money to put down a good deposit for a place of your own.'

'What – a pokey flat in town?'

'It would be a start, yes!'

'But I like *this* house.'

'Yes, but you can't afford this one.'

'You're just being greedy, Alice. You just want your half of the money. You're not even thinking about me.'

That seemed to do it for Alice. She was fed up of Stella accusing her of things she wasn't guilty of and she wasn't going to take it any more.

'You're right,' she said. 'I'm not thinking of you and you know why? Because I'm going away.'

'Going where?' Stella sounded panicky.

'Kethos.'

'Kethos? What on earth are you going there for?' Stella asked and then she rolled her eyes. 'Oh my God! You're going back to that guy, aren't you?'

'No, I'm not going back to that guy.'

'Then why on earth else would you bother going back there?'

Alice bit her lip. What could she say? 'I'm going back—'

'Yes?'

'Because—'

'What?'

'I have some private business there.'

Stella's face screwed up in disbelief. 'You're so weird, Alice. I'll never understand you.'

'No, you won't,' Alice said, 'because you never make an effort. Everything is always about you, isn't it?'

'What?' Stella said, her face creasing up in consternation.

'The whole world has got to revolve around you all the time, but it doesn't, Stella. It *doesn't!* There are other people on this planet too – people with dreams and worries – people who have feelings! Only you don't seem to notice because you're too wrapped up in your own selfish ways.'

'Selfish? *I'm* selfish?' Stella said, her face reddening and her eyes blazing with indignation at being scolded.

'Yes – *you!* You think it's fine to spend money that isn't yours on things you don't need and then you expect somebody else to tidy up the mess. Well, the world doesn't work that way and the quicker you learn that, the better, and I won't always be around to sort things out for you!'

'Alice – I—'

'And don't try to sweet-talk me, or flatter me or make me feel guilty about something because that isn't going to work again. I've had enough, Stella.'

Stella's mouth dropped open but – for once in her life – she didn't have a smart comeback nor did she break down in tears, and Alice used the moment to leave the house and get as far away from her as was possible.

Chapter 34

Milo was pacing up and down the harbour, wondering what to do. It felt like he'd paced the whole of Greece in his anxiety over Tiana but he just couldn't keep still whilst she was missing. He'd been in and out of every shop on the harbour front, asking if they had seen her. One woman had taken her time in replying, her eyes scanning the ceiling. Milo had waited, his heart thudding in his chest, and then she'd given him a look as if to say he was completely mad and that, of course, she hadn't seen a little girl.

He asked the row of fishermen who seemed to live on the harbour wall but they never saw anything that wasn't directly under their nose or under the water.

When he found himself at the bus stop, he decided it was best if he got himself home and be there if that was where Tiana was making her way back to. He was just fishing around in his pockets for some change when he saw her. It was a girl with long dark hair on the other side of the street. She was looking in a shop window with her back to him. Milo tried not to get excited. After all, most of the girls in Greece had long dark hair.

'Tiana?' At first, her name came out as a whisper but then the dark-haired girl turned around and he saw that it was *his* dark-haired girl.

'TIANA!' he cried, her name carrying above a sea of tourists between them. She turned and saw him and he breathed a sigh of relief, tears filling his eyes as she smiled and began to run towards him.

'Milo!' she shouted, her feet flying over the pavement.

Milo's arms opened wide as she crashed into him. 'Oh my God, Tiana! I was so worried about you.' He stroked her long hair and breathed in the scent of her in relief. 'I've been looking all over Athens for you. I didn't know where you were!'

'I was here,' she said. 'Well, I've been here a *little* while.'

'I've never been so worried in my life!'

'But I was fine,' she said. 'You shouldn't worry so much. I can look after myself.'

He cupped her face in his hands and looked down at her. 'Yes, well I can see that now but what if something had gone wrong?' he asked. 'What if you'd taken a wrong turn down a street or somebody had abducted you or you'd fallen into the sea?'

She laughed. 'But I didn't!'

Her calmness suddenly angered him. 'You mustn't *ever* do anything like that again.'

Her smile vanished. 'But I thought you'd worry if I stayed with Georgio and Sonya. I thought you wanted me to live with you.'

'I do! But you should have stayed where you were. I would have come to collect you.'

'I didn't want to stay there. It didn't feel right.'

'But you were safe there, Tiana.' He saw the sadness in

her eyes and suddenly felt terrible at having shouted at her. She was safe now and that was all that mattered so he hugged her to him again. 'How did you get back, anyway?'

Tiana looked a little uneasy for a moment. 'I took some money,' she said. 'But I'll pay it back!'

'Where did you get money from?'

'Sonya's handbag.'

Milo laughed. 'I think she'll forgive you.'

'But I ran out of money here so I couldn't get the bus home.'

'So, what were you planning to do, then?' Milo asked, trying to sound serious.

'I guessed you'd come looking for me so I thought I'd wait around here for a bit.'

'Oh, really?'

'Yes,' she said philosophically. 'I knew you'd be here sooner or later.'

'You did, did you?' he said, getting her in a gentle headlock in the crook of his arm.

'Owww!' she cried but she was laughing at the same time.

'Knew I'd come for you, eh? Knew I'd bail you out of any trouble you managed to get yourself into?' He ruffled her hair and then kissed the top of her head. 'Come on, let's get back to the bus stop and get you home.'

They walked hand in hand.

'I guess I won't be going to school today,' Tiana suddenly said.

'I guess not,' Milo said.

'It was really horrible when they took me. I screamed all the way to the boat and then cried for the whole journey too.'

Milo smiled with pride but he didn't think it wise to praise her for such behaviour even though he secretly applauded it. They were going to have to build some sort of ongoing relationship with Georgio and Sonya, after all.

'I've been thinking,' Milo said after a moment, 'and I was wondering if you might like to spend more time with Georgio and Sonya.'

Tiana stared at him with bewilderment in her eyes. 'What do you mean? I thought you didn't want me to live with them. I thought you said—'

'I don't want you to live with them!' Milo said. 'I'm not talking about you moving to Athens. I'm just thinking you could stay there every now and again – like a little holiday.' He knew he wasn't selling the idea very well because his heart really wasn't in it but he had to think about Georgio and Sonya and he remembered the fear he'd seen in their faces when they'd thought something might have happened to Tiana. 'You've got your own room there and everything, and they love you, Tiana! They really want to spend more time with you.'

Tiana's eyes filled with tears. 'Do I have to?'

'No, you don't have to but it would be really kind if you did.'

She looked thoughtful for a moment as if weighing up all the pros and all the cons and then she nodded solemnly.

'Good girl,' he said, ruffling her hair. 'Now, I'd better give Georgio and Sonya a call and let them know you're okay and it would be very nice indeed if you spoke to them too.'

'But what would I say?' she asked.

'That you're sorry.'

'Do I have to?'

'No, but it would be very nice if you did that too,' Milo said, his eyebrows raised as he awaited her response.

'Oh, all right then.'

'Good girl,' he said and he ruffled her hair once more for good measure.

* * *

It was a strange feeling to be going back to Greece, Alice thought as she stared out of the plane at the wispy white clouds that threaded by her window in eerie skeins. She couldn't help feeling a deep sadness when she thought about all that had happened since her last trip there. She felt like a different person now. For a start, she was an orphan. That was probably being a bit overly dramatic at the age of twenty-eight, she thought, but she couldn't help it. She no longer had a mother or a father and the thought made her intensely sad.

Arriving in Athens, Alice thought about a conversation she'd had with Milo. He'd lost both his parents some years ago. He'd mentioned it briefly – as if it didn't matter – but she'd seen the sadness in his eyes and she'd wanted to know more.

She shook her head. This trip wasn't about Milo. She wasn't going to think about him or their unfinished conversations. It didn't matter what he thought about his parents because he wasn't a part of her life. The only part he might play in it was to help her undo this wish which was his fault in the first place. If he hadn't told her about that silly statue, none of this would have happened. She'd have left the villa that day in blissful ignorance as plain old Alice Archer and would be living quietly at home, and Bruce, Wilfred, Larry, Mr Montague and Ben would never have batted an eyelid at her.

Leaving the airport in a taxi, Alice looked at the streets which led up to the Parthenon and wondered if she'd have time to visit it on her trip. She'd booked five nights because there'd been a deal on and she thought she could probably do with some time away from work and home, some time to call her own. However, thinking about the Parthenon, it probably wasn't a good idea. There were no doubt dozens of statues of gods and goddesses up there amongst the ruins and Alice didn't want to be tempted by any of them. Heaven only knew what would happen if she had a close encounter with Zeus or Athena.

She couldn't afford to book the villa she'd stayed in with her sister and she couldn't find any other places available on the island at such short notice. Holiday season was in full swing and Kethos was fully booked. So she made do with a room in a characterless hotel on the mainland just outside Athens and near enough to the ferry crossing to get her over to Kethos with the least fuss possible.

Arriving at the hotel after giving an amorous taxi driver the brush-off, she dumped her suitcase and walked across to her second-floor window. She could see the sea if she stood up on tiptoe and craned her neck. She tried to imagine the little heart-shaped island of Kethos beyond the indigo waves.

What would Milo be doing, she wondered? How many children would he be tucking into bed that night? And would he be making more with his beautiful Greek wife who had no idea about his romantic liaisons with tourists?

As Alice gazed out across the little patch of visible sea, she only hoped that she could get over to Kethos and back again without running into Milo the married man.

Chapter 35

The next morning was business as usual for Milo and Tiana. She got ready for school and he got ready for work. The only difference was that Milo was going to work on an ancient moped that a neighbour had lent him. It really was a terrible vehicle and Milo would probably have got more speed out of a mule but, until he replaced his old moped, he didn't have much choice.

All that morning, he couldn't take his eyes off Tiana. She sat like a little miracle in the middle of their kitchen, the sunlight flooding through the window and making her skin glow.

He'd packed her lunch as he always did, checked that she had all her books and had written a note to the teacher explaining why she'd been absent the day before and why she hadn't had time to do her homework.

'She won't believe us,' Tiana said.

'Probably not,' Milo agreed.

Now, riding the ancient moped to work, he thought about the conversation he'd had with his brother the night before. Georgio called after ten when he was sure Tiana had gone to bed.

'Is she all right?' he'd asked anxiously.

'Well, she's not crying herself to sleep if that's what you're worried about.'

'There's no need to be so cruel.'

Milo had sighed. There was still a part of him that wanted to punish Georgio for what he'd done but another part of him – the gentler part – wanted to sort things out between them all. He might not be able to understand why his brother had acted the way he had but knew that it was because he loved Tiana, and he told him his idea about her spending more time in Athens with them.

'Are you serious?' Georgio said.

'If you promise to take good care of her and not emigrate or something.'

There'd been a pause. 'You can trust us. We won't do anything like that again. Sonya's really shaken up. She didn't – *we* didn't – realise how much she loved her home.'

'She's an islander, Georgio, like me,' Milo said and he heard his brother exhale slowly.

'I can see that now.'

'She'll never leave,' Milo told him.

'I'll never try to force her to.'

There'd been a silence that was neither awkward nor uncomfortable. It was as if the two brothers were letting something settle between them and, when they said good night, it was understood that what had passed would not be spoken of again. Apologies had been accepted and punishments received.

Now, turning off the main road towards the Villa Argenti, Milo was glad that it was all behind them. He'd known things

294

had been building up for some time but hadn't known which direction they would take.

Lander was there by the gate when Milo arrived. 'You all right?' his colleague asked him, giving him the once-over.

'I think I'll survive,' Milo said, getting off the moped and taking his helmet off.

Lander peered closely at his face. 'You been to the hospital for that cut?'

'What cut?'

'The one below your hairline.'

Milo's hand flew up to his head and felt the scab that was forming there. 'It's nothing.'

'You're limping too,' Lander pointed out as Milo walked into the garden.

'I'm fine. I just want a nice quiet day without any incidents,' he said and he disappeared into the garden to enjoy the solitude before the first of the tourists arrived.

Alice had never seen such bright water in her life. At once, she remembered Milo saying that the sea was 'six shades of blue' but she was sure she could see far more than that and it dazzled her eyes. There was clear aquamarine, dancing turquoise, there was indigo and navy, sapphire and lavender and so many shades in between.

Her fingers clenched the railings as she looked down into the water, marvelling at the foamy white wake behind the ferry which widened like a gigantic tail over the thousands of shades of blue and green. It would be easy to believe in mermaids on such a day or even believe that the mighty

Poseidon lived in the watery depths, his trident ready and waiting to capture any unsuspecting tourist. And hadn't Aphrodite been born from out of the sea? Alice remembered reading about a god having his unmentionables cut off and flung into the sea and the goddess of love rising up out of it.

Alice shook her head. Why was she always thinking about gods and goddesses? It was far more likely that there'd be nothing but jellyfish and the occasional flip-flop in the water below but she couldn't shake the notion that if her statue of Aphrodite had had the power to grant wishes then what else was true from the world of myths and legends? Were there winged horses flying around the Greek mountains? Had Medusa been real? Alice felt so confused with it all but decided to dismiss the mythical beings for now and focus on getting herself to the Villa Argenti.

She walked to the front of the boat and watched as they approached Kethos. The familiar sight of the harbour made her feel nervous all of a sudden with its rows of white buildings and brightly-painted shutters. As they got closer, she could see the little row of fishermen on the harbour wall and could well believe that they'd been sitting there without moving since she'd last seen them.

Narrowly avoiding being proposed to by an Italian tourist who was quickly dragged away by his furious girlfriend, Alice walked to the bus stop and waited for the island bus to take her to her destination. There were about a dozen or so other holiday-makers standing in line that morning and she guessed that a fair few of them would be accompanying her to the villa.

The bus ride felt like something from a dream – a half-remembered thing that she thought she'd never encounter again and she couldn't help but let a little part of her float back to that first week on Kethos when everything had been so beautiful and she'd been falling in love with Milo.

She looked out of the window as the bus turned a corner and the earth fell away towards the sea. There were gasps from the other tourists who had never seen the view before and Alice couldn't help feeling just a little bit territorial because this was her special place.

Getting off at the Villa Argenti, Alice sighed at the number of people who accompanied her down the long sweep of driveway. Didn't they have anywhere else to go? Must they all be here today? She'd be lucky if she got a private moment with Aphrodite at all, especially if everybody knew about the wish. They'd be queuing up for hours to place their hands on her magical body.

Alice decided to make her way towards the Goddess Garden straightaway in an attempt to beat the crowds. She wanted to get this over and done with as quickly as possible.

The garden was quite different from when she had last seen it. Everything seemed so much bigger and greener and there were flowers in dazzlingly exotic colours and a border filled with old-fashioned roses in pinks and creams. A part of her wanted to linger and take it all in but she was too anxious to deal with business first and so directed her gaze straight ahead.

Her feet crunched along the gravel towards the Goddess Garden and she saw a few familiar faces. There was Demeter with her sheaf of wheat and there was Artemis with her hounds. Alice stopped. One of the hounds had a large crack around his neck and there was something amiss with Athena too – she'd lost an arm. *How on earth had that happened,* she wondered?

Alice walked on towards the sheltered corner of the garden that was home to Aphrodite. Red roses were in bloom around her feet and Alice took in a deep breath of relief that she was finally there. She'd made it and she was going to change things back to the way they had been before she'd made the wish. Everything was going to be all right.

But, as she looked up into the beautiful, serene face of the goddess, she knew that something was wrong. There was something about her face that didn't look right. It was her and yet it wasn't her. Alice blinked and tilted her head to one side as if that might make a difference but it didn't. It *wasn't* her, was it? It wasn't the same statue. She knew it was Aphrodite – a representation of her, at least – but it wasn't *her* Aphrodite.

She looked around the garden as if somebody was playing a trick on her. What was going on? She couldn't ask anything of this statue, could she? That wouldn't work. This Aphrodite was an imposter. She had no right being in the garden. And what about Artemis's hound and Athena and her missing arm? Something had happened here and Alice's mind raced as she realised what it might mean for her.

In another corner of the garden, Milo was watching a tourist who was hovering awfully close to a perfect pink rose, eyes looking askance as if to see if she was being observed.

'I don't believe it!' he whispered to himself a moment later when the tourist snapped off the head of the rose between two vicious-looking fingernails. He cleared his throat and stepped out of the shadows but didn't look directly at her. He was just letting her know that he was there and that any future rose-plucking would be dealt with less kindly.

He found it all rather amusing, actually. It was a compliment to the garden that people wanted to take a little bit of it away with them but, if every tourist had the same idea, there wouldn't be a garden left. He'd once seen a man bent double in one of the borders actually attempting to dig a whole plant up – roots and all. He'd escorted him to the gate and told him not to come back and that the goddess, Artemis, would send her hounds in pursuit of him if he were ever seen there again.

Now, Milo was making his way to the Goddess Garden. He wanted to check on the new rose bushes that had been planted in the winter and were looking their very best now. The red roses around Aphrodite were particularly striking and he wanted to make sure they were in perfect condition. Mr Carlson was due back any day now from yet another business trip and, if the roses were looking good, it might take his mind off the fact that his favourite statue had been lost to the earthquake.

His feet crunched down the pathway. Only one tourist had reached this part of the garden already and Milo watched her for a moment. She was hovering around the statue of Aphrodite, pacing up and down as if in distress. He thought it was amusing at first. After all, he'd seen all kinds of goings-on as far as tourists were concerned.

It was only when she turned around that he stopped smiling because the figure that had been pacing up and down wasn't just a tourist. It was Alice.

Chapter 36

'Alice – you came back.'

Alice froze. She didn't need to turn around to know that Milo was standing behind her.

'Alice?' he said again. She took a deep breath and turned to face him.

'What?' she said.

'I wish I'd known you were coming. I could have met you at the boat.'

'I didn't come here to see you, Milo,' she said abruptly.

'Oh,' he said, looking thoroughly deflated at her declaration.

'I needed to see the statue again.'

Milo looked puzzled. 'What do you mean?'

'Where is she?' she asked.

'Where's what?'

'*Aphrodite*, Milo! Where is she?'

'Oh, she got damaged. We had an earthquake.'

Alice stared at him. 'An earthquake?'

'Yes. Aphrodite got broken and Athena lost an arm. You should've been here. It was really dramatic.'

'Oh, God!' Alice exclaimed.

'It's all right,' Milo went on, 'nobody was hurt.' He gave a little smile and she suddenly felt guilty for not asking him if he was okay although, looking at him now, he did seem as though he'd sustained some injuries. He saw her looking at him. 'Oh, this wasn't the earthquake. I came off my bike.'

'Are you all right?'

'Just a few scuffs and sprains.'

'What happened?' She inwardly cursed herself as soon as the question was out there but she couldn't deny that there was still a little part of her that cared about this man.

'I was going too fast – not paying attention to the road.'

'I see,' she said, wondering if he realised how stupid that was when he had a family to look after. He really shouldn't be tearing around the island roads like a boy racer when he had responsibilities.

'You said you came back because of the statue?' Milo prompted her.

Alice nodded and began pacing up and down the path again.

'I've got to find her – the one that was here before. Where is she?'

Milo shook his head. 'I told you – she got smashed in the earthquake. We had to send her away.'

'Send her where?' Alice's eyes were wide and wild.

'There's a man on the island who does repairs. He came to collect her but I really don't think there's much he can do. She was in really bad condition. So we got another one so as not to disappoint the tourists.' He paused. 'Why's this so important to you?'

'I've got to find her,' she said, her words firing out of her mouth in staccato desperation. 'She's the only one who can

302

help me now. I've come all this way. I've *got* to find her.'

Milo looked concerned now. 'Calm down. You're not making any sense.'

She stared up at him, anxiety in her blue eyes. 'But you don't understand how important this is.'

'No, I don't,' he said, 'and I wish you'd tell me what's going on.'

Alice sighed. 'I made a wish on this statue – the other statue – the one that was here when I was on holiday. You told me that it granted wishes and I was silly enough to make one and it came true and it's caused nothing but trouble. I've got to undo it.'

Milo's mouth dropped open and he didn't say anything at first but Alice felt sure he was doing his best to stifle a laugh. 'Alice, have you *any* idea how mad that sounds?' he said at last.

'Look, you can stand there and laugh at me or you can try and help me.'

'Of course I'll help you.'

'It's your fault that it happened at all. I'd never have made a wish in the first place if it hadn't been for you.'

Milo scratched his chin. 'What exactly happened to you? Alice?' His hand was upon her shoulder and he guided her towards a nearby white bench where they sat in the dappled light of a fig tree. It was the same bench on which they'd sat together the first time they'd met. 'Tell me what's going on.'

Alice took a deep breath. Her mind was buzzing with fear and confusion and she knew she had to try and calm herself down if she was going to sort anything out. So she told him everything that had happened since she'd left Kethos and, indeed, the things that had happened to her when she'd been on the island.

'The pelican?' Milo said incredulously once she'd finished.

'It was male, wasn't it?' Alice said.

'And you're sure it was the statue that did all these things to you?'

'What do you mean? What else could it have been?'

Milo shrugged. 'Your natural charisma and beauty?'

'Oh, don't be soft,' Alice said. 'Nothing like this has happened to me before and it all started after my visit here.'

Milo shook his head. 'I think you've made some mistake.'

'But you're the one who told me she could grant wishes.'

'Yes, but that's just something I say to the tourists. It's just a bit of—' he hesitated, looking for the right word, '*fun*.'

'Well, it wasn't much fun for me, I can tell you,' Alice said, 'and I'm not the only one, you know. There's a whole website forum full of people who have had their wishes granted.'

'Oh, that's just holiday fun!'

'Well, if you're not going to help me then I shall do this on my own.'

'I didn't say I wasn't going to help you. I just said that it all sounds very—' he paused, searching for the right word, 'unlikely.'

'Well, you try getting to sleep when your ancient neighbour's serenading you at your window or getting a day's work done when your boss keeps trying to corner you.'

Milo looked thoughtful for a moment. 'Look,' he said at last, 'I believe anything you say, and I want to help you if you really think that the statue holds the answer to all this.'

'Of course I do!'

'Okay,' he said. 'Then we'll find her and we'll sort it out.'

Milo knew that he owed Lander big time. Leaving Alice at the gate, he went in search of his work colleague, finding him deep in a shrubbery tackling some out-of-control ivy.

He cleared his throat. 'I've got a favour to ask you.'

Lander was brilliant. As long as Mr Carlson was away, the two of them could pretty much make their own rules up and Milo could go off on a wild-goose chase around the island with his mad Englishwoman if that was what he wanted to do. Goodness, Lander had even let him borrow his car.

'Now, don't get any ideas, will you? I'm not driving around on that dreadful moped of yours longer than I absolutely have to,' he told Milo.

Milo thanked him profusely and walked back to the gate where Alice was pacing like a caged animal.

'We've got a car,' he told her.

'What happened to your bike?'

'Went over the cliff – like me,' he said with a grin. Alice gawped at him as if he was quite mad.

Milo didn't often get a chance to drive a car. He'd learned to drive, of course, and his brothers had shared a car for a while until Georgio had left Kethos and taken it with him. Milo hadn't really missed it. He adored the freedom of his moped with the wind in his face and the close contact with the land although he'd had rather too much contact with the land in the last few days, he had to admit.

Getting in the car with Alice felt strange. They were

suddenly enclosed together in a small space and didn't have the distraction of the garden around them any more. He cleared his throat. Alice looked pale and distant and he desperately wanted to reach out and take her hand in his but he didn't feel it would be right. There was too much that had been left unsaid so he drove out onto the main road in silence.

Lander's car, although pretty old, was a surprisingly smooth drive and took the hairpin corners of the island well. It was a pleasure to handle but it wasn't such a pleasure to sit in stony silence with his travelling companion.

Milo's fingers clutched the steering wheel, his knuckles turning white as he wondered what to do. Would now be a good time to tell her everything? After all, hadn't he been going to do that on the day she had left Kethos? He was going to be open and honest with her because she deserved nothing more than the truth. Besides, he *wanted* to tell her. If they were to stand any chance of a future together, she had to know what his situation was.

But she didn't come back here to see you, a little voice reminded him. *She came to see Aphrodite. You weren't even on the agenda.* He groaned at the realisation. That didn't mean he couldn't still tell her the truth, though, did it? And how he felt about her.

He threw a quick glance her way. She was staring resolutely ahead as if into some horrible abyss.

'Alice,' he said, swallowing hard.

'What?' Her one word was cold, sharp and uninviting.

'There's something I need to tell you,' he said, desperate to clear the air between them and frustrated that she was so uncommunicative.

'Can it wait? I mean, if it's not about this whole Aphrodite business.' She turned to look at him. 'Well, is it?'

'No,' he said. 'It isn't.'

'Okay, then,' she said. 'Let's just focus on that for now.'

Chapter 37

Milo had a vague idea where he was going. Lander had given him directions but he only half-recognised the road out of Kintos. It was a part of the island he didn't get to very often but he slowed down as they reached the top of a hill, descending slowly until they came to a high wall.

Milo turned into a driveway and gazed at the sight that greeted them. There was a one-storey white house that was typical of the island but it wasn't that which made Milo's mouth drop open but the large swimming pool to the left-hand side. There was no water in the pool but it was full all the same – with the broken bodies of hundreds of statues. There were legs, heads, arms and torsos all over the place. It was a startling sight – as if they were victims of some great war.

Milo parked the car and Alice was out before he'd even switched the engine off. He joined her by the side of the body-filled pool.

'Do you think she's in there?' she asked.

'I don't know,' Milo said. 'She could be, I suppose.' His eyes scanned the stone stumps. He recognised a couple of Poseidons with broken tridents but he couldn't see his Aphrodite anywhere. 'Maybe she's in a workshop somewhere,' he said, trying to keep Alice's hopes up.

They left the pool of broken bodies and walked round the back of the house where a large barn-like structure stood. There was the sound of some vicious machinery whirring and Milo held Alice back before she could run headlong into the dark interior. He didn't want her broken body being chucked into the swimming pool.

'Hello?' Milo called in both English and Greek, taking slow steps into the barn. Alice followed him and they saw a man standing at one of the machines, head down in concentration. They waited a moment, not wanting to startle him. A minute later, he lifted his head up, saw them both standing there and stopped the machine. Silence descended.

The dark-haired man lifted his goggles from his face and stared at the intruders. Milo stepped forward, his hand extended in greeting and the man wiped his own dusty one on the front of his trousers and shook, saying something in Greek.

Milo made a bit of polite conversation, telling him about the Villa Argenti, and the man nodded.

'I believe you were going to try and fix the statue of Aphrodite,' he said, continuing the conversation in Greek. 'She's a particular favourite of the tourists.'

The man shook his head solemnly. 'She was irreparable. You must have known that.'

Milo nodded. In his heart, he'd known but he hadn't wanted to admit as much to Alice.

'What's he saying?' Alice asked.

Milo turned round to face her. 'I'm afraid she couldn't be

fixed,' he said.

'So that's it?' Alice said, her voice rising hysterically.

'It looks like it,' Milo said.

'But the statue still exists, doesn't it? Even if it is in pieces? I need to see it. Tell him that I need to see it, Milo.'

'He didn't keep it,' Milo told her.

'What?'

'It's gone,' Milo said.

The dark-haired man was still babbling on.

'Hang on a minute,' Milo said, listening to him. 'He's saying that, apparently, it's a very special statue. The sculptor is well-known here and he says he got in touch with him.'

'And?' The conversation was going far too slowly for Alice's liking.

'The sculptor wanted it back.'

'It's with the sculptor?' Alice asked.

'Yes.'

'And where is he?'

Milo sighed. 'I'm afraid we can't get in touch with him.'

'What? Why not?'

'He's Yanni Karalis. He's a recluse and he hates people.'

'But this man got in touch with him.'

'That's different. This man had something that Mr Karalis wanted. He obviously made an exception so he could get this statue back.'

'But we've *got* to see him. Where does he live? Is that the problem? Is he miles away?'

'Oh, no – he's right here on Kethos.'

'Then I don't see what the problem is.' Alice turned and

310

marched out of the barn, her strides long and purposeful as if she was not going to stop walking until she'd found the statue. Milo thanked the man and followed her.

'Alice,' he said, 'I think we're going to have to admit defeat here.'

Alice had reached the car and opened the door, sinking heavily into the seat, her face even paler now. 'I can't give up,' she said, looking directly ahead through the windscreen rather than at Milo.

'But this sculptor is famous for not seeing visitors. We've bought statues from him in the past and – believe me – we've spent a lot of money. They're the best statues in the world. But he doesn't have anything to do with anyone.'

'But we've got to try.' She turned to face him. '*Please*, Milo.'

He looked pensive for a moment. 'Well, I don't suppose it'll do much harm to visit him,' he told her, 'but don't get your hopes up'.

They drove for about twenty minutes before the road started to narrow and climb steeply. They'd turned away from the coast and noticed how quiet it was. They hadn't passed another vehicle for miles. This was a part of Kethos that the tourists rarely saw. It was bare and barren but there was a strange beauty to it. It was a place where myths seemed to hang in the air and the scent of wild flowers was everywhere.

Milo glanced at Alice to see what she made of it but she still had that strange, wild look on her face which told him that a beautiful landscape was probably the last thing on her mind at the moment.

The road curled round to the right and Milo dropped

down a gear and started looking out for a likely house. It was the perfect setting for a recluse. No wonder the tourists never made it to this part of the island, because the locals didn't either, he couldn't help thinking. How much of his island he had yet to explore. Just when he thought he knew it, a beautiful surprise awaited him round an unexplored corner.

It was after they'd passed a small herd of goats grazing at the side of the road that they saw the place. Milo pulled over and they got out of the car.

'Well, this looks like it,' Milo said, peering in through an oppressively massive pair of iron gates which were double padlocked.

From out of nowhere an enormous dog came bounding across the bare earth, teeth bared as it barked furiously.

Alice screamed and Milo sprang back.

'Right,' he said. 'I don't think we're going to get in that way.' He took a deep breath. 'Hello?' he cried in through the gate, setting off the dog again. He noticed there was no bell and no intercom but, if somebody was home, surely they would have heard the dog. He thought about sounding his horn but it probably wouldn't be heard over the barking.

He stood back to look at the property. An enormous wall ran around the perimeter. It all looked foreboding as well as impenetrable and he shrugged his shoulders. 'I think we're going to have to come back tomorrow,' he said.

'Oh, Milo – no!'

'There's nothing we can do if there's nobody around.' He watched Alice's response and couldn't help feeling sorry for her. She looked thoroughly dejected with her slender shoulders slumped and her head hung in sorrow.

'I'm so sorry,' he said.

'You didn't even try,' she said as they headed back to the car.

'What do you mean? I drove out all this way with you and nearly got attacked by that wolf.'

'I don't mean today.'

Milo frowned. So, they were no longer talking about today, were they? The conversation had shifted when he wasn't looking. He sighed. Why were women so complicated?

'I mean, you never tried to see me before I left Kethos. You never tried to explain.'

Milo scratched his chin. 'But I *did* try to see you. I came to the villa as soon as I could but you'd gone.'

'I had to go home,' she said, glaring at him as if he was an idiot. 'I came to see you at the Villa Argenti but your colleague told me you couldn't work that day and there was no way of contacting you. I didn't know what to do.'

'I'm so sorry, Alice. Something came up and I couldn't reach you.'

She looked at him and he felt as if he were being punished with the fierceness of her stare.

'What is it?' he asked.

'Nothing,' she said. 'I just thought you might have something to say to me.' He wasn't sure what she meant and so he wasn't sure what to say to her. He held her gaze, wondering if she was going to say anything else but she remained silent, the coolness of her eyes seeming to say so much but in a language which he didn't understand.

313

'Look,' he said at last, glancing at his watch, 'the last ferry leaves for the mainland in an hour and we'd have to break our necks to get there in time. Stay with me.'

'What?'

'I have plenty of room and you'd be very welcome and we can get up early and make a good start by coming back here and trying to find the statue.'

Her blue eyes seemed to double in size and her mouth had opened in a perfect little circle. 'But—'

'But what?' he asked, his head cocked to one side.

'What are you talking about, Milo? I can't stay at yours.'

'Why not?' he asked, looking puzzled.

'Because – because you have a family!'

He looked startled for a moment. 'How did you know about that?'

'Oh, Milo!' Her hands flew up in the air in exasperation. 'I saw them! You have a wife – a *family!*'

'Wife? Hang on a minute! What do you mean, *wife?*'

'Please don't lie to me any more. I came to your house.'

'What? When?'

'When you weren't at the villa, I asked a few people where you lived. I wanted to see you again before I left but, when I got to your house, I saw—' she stopped.

'What?' he said, anxiety filling him with fear. 'What exactly did you see?'

'I saw you pegging out washing in the garden. Children's clothes.'

'Oh, God!' Milo said, shaking his head. 'Do you know who those clothes belong to, Alice? They belong to my sister!'

'Your sister?'

'My little sister – Tiana. I wanted to tell you about her and I was going to. I tried on the morning you were leaving but it was too late and we couldn't make it to the boat in time. Tiana was unwell. That's why I couldn't get in to work. There's a lady who takes care of her after school but she was ill too so I had to stay at home.'

'You have a little sister?'

He nodded. 'Our parents died. I'm the one who looks after her.'

Alice looked dumbstruck. 'Why didn't you tell me all this?'

'I was going to only I didn't get the chance and there was no point mentioning her when we first met,' he said. 'I mean, would you really want to see somebody who has a little sister to take care of?'

'You should have let me be the judge of that,' she told him.

'I know,' he said. 'But I thought we were just going to be a holiday romance. When I first met you, I didn't know how you felt about me and I always thought you'd forget about me and this place as soon as you left. I didn't feel you needed to know everything about my life here.' He looked at her and her face softened a little. 'I'm so sorry I didn't get the chance to explain things,' he said. 'I really care about you and I felt so bad letting you go like that without explaining. I don't know what you must have thought.'

'You *really* don't want to know,' Alice said.

'I'm sure I don't,' he said, giving her a tiny smile. They left the forbidding gate and the barking dog and drove back through the wild island landscape.

Milo kept giving Alice little glances. Her shoulders had lost some of the tension that had been held in them for the whole of that day but she still looked sad – as if something was missing from her existence. 'Are you okay?' he said at last.

She nodded but didn't say anything.

'You must be hungry,' he said. 'I know I am. We haven't eaten for hours.'

She nodded again. 'I guess I lost track of time.'

'It seems to me that you've been thinking about nothing but this statue,' he told her. 'Am I right?'

She looked at him as he slowed to take a corner. 'It's been an odd time,' she said and then, suddenly, her eyes filled with tears.

'Alice!' he cried, pulling over to the side of the road. 'What's the matter?' For a few moments, she didn't say a word but just sat there, tears streaming down her face, her little nose rapidly turning red.

He took his seatbelt off and inched closer to her, resting a hand on her shoulder. He couldn't bear to see her like this and he couldn't help but feel partly responsible. 'It's my stupid behaviour, isn't it?' He groaned. 'I should have told you. I *knew* I should have.'

She shook her head. 'It's not you,' she said in a tiny voice.

'What is it, then?'

She turned to look at him and her eyes were rimmed with red. 'My father,' she said. 'My father died.'

'Oh, Alice! I'm so sorry.' Without thinking, he took her hands in his and squeezed them whilst fresh tears fell as she told him what had happened.

'God,' he said when she finished. 'You've had a really bad time.'

'I guess I've been holding on and holding on – just trying to get on with things and sort everything out.'

'When what you really needed to do was to sit down and have a good cry,' he said. 'Look, let's get you back to my place. You can take a shower, have a rest, do anything you like and I'll cook us dinner. We've got a spare bedroom with clean sheets and you're welcome to stay as long as you need. How does that sound?'

'But I don't have any clothes or my toothbrush or—'

'I'll lend you some clothes,' he said, 'and there's a brand new toothbrush in the bathroom cabinet. Come on. Let me take you to my home.'

Chapter 38

Alice's mind was reeling from what Milo had told her. For all those weeks, she'd thought of him as nothing more than a no-good cheating husband when he had, in fact, been a single man struggling to take care of his little sister whilst holding down a job.

As he skirted the town of Kintos and headed to a part of the island she didn't know, she glanced at him. His face was dark with his long hours of exposure to the sun and the little cut below his forehead looked red and raw and she wanted to reach out and touch it gently with her fingertips. His dark eyes were focused on the road and his dark green shirt sleeves were rolled up to reveal his tanned forearms. Alice swallowed at the sight of them and she tried not to think about the way that they had held her as he'd made love to her.

That moment seemed such a long time ago now. She felt as if she'd been a different person then and it felt strange sitting so close to Milo now with all that had happened between them and yet they hadn't talked about the time when the world had closed around them and nothing had been more important than the two of them.

She couldn't help wondering if he was thinking about it too or if his mind was purely on negotiating the treacherous coast road that they were now driving along. Whatever he was thinking, he kept to himself and they drove on in silence together.

When they reached Milo's, Alice recognized the little house and saw the washing line which had caused so much trouble between them. He parked the car and turned to look at her.

'Well, here we are,' he said.

Alice nodded. 'Where's your sister?'

'Oh, she's inside. There was a party after school today and a friend said she'd bring her home and sit with her until I got back.' Sure enough, a young woman came out of the front door and waved at Milo. He got out of the car and greeted her and they chatted away for a few moments before she turned to leave.

'She wanted to know who the pretty girl was,' Milo said as he opened Alice's door for her.

'And what did you tell her?'

'I told her absolutely nothing because it would be all over the village before we sit down to dinner.'

'I think it probably will anyway,' Alice said as she got out of the car.

'You're probably right.'

They walked towards the house together.

'Does Tiana speak English?' Alice asked nervously.

'Yes. I've been teaching her,' Milo said as he opened the door for her. 'I think she speaks better English than me now!'

Alice stepped inside and was immediately greeted by a girl with huge dark eyes and long dark hair. She was standing in the doorway of the kitchen and she had a big smile on her face. 'Hello,' she said.

319

'Hello,' Alice said, smiling right back at her.

Milo cleared his throat and stepped forward. 'Tiana – this is Alice,' he said in English.

The little girl cocked her head to one side in a manner that was uncannily like her brother. 'ALICE!' she suddenly shouted.

Alice laughed at the explosive cry. 'Yes,' she said.

'You came back.'

'I did.'

'You came back to see Milo,' the little girl continued.

'Er – no,' Milo interrupted.

'Then why?'

'Alice has business on the island.'

'Business?' Tiana said, sounding out the word as if it was something disagreeable in her mouth. 'What business?'

'Private business that has nothing to do with little girls,' Milo said.

'Oh,' she said, obviously disappointed, and then she turned her big brown eyes on Alice as if she might want to contradict Milo and tell her why she was there.

'I think you have homework to do,' Milo prompted her.

'Oh, no. Not tonight,' she said with a light smile. 'I can stay and talk with Alice *all* evening.'

Milo's eyes widened in alarm. 'But not before you've tidied your—'

'My room's tidy,' she said.

'And put all your books into alphabetical order.'

'What?' Tiana said in alarm.

'Go on – you know I've told you that's how Mama liked them.'

She stood stunned for a moment but then gave in.

'Okay!' she said with a sigh.

They watched as she walked as slowly as was humanly possible down the whole length of the hallway to her bedroom at the end.

'Sorry about that,' Milo whispered. 'She can be a little demanding.'

'She's lovely,' Alice said. 'I wish my sister was as adorable.'

'How is she?' he asked, leading her through to the kitchen.

'Oh, she's her usual self.'

Milo nodded in understanding. 'And how has she taken your father's death?'

'Not well,' Alice said. 'She's been living in the family home, and she doesn't want to leave now but it's a condition of the will. The house is going to be sold, you see, and everything paid for and then what's left will be split between us.'

'That sounds fair enough,' Milo said.

'She doesn't see it that way, I'm afraid.'

'I take it she's been living rent-free all this time?'

Alice nodded.

'Then it all sounds more than fair to me.' He pulled a chair out at the dinner table and Alice sat down as Milo busied himself around the kitchen preparing dinner. 'So, what will you do with the money?'

Alice cast her eyes up to the ceiling. 'I guess I should put a deposit down on a house of my own. I've been renting for years now.'

'So, you're going to stay in the UK?'

She looked at him. 'That's where my job is.'

He nodded and Alice swallowed. She had the feeling that he wasn't saying everything in his mind and was aware, once again, that the closeness they'd briefly shared seemed to have evaporated.

'Anyway,' she continued, 'we'll have to wait and see.'

'Have you any idea how much it will be? If you don't mind me asking.'

'Well, I've not worked it out in detail yet but there was no mortgage on the property and it should get a good price. I guess we're looking at six figures.'

Milo looked as if he'd been slapped in the face. 'Six figures?'

'Very low six figures,' Alice said.

'Each? In pounds?'

'Yes! Why? Does that seem a lot to you?' Alice said in surprise.

'You mean, it doesn't seem a lot to *you*?' Milo said.

'It seems an absolute fortune to me but it won't buy much in the UK.'

'My God!' Milo said. 'You could buy a mansion with grounds for that here.'

'Really?'

'Yes!' Milo said, his voice sounding hysterical. 'Not as grand as the Villa Argenti, you understand, but a really nice house and plenty of land.'

Alice found that she was smiling in spite of herself. 'But that's here, and here is miles away from anywhere, in a country that gets earthquakes.'

'Well, we might not be perfect but our skies and sea beat yours for blueness.'

Alice smiled and watched as Milo reached into a cupboard and produced two large wine glasses which he filled with a local white wine.

'If I had six figures, I would buy the *biggest* plot of land I could afford,' he said, passing a glass to Alice and taking a sip from his own. 'It wouldn't matter what the house was like as long as it had rooms and walls and things. Then I would create the most beautiful garden Kethos has ever seen. The Villa Argenti would be *nothing* in comparison!' His dark eyes shone as he spoke. 'I would choose all my favourite plants and put them exactly where I wanted them. There would be all the bright and brilliant Mediterranean flowers and the herbs that our island is so famous for and I would raise my own plants from seed and take cuttings – even do a bit of experimenting.'

'But don't you do all that already at the villa?' Alice asked.

'I have a certain amount of freedom with the plants, of course, but it's Mr Carlson who has to tick everything off. The garden is his, after all.'

Alice nodded and smiled at the faraway look in Milo's eyes. He was a dreamer, wasn't he? She liked that about him. Why couldn't she be more like that? She was so stuck in the here and now, worrying about practicalities like work and rent and bills. Why couldn't she just let her mind soar like Milo and dream of a future filled with flowers?

'Anyway,' he said, snapping himself back into the present, 'that's not likely to happen and – well – I love the Villa Argenti – I really do but—'

'You'd like to be your own boss?'

'Exactly!' He grinned like a young child and then turned his back to her as he prepared dinner. Alice watched him moving around the kitchen with graceful ease. He looked so at home amongst the pots and pans as if he genuinely enjoyed the whole experience of cooking rather than getting on with it simply because he had to eat.

'Anything I can do?' Alice asked.

'No, no,' he said lightly, waving a hand in the air. 'Have yourself another wine.' So Alice did.

She wasn't sure whether it was the wine or the rhythm with which Milo moved around the kitchen but she soon began to feel pleasantly mellow. It was as if all the tension of the last few weeks was finally draining away from her. Maybe it was the fact that she was back on Kethos too. After all, it had been the last place where she'd felt truly relaxed.

Before she knew it, she was being presented with an array of pretty plates and bowls all filled with food.

'It's just a simple supper,' Milo said, almost apologetically, as he laid everything out on the table. 'It's called *meze*. It's food to pick at whilst you're drinking ouzo but we like to eat it together for supper. Tiana likes it – I guess it's what you might call *finger food*.'

Alice nodded in approval as she recognised pitta bread, houmous, haloumi, calamari and scampi. 'It all looks amazing,' she said, and she couldn't help comparing the exotic spread before her to her own dreary suppers at home of tinned soup and toast or some breadcrumbed concoction from out of the depths of the freezer.

'Dinner!' Milo called and Tiana came racing through to

join them. 'Have you cleaned your hands?'

She nodded. 'Yes!'

'And sorted all your books?'

'*Yes!*'

'Okay,' he said with a smile as his little sister sat herself at the table.

The food was simple and delicious – just what Alice had needed and, for a while, they all ate in silence, happily picking and munching away together like a little family. But Alice couldn't help feeling a pair of eyes upon her the whole time she was eating and finally glanced up to meet them. Tiana grinned at her.

'You're pretty,' she said.

Alice choked on a mouthful of pitta bread. 'No, I'm not,' she said. '*You're* pretty.'

'Thank you,' Tiana said.

Milo laughed. 'You see! You should learn how to accept a compliment, Alice – like Tiana.'

'But she *is* pretty,' Alice said.

'And so are you, isn't she, Tiana?' Milo said.

'I just said so,' Tiana said, looking confused.

Milo laughed. 'You did and she is and that's the end of it.'

Alice shook her head and continued eating – this time, with two pairs of eyes fixed upon her. When she looked up again, she caught Milo's eye and he grinned at her. She gave him a warning look and he cleared his throat.

'Get on with your dinner, Tiana,' he said, 'you're putting Alice off.'

They ate the rest of their meal with furtive glances and

funny little giggles doing the rounds of the table. Finally, the food was finished and Milo told Tiana to return to her room.

'Can't I stay and talk to Alice?' she asked, her eyes big and soulful.

Milo shook his head. 'She's had a long day,' he told her. 'You can chat to her in the morning. Go to your room. I'll come and tuck you in later.'

With a resigned look on her face, she left the room.

'Night, Tiana,' Alice called after her. 'She's wonderful,' she told Milo.

'Yes, some of the time,' he said with a little smile.

'You must adore her.'

He nodded. 'I can't imagine life without her.'

'It must be hard, though, raising her on your own.'

'It's no more than I can handle,' he told her and a serious look crossed his face.

'What is it?' Alice asked, feeling that she had touched a nerve.

He shrugged. 'We've had a bit of a rough time recently. Family stuff. You don't want to hear about it.'

'Yes, I do,' she said. 'I've told you all about my family. I'd like to know more about yours.'

Milo sat down at the table again and poured some more wine for them both and then he told her about Georgio and Sonya and what had happened over the last few days.

'They just took her?' Alice said in shock.

'It had been building up for some time,' Milo told her. 'But I hadn't realised just how desperate they were to have her.'

'Will they try it again?'

326

'I don't think so. I think they got a bit of a shock at how unhappy Tiana was about it all, but what did they expect? All she's known is this island. You can't just drag a child away from her home and expect her to be happy about it.'

'You must have been so worried.'

'Well, I crashed my bike trying to get to her.'

'Ah,' Alice said. 'I didn't think you'd been tearing round the roads just for the sake of it.' She looked at the cut on his head. 'Is that going to scar?'

His fingers brushed it. 'I don't know. Perhaps it should as a reminder of what's important.'

Alice nodded and then stood up and began clearing the table.

'You don't need to do that,' Milo said.

'But I'd like to. You've gone to all this trouble—'

'It's no trouble,' he told her. 'Please, go and sit down.' He motioned to the sitting room next door and Alice relented, leaving the kitchen and sinking down onto a sofa.

It felt funny to be in somebody's house not doing anything. She didn't even have a book to read. She looked around the room for a moment. There was a row of novels on a little shelf near the television but they were all in Greek. Anyway, she didn't really feel like reading. She was too tired to concentrate. In fact, her eyelids were feeling very heavy. She'd just close them for a bit.

'Alice?' a little voice came from a long way away. 'Alice?'

She opened her eyes. 'Oh!' she cried. 'Was I asleep?'

'I think so,' Milo said, sitting down next to her. 'Can I get you something? A cup of coffee?'

327

'Oh, no, thank you. I guess I'd better call it a night.'

He nodded. 'I'll show you your room.'

They walked down the hallway together and Milo opened a door to the right. The bedroom was small and simply furnished with a small double bed, a bedside cabinet on which stood a pottery lamp, and a large wardrobe in the corner. Milo stepped inside to draw the curtains.

'You'll love the view in the morning,' he told her. 'You can see right down to the sea.'

She nodded and noticed that there was a towel and a brand new toothbrush on the bed together with a T-shirt and a pair of socks.

'Just in case you get cold,' he said, noticing that she was looking at the socks. 'Tiana is always complaining about cold feet.'

Alice smiled. 'Thank you.'

'The bathroom's along the hall on the left.'

'Okay.'

'Is there anything else you need? Anything else I can get you?'

She looked up at him. He was standing awfully close to her now and she could feel his warm breath on her face. This was the man she had swum naked with in the sea. This was the man whom she had made love with in the ruins of an ancient temple. She swallowed hard.

'I'm fine,' she said.

'I'll be next door if you need anything,' he said, his eyes dark and warm.

'Thank you,' she whispered, watching as he left her room

and closed the door.

What was she doing here? She was sending out all the wrong signals by staying here and yet she didn't feel awkward at all. In fact, she'd never been made to feel so welcome anywhere in her life.

She sat down on the bed and picked up the pair of perfect woollen socks. He had a little sister, she thought to herself. That was the big secret he'd been hiding. He hadn't been married with six children. She had painted him as a total villain when he had, in fact, been – what? The perfect man?

She shook her head. The perfect man, she thought. She had thrown away her one chance of happiness with the most perfect man she had ever met and, yet, how else could it have ended? Even if he was perfect, their relationship had been nothing more than a holiday romance, hadn't it? It didn't have a future.

Unless…

Alice switched the little pottery lamp on by the bed and gazed at the warm pool of yellow light it cast, her mind whirling with sudden, unexplored, unanticipated thoughts.

She'd never thought very much about the future before because she'd been so resolutely stuck in the present with her job and her rented house, but the inheritance from her father might give her the chance to *choose* a future for herself. It might just allow her to make a decision that would change her life forever, she thought.

'If I have the courage,' she whispered to herself.

Chapter 39

Milo hovered around Alice's door for a while after having closed it, wondering if she would think of something that she needed. He wished she'd stayed and talked to him a little longer. It seemed too early to say good night.

Finally, he walked back through to the kitchen and tidied a few things up and prepared Tiana's packed lunch for the next morning. It was as he was crossing the hall to the sitting room half an hour later that he saw Tiana. She was standing in the doorway to Alice's room.

'Tiana! Come away. What are you doing?' he hissed.

'Just watching her,' Tiana whispered back. 'She looks so sad. I think she's been crying.'

'You shouldn't have opened her door.'

'It just came open,' she said.

Milo sighed but couldn't resist joining Tiana at the bedroom door and looking inside, the hallway light falling softly on Alice's face as she lay in bed.

'She does look sad,' he said.

'What's she so sad about when she's here with you?' Tiana asked.

'She has a lot to think about at the moment.'

'Like what?'

'Well, her father's just died and there are other things too.'

'And she doesn't have a big brother to take care of her like I do?' Tiana asked.

'No, she doesn't.'

'So you're looking after her instead?'

Milo cleared his throat. 'Something like that. Now, you should be in bed, young lady.'

'Can I kiss her good night?'

'No, you can't.'

'Are you going to?'

'Go to bed,' he said.

He escorted her back to her bedroom and, once she was tucked up in bed with the promise that she wouldn't go wandering into Alice's room in the middle of the night, Milo retraced his steps and popped his head around the door again and gazed at the pale face of Alice asleep in the bed. It was strange to think of her wearing his T-shirt and socks. Strange but rather wonderful.

'Good night, Alice,' he whispered, and gently closed the door and walked silently to his own room next door.

Alice awoke in the strange bedroom and looked across at the pale blue curtain through which the sunlight streamed. She had no idea what the time was so leapt out of bed and grabbed her watch. It was after ten. She'd slept for twelve whole hours.

As she drew back the curtain, she was instantly drenched in sunlight. Milo had been right about the view – it was breathtaking. The land rolled away in gentle hills and, there beyond a silver-bright olive grove, was the sea. Today, it was a deep sapphire-blue that almost hurt the eyes to look at it but Alice couldn't tear her gaze away from it. It was mesmeric and she could easily imagine becoming obsessed with such a view and spending endless hours staring at it.

What must it be like to live somewhere like this, she wondered? To be able to look at the sea whenever you wanted to and to observe its changing nature, its myriad colours and its volatile moods swinging from calm and glassy to stormy and savage. No wonder Tiana and, indeed, Milo didn't want to live anywhere else. Alice could totally understand that. A place like this became part of a person. It was the very breath you took, it was what filled your mind and your heart. It was an emotional anchor that gave you a true sense of who you were and where you belonged. That, Alice thought, must be one of the most satisfying feelings in the world and it was one that she'd never had.

Nipping quickly into the bathroom, she took a shower and got dressed. There was an old mirror above the sink and Alice glanced at her reflection. Her skin had paled since her last trip to Kethos and her hair had lost the warm highlights that the sun had graced her with, and her eyes were more pink than blue after her crying the night before.

Walking back through to the bedroom, she sat on the edge of the bed for a while thinking about all the possibilities that the future held and then she felt incredibly sad because the very thing that was giving her such opportunities had been the death of her beloved father and she wouldn't have wanted that for the whole world.

She took a deep breath. She was going to get through this.

She was going to sort out this whole Aphrodite business and then she would sort out her father's estate. Then, she promised, she'd do something wonderful for herself.

Leaving the bedroom, she ventured through to the kitchen where Milo was making a cup of coffee.

'Good morning,' she said. 'I'm sorry I slept so long. You should've woken me.'

'I didn't want to,' he said. 'I guessed you'd be exhausted after yesterday.'

'Where's Tiana?'

'She's left for school.'

'Oh, of course,' Alice said, realising it was a weekday.

'Did you sleep all right?'

'Yes, thank you.'

'There's plenty of breakfast,' he said and Alice sat at the table and began to eat.

'Don't you have to go to work?' she asked.

He shrugged. 'The boss is still away and Old Costas is taking some leave so he can't tell on me and I can catch up with things another time. Lander's covering for me,' Milo said.

'I'm sorry I'm causing you so much bother,' she said.

Milo shook his head. 'You're not,' he said. 'I told you I'd help you and I will.'

'So, we're going back to the sculptor's house?'

'As soon as you're ready.'

Alice nodded and then she suddenly felt nervous which was silly, really, because this was the day she'd been so longing for – the day when everything would be back to normal. No more ridiculous male attention, no more bizarre declarations of love from complete strangers. She was going to return to her true self. The real Alice Archer.

'You okay?' Milo asked her.

Alice nodded. 'I just want to get this all over and done with.'

'And get home again?'

She looked up at him. 'I – I guess,' she said.

'You've got a lot to sort out, haven't you?'

'Yes,' she said.

He nodded again. His face was solemn and she couldn't help wondering what he was thinking. He'd probably be glad to see the back of the strange English girl who kept yo-yoing in and out of his life. She'd done nothing but cause trouble and she wouldn't blame him if he never wanted to see her again.

'Okay,' he said, his voice flat and devoid of emotion and his face a perfect blank. 'Let me know when you're ready to go.' He left the room and Alice blinked in surprise. What had just happened there? Had she said something to upset him? She finished her cup of coffee and walked down the hallway to his bedroom and knocked lightly on the door. He appeared a moment later. 'Ready?' he asked.

'I'm ready,' she said and, like two strangers, they left the house in an uncomfortable silence.

How she longed to talk to him on the journey back to the sculptor's house. There was so much she wanted to know about him but she felt as if he'd somehow closed down on her. Maybe it was because she'd said she was going home but what else could she do?

334

She looked out of the window at the barren, rock-strewn landscape. The road climbed higher and, for a few moments, the sea was lost to them. She opened her window and breathed in the sweet thyme-scented air. She wanted to say something – to share the moment – but Milo seemed so distanced from her that she remained silent.

When they reached the home of the sculptor at last, they saw that, once again, the gates were closed and padlocked. Nevertheless, they got out of the car.

'Hello!' Alice shouted and immediately set off the dog. She noticed that it was on a long lead today and she was thankful that it didn't get any closer to her than it did. 'Sound the horn,' she told Milo.

He returned to the car and gave three blasts. It sounded so horribly loud in the silence of the countryside and it started the dog off again.

'How are we going to get in?' Alice asked.

'I don't think we are.'

'There must be a weak spot somewhere,' Alice said.

'What do you mean?'

'I mean – let's get in there. It's obvious we're not going to be invited in so let's find our own way in.'

'What – with that enormous dog?'

'He's tied up.'

'But he might break free!' Milo pointed out.

Alice shook her head and started walking around the perimeter of the wall. The ground was dusty and stony and Alice twisted her ankle at one point. Milo rushed forward but she waved him away.

'I'm okay,' she said. 'Let's keep going.'

The wall stretched interminably and it soon became obvious that there was no entrance other than the one that was padlocked and guarded.

'I'm sorry, Alice,' Milo said, 'but it looks like this isn't going to work out as we'd hoped.'

Chapter 40

Alice looked down the long length of wall. She'd come all this way and she wasn't ready to give up yet. There must be a way inside. There *must*. It was then that she saw the tree.

'Milo – look!'

'What?'

'The tree.'

The olive tree looked centuries old and was good and sturdy. Alice ran over to it and Milo gave her a leg-up and she was hoisted into its silvery-green depths. Its bark was ridged and gnarled and felt rough against Alice's legs and she wished she hadn't worn a dress but had chosen something more practical to wear.

'You okay?' Milo said, climbing up the tree after her.

Alice shimmied her way along a thick branch towards the top of the wall. 'Nearly there,' she said, releasing the hem of her dress from where it had caught on a rough bit of bark.

Finally, she made it to the wall and positioned herself on its top, gazing down at the ground beneath her. She took a few steadying breaths before launching herself into the air and landing with a great thud that she felt sure would start another earthquake. It was much more of a drop than she'd thought and she wondered how on earth they were going to climb back up and get out but she wasn't going to worry about that just yet.

A second later, Milo thudded to the ground next to her. 'Well, we're in,' he said, dusting himself down. Alice looked at him and he gave her a little smile and then they began walking towards the villa, careful to go round the side that was furthest away from the dog.

'Gosh, there's acres,' Alice said a few minutes later as they surveyed the grounds.

'Don't worry. We'll find her,' Milo said as if reading her mind.

'What if we don't?'

He looked at her. 'You'll just have to get used to being irresistible to men for the rest of your life.'

'That's not funny, Milo,' she said.

'I can think of worse fates.'

She took a deep breath. 'I've got to do this.'

'I know,' he said. 'Look, the sculptor's bound to have kept the statue close to the house if he was going to try to repair it. There must be a workshop somewhere. She's probably in one of those.'

Alice nodded. 'Yes,' she said hopefully.

Skirting the villa, they soon found themselves in what was obviously a stonemason's yard. It was full of pieces of rubble from tiny fragments to great boulders but there weren't any statues around.

Milo nodded towards a strange sort of outbuilding that looked like a cross between a garage and a church. It soared up from the ground and its great arched wooden doors stood

338

open. They approached it slowly, almost reverentially, their footsteps hushed as they entered. They allowed their eyes to adjust slowly and, when they did, they saw the most amazing sight. They were completely surrounded by statues. They were everywhere, making a semicircle of stone around them.

'Why do you think they're lined up like this?' Alice asked.

'I don't know,' Milo said. 'Maybe Mr Karalis likes to stand in the middle and look at them for inspiration. It's a bit like a museum, isn't it?'

'It's more like a strange sort of charnel house,' Alice said with a shudder. 'You know – where they keep skeletons that have been dug up from graves?'

Milo nodded.

'Look – not one is complete,' Alice said.

They gazed with a mixture of wonder and horror at the statues. There were the usual missing arms and noses but some didn't even have heads and some were just bare torsos on plinths.

'Poor things,' Alice said, as if the statues were alive and might actually be missing their various misplaced body parts.

'Hey!' Milo said, nodding towards the far side of the room. Alice followed his gaze and that's when she saw her – Aphrodite, her beautiful broken body lying on the floor of the workshop.

'She looks so sad,' Alice said, walking over to her and placing a reverential hand upon her.

'What are you going to do?' Milo asked.

'I don't know. How do you undo a wish?'

Milo shrugged. 'I have no idea,' he said.

Alice knelt down on the floor beside the statue and took a deep breath. 'I'm not quite sure what to say,' she said.

'I'll give you some space,' Milo said, walking out of the building. Alice watched him go, his figure silhouetted in the arched doorway by the bright sunshine, and then she turned back to Aphrodite.

'Hello,' she said, and then smiled to herself. It felt funny talking to an inanimate object, especially a broken one, but wasn't that exactly what she'd come so far to do? A part of her couldn't help thinking that the whole thing was ridiculous. What if this didn't work? What if Milo was right and Alice was completely mad? But she hadn't imagined it all, had she? How else was she to explain all of the male attention she'd received? No, this statue had a lot to answer for and Alice was jolly well going to put a stop to it now.

She placed her hand on Aphrodite's right shoulder and closed her eyes.

'I don't know what to say to you but I'm hoping you can help me,' she began. 'I made this wish to be noticed by men and I realise now that I didn't want that at all. It was a silly thing to do and it was nothing but a nightmare so can you undo the wish? I wish to be just me again – just the Alice Archer who arrived here on Kethos before making the wish. Is that all right? Can you do that for me, please?'

She took a deep breath and opened her eyes. Had it worked? Had things returned to normal? She wasn't sure and guessed she wouldn't be until she ran into a few men but, kneeling there on the floor next to Aphrodite, Alice felt the urge to keep talking.

'Do you grant other wishes, Aphrodite?' she asked in a voice little above a whisper. 'I think it would be greedy of me to make another wish and I know I really shouldn't but I can't help wishing that I could stay here on Kethos. I'm not going to wish that Milo falls madly in love with me – that would be wrong – but I wish I knew how he felt about me. As soon as I saw the island again, I felt so happy. I love it so much – the colours and the smells and the light and the air. I don't think I want to be anywhere else and I've been thinking – really thinking – that I could make a go of things here. I mean, I'm not sure what I'd do yet but I've got some money now and I've got some time to work things out, haven't I? I've never done anything adventurous in my life and I can't help wanting to change that. I keep thinking of my father and how happy he was to spend all his life in the same place but I no longer think that's right for me and – no, I'm not going to keep wishing. I—' she paused. 'I'm going to go now.'

She lifted her hand from Aphrodite and stood up. For a moment, she looked down at the beautiful face and couldn't help wondering if her words had been heard. 'I do hope so,' she said to herself before leaving the workshop.

Blinking in the bright sunshine as she stepped outside, she looked around for Milo and saw him standing next to a low wall that looked out across an orchard. He turned round at her approach.

'Hey!' he said. 'How did it go?'

Alice shrugged. 'I really don't know.'

'Do you think it's worked?' he asked.

'I hope so,' she said and part of her was desperate to ask

him if he still found her attractive but it would be too awful to ask him such a question. Besides, she seemed to have her answer when his gaze moved from her to the orchard.

'Look at the size of this place,' he said. 'Just imagine the garden you could make here.'

Alice looked around her. Beyond the orchard, the land rolled away into a boulder-strewn hillside which tumbled towards an azure sea. It was stunningly beautiful and she tried to picture it through Milo's eyes with borders filled with flowers and herbs and pretty pathways leading to secret fountains.

'Well,' he said a moment later, 'I suppose we'd better get out of here before we're caught trespassing.'

Alice nodded. She'd forgotten that they were on private property and that they'd climbed over a wall to get in.

Sneaking back around the villa, they retraced their footsteps and Milo gave Alice a leg up the wall before managing to clamber up it himself, hooking his fingers into the crumbling brickwork. They eased themselves down the olive tree and ran back towards the car, instantly waking the dog who gave a volley of vicious barks.

'I can't thank you enough,' Alice said once they were safely inside the car. 'I'm sorry I put you through all that.'

'I wouldn't have missed it for the world,' he said with a little smile and then a strange silence fell between them. Finally, Milo cleared his throat. 'I guess you want me to take you to the ferry now?'

There was a pause before Alice answered. 'I guess,' she said in a voice that was barely audible.

'Okay,' he said and he started the engine.

Chapter 41

Milo was at war with himself. Alice wanted to go home. She was leaving Kethos for the second time and he didn't know how to stop her. He thought about the week they'd shared together a few months ago back in the spring and then he thought about how – just last night – they'd talked and talked like old friends. There'd been such an ease in their togetherness – a closeness that usually comes over time. It had been so natural and he didn't want to give that up because he truly believed that he'd never find it again.

So, what if he told her all these things now? What if he asked her to stay?

But she doesn't want to hear what you have to say, a little voice told him. *You lied to her. You deceived her. She only came back because of the statue – it had nothing to do with you.*

Milo sighed. None of that seemed to matter, though. What mattered was that he had a burning sensation in his gut and he just had to tell her how he felt about her otherwise he was quite sure he would spontaneously combust.

They reached a crossroads where a pair of hairy goats were grazing and he stopped the car.

'What is it?' Alice asked, looking at him. 'Are we lost?'

'No,' he said. 'We're not lost.' He cleared his throat. He had to do this, he told himself. 'There's an amphitheatre near here,' he said. 'I've just remembered it. I've not been there for years. Do you want to see it?'

Alice looked surprised. 'What about the ferry?'

'You can get a later one.'

They locked eyes for a moment and Milo silently willed her to stay. *Say yes*, he silently pleaded. *Say yes!*

'Okay, then,' she said.

He smiled. 'You won't regret it,' he said.

He turned right and followed the road up into the mountains, watching out of the corner of his eye as Alice wound her window down. The warm air pushed its way into the car and the breeze caught her hair and tangled it around her face and she smiled.

How could she leave all this, Milo thought to himself? How could she choose to return to the country of grey skies and stormy seas – a country so far away from him?

She hasn't gone yet, a little voice told him. *Don't give up now*.

The road suddenly dropped down into a little valley and Alice gasped as she saw the amphitheatre for the first time. The semicircle of stone was set perfectly into a great scoop in the landscape and looked as if it had been there forever.

'It's not the grandest in Greece,' Milo said as he parked the car. 'It's probably one of the smallest.'

'It's wonderful,' she said. 'I can't think how I overlooked it before.'

'Because you rushed back to England before you gave this place a chance to work its magic on you.'

'What do you mean? It *did* work its magic on me!'

Milo shook his head. 'I don't mean the wish – I mean – this *place!* It's a place you feel in your very soul.'

They got out of the car and walked across the stony ground, entering the amphitheatre at the top and gazing down the steep rows of seats to what would have been the performance area below.

'Isn't it amazing?' Milo said, his dark eyes shining with pride. 'I often wonder if my ancestors came here to watch plays and be entertained.'

'Is it used now?'

'Not often. Just the occasional play in the summer for the tourists and firework displays at New Year.' Milo walked along one of the rows of seats and Alice followed him. *You're going to do this,* he told himself. *Just keep calm and work out exactly what you want to say.*

He stopped abruptly and Alice crashed into him.

'Oh!' he said, turning round and facing her, a blush colouring his face. 'Sorry.'

'Milo, what is it?'

'Nothing,' he said.

'You're all angsty and jittery.'

'Am I?'

'Yes, you are,' Alice said, and her hands were on her hips. 'Milo – why did you bring me here?'

He looked into her soft blue eyes and noticed the little wrinkles in her forehead as she tried to work out his motive. 'Why did I bring you here?' he said, repeating her question.

'Yes,' Alice said, staring at him hard.

'That is a direct question and it deserves a direct answer.'

345

'Right,' Alice said.

Milo took a deep breath. 'I brought you here because I want to tell you something.'

'Okay,' she said encouragingly.

He paused before beginning, kicking one of his shoes against the other like a nervous schoolboy. 'Alice,' he said, 'I don't want you to leave.'

She frowned. 'You don't?'

'Of course I don't! You've already left once and it almost broke me. I can't bear the thought of you going again and I will hold you fully responsible for my actions if you do go.'

'But I thought—' she stopped.

'What?'

'I thought you hated me because of the conclusion I'd jumped to about you being married.'

'I don't *hate* you!' he said aghast.

'But you didn't talk to me this morning. At breakfast, you just stared at me and froze me out completely and I didn't know what to think.'

'Alice – I'm so sorry,' he said. 'I was trying to work out what to do. You said you were leaving and I knew I had to stop you but I didn't know how you felt about me any more. I know you only came back to Kethos to see the statue and—'

'Well, I—' she paused, tears in her eyes. 'I'm so sorry, Milo. I've had so much on my mind lately.'

'I know you have,' he said gently.

'My father, and the wish and – well – I didn't really know if you were interested in me. I mean, *really* interested in me or if it was because of the wish I'd made.'

'Oh, Alice! And then I go and make a huge mess of everything between us,' he said. 'Look, I have no right to expect you to forgive me after I lied to you. I should have told you the truth about Tiana and I'm sorry I didn't.'

'But Milo – it should be *you* forgiving *me*,' she said.

'There's nothing to forgive,' he said, taking a step closer to her. 'I just wish—' he paused and laughed. 'Maybe it would be better not to wish but I can't help wishing that I'd done things differently.'

'But you did what you thought was right for Tiana,' Alice said. 'You were right to protect her. You had no idea how things would be between us and it would be unfair to bring all of your girlfriends home and confuse her.'

'But you're the only one I've ever brought home,' he said and their eyes locked for a moment. 'You won't leave, will you? I mean, I know you'll have to go home and do whatever you have to do but you will come back, won't you?'

Alice smiled and her whole face suddenly lit up with joy. 'I want to tell you something,' she said.

'Okay,' Milo said, his face filled with anxiety.

'I'm not planning on leaving,' she said with a little laugh.

'What?' Milo's eyes almost popped out of his head.

'I've been trying to think this all through,' she said. 'I know it's a little bit crazy but I really want to have some crazy in my life now. I've always done the sensible thing, you see – I got a job, I rented a house, I've tried to save up for a place of my own and yet none of it's brought me any happiness. But, when I came here, it was as if the world suddenly switched from black and white to colour and I was just dazzled by it

347

all. I know I got a bit distracted by the wish and everything and – well – all the chaos it brought when I went home, but I couldn't get this place out of my mind. I'd sit staring at my computer at work and yet it wasn't the computer I was seeing but the Villa Argenti or that little beach you took me to. I'd see a pigeon sitting on my garden wall and I'd think of Pelagios the pelican.'

Milo laughed.

'Oh, dear, I'm rambling now, aren't I?' Alice said.

'You're not rambling.'

'But I thought I might have to find myself another island if you didn't want me on this one.'

'But I *do* want you on this one! You should have told me what you were thinking! Why didn't you tell me?'

'Because you seemed so distant today. I didn't know what you were thinking.'

'What I was thinking? I was thinking of *you!* I haven't been able to stop thinking of you since I first met you. Since I first *saw* you.'

'Really?'

'Yes, really!' He laughed. 'You still don't believe me, do you? Stay right there,' he said and, suddenly, he was racing down the steep stone steps towards the centre of the amphitheatre.

'Milo – what *are* you doing?' Alice called after him.

'Wait there!' he said excitedly. His feet almost tripped over themselves as he ran but then he reached the bottom and he stood perfectly still right in the middle of the performance area. He gazed up at Alice high above him. She was shielding her eyes from the sun with her hands.

'Alice?' he said, testing out his voice in the immense space.

'Yes?' she called back.

'I love you,' he said in a voice barely above a whisper.

'What?' she said.

'You heard me!' Milo said. 'The acoustics in here are the best in the world.'

'Yes, but I want to hear it again just in case I imagined it.'

'All right then – I LOVE YOU!' This time, he shouted his declaration and his voice filled the whole amphitheatre and seemed to spread far beyond to the very heavens. 'I've loved you from the first moment you walked into the gardens at the villa and it had nothing to do with your blue eyes or your hair or what you were wearing. I loved you because you were *you!*' he said. 'Because you were *Alice!*'

'But you didn't know me then,' she said, slowly walking down the steps towards him.

Milo shook his head. 'But I did! I knew you straightaway. I could *see* you, Alice. I could see you for the person you really were.'

'But how do I know it's not because of the wish?' She was halfway down the steps now.

'Because I saw you getting off the boat that day – the very moment you arrived on Kethos – *long* before you made that wish. You were with your sister but it was you I was looking at. I couldn't take my eyes off you, Alice. You looked so happy to be here – on my little island – and I so wanted to get to know you and then you came to the gardens and we talked. Do you remember that? You told me all those things about your life and I loved listening to you. And that – *all* that – was

349

before you made that silly wish.'

Alice had reached the centre of the amphitheatre and he could see that her eyes were shining with tears.

'I love you,' he said again. 'And I know we've only just met and I know it seems crazy to say such a thing but I just can't help it.' He gave her a smile, relief and joy surging through him at having told Alice how he felt.

'Oh, Milo,' she said. 'I love you too.'

'Really?'

'I think so,' she said and they both laughed.

'And I know it has nothing to do with Aphrodite,' he said.

Alice nodded. 'You're right. It doesn't. But I do have something to confess.'

'What's that?'

'I might have made another wish on her.'

Milo looked surprised. 'What was it? What did you wish for?'

Alice looked up at him and her eyes were soft with adoration. 'I wished that I could stay here on Kethos.'

Milo sighed with great satisfaction. 'You didn't need Aphrodite to make that wish come true. I would have granted it for you.'

One Year Later

The sea was the colour of aquamarines. Alice shielded her eyes as she looked out over the orchard towards it. It was going to be a glorious summer on Kethos. She could smell the thyme and lavender which Milo had planted in the new garden he was creating and the rich lemony scent of the little flower which only grew on Kethos and whose name Alice had forgotten. Still, there was plenty of time to learn it. She wasn't going anywhere.

She still couldn't believe what had happened over the course of a single year. Her father's house had been sold and Stella had paid off her debts and put down a deposit on a little flat in Norwich and had even got herself her first full-time job.

'It's so tiny!' she'd complained when Alice had visited her.

'Stella, you have two en suite bedrooms, a brand new kitchen and a balcony all to yourself!' Alice told her, shaking her head in despair. Stella would never be happy and Alice had finally realised that there was nothing she could do to change that. But *she* could be happy.

'And I am,' she said to herself now as she gazed into the silvery green olive trees where Tiana was playing.

It seemed an age since she'd handed in her notice to a perplexed Larry Baxter.

'Greece?' he'd said. 'You're going to live in *Greece?*'

Alice had nodded. 'I'll send you a postcard!' she'd told him.

Ben had found out about her plan and had come down to the department to wish her well on her last day. It was a moment laced with awkwardness and Alice had wondered what she'd ever seen in him and she had the feeling that he was thinking exactly the same thing about her.

And then the villa had come up for sale. Alice and Milo couldn't believe it. The sculptor, Yanni Karalis, had retired. He was ninety-two, after all, and had been persuaded by one of his sons to sell up and move to the mainland.

Mr Karalis's statues were all sold before Alice and Milo took possession of the property. All apart from one. Alice had made sure that one very special statue was left as part of the deal and she was looking at her right now.

They'd managed to find a sculptor who had done his best to piece back Aphrodite's broken body and she now stood in a shaded corner of the garden, overseeing the work that they were doing. Alice would plant roses around her one day and make that little corner of the garden fit for a goddess.

She smiled as she remembered that it was because of Aphrodite that she was here right now. The foolish wish she'd made seemed to have been reversed and Alice's life had returned to normal – if she could call finding her true love and living happily ever after *normal*.

For a moment, she thought about the wedding ceremony in the tiny white church at the top of the hill and the reception afterwards which had been full of laughter and the most delicious home-cooked food Alice had ever tasted. All of Milo's brothers had been there and it seemed like the whole of Kethos had turned up too. She'd never been made to feel so at home in her life and she had Aphrodite to thank for that. If it hadn't been for the statue, she would never have returned to Kethos.

'Hello, beautiful,' Milo said, appearing on the terrace with two glasses of homemade lemonade.

Alice had stopped telling Milo that she wasn't beautiful because she really believed him now and it wasn't because the sun had banished her pale face and limbs or because it had highlighted her hair – it was because she was in love and love, she realised, had made her truly beautiful.

He handed her a glass of lemonade and they watched as Tiana clambered up one of the olive trees in the orchard.

'Careful!' Milo shouted, and they looked on helplessly as Tiana's grip suddenly loosened and she fell from one of the lower branches with a great thud.

Alice sprang out of her chair in an instant but Milo's hand reached out and grabbed her shoulder. 'Wait a moment,' he told her.

'Tiana?' Alice called. 'Are you all right?'

Tiana got up from the dusty ground and brushed herself down. 'It's okay!' she shouted back. 'I'm fine!'

Alice breathed a sigh of relief.

'You've got to learn to relax,' Milo told Alice, kissing the top of her head.

'If our child is going to be *half* as energetic as Tiana, I doubt I'll ever relax again!' Alice said with a laugh.

Milo placed a hand on her belly. 'How is he?' he asked.

'Milo! It might not be a *he* at all. It might be a little *she*.'

He shook his head. 'It's a boy. I can feel it!'

She smiled at his certainty. 'You're going to be so disappointed if it's a girl.'

'How can you say that? I'd *love* a little girl. In fact, we're going to have lots of little girls too but this is a little boy!'

'How many children are you planning, exactly?' Alice asked. 'I mean, I've already got the barn conversions under way for the holiday lets and—'

'Alice, I don't want you working so hard. Not if we're going to have three boys and three girls to take care of.' He grinned at her as her eyes doubled in size. 'Well, let's just take it one at a time,' he said, bending down to kiss her.

Alice smiled in contentment. She was living on a beautiful island with the man she loved and they were going to make a family together.

She really couldn't wish for anything more.

Read on for an exclusive Q&A with Victoria Connelly.

Where does your inspiration come from?

Anywhere and everywhere really. I'm mostly inspired to write about things I'm passionate about so my Austen Addicts' Trilogy came about because of my love of Jane Austen's novels. *Molly's Millions* was inspired by junk mail - we used to live in a house in the London suburbs and we got so much junk mail and, one day, I thought, wouldn't it be lovely if somebody pushed a £50 note through the letterbox instead of yet another flyer trying to sell us something? That thought inspired the heroine in *Molly's Millions*.

The Runaway Actress explores the fantasy that I think a lot of us have had – what if your idol turned up at your home? And *Wish You Were Here* was a 'what if' novel when I asked myself, what if wishes came true?

Have you always wanted to be a writer?

Yes! I started writing my first novel when I was at high school and I've been writing ever since. Of course, getting published can take years and so I've had many other jobs as well. When

I was a civil servant, I used to write my novels under the desk and use the office photocopier mercilessly! And, when I trained to become a teacher, my primary thought was that the long holidays would enable me to write.

What's the strangest job you've ever had?
I don't think I've had any really *strange* jobs but I've had some pretty dreadful ones including supply teaching in inner-city Leeds and Bradford – scary!

And I once had a holiday job as a courier for SAGA Holidays which was enormous fun and meant taking coach trips out to amazing places, doing the spiel on the microphone and taking part in the evening entertainment. It was probably the hardest I have ever worked and, despite eating masses of fantastic food, I lost half a stone during the summer holidays because I was on the go from eight in the morning until 11 o'clock at night!

When you're not writing, what are your favourite things to do?
Like most writers, I love reading and I adore watching films - anything from a 1930s gangster flick, an MGM musical or the latest romantic comedy. I also love baking, gardening, long walks in the countryside and visiting historic houses.

We recently moved from the London suburbs to a cottage in rural Suffolk and I'm filling the garden with old-fashioned roses. They've become a bit of an obsession of mine – they're so beautiful and have such gorgeous names like *Comte de Chambord*, *Honorine de Brabant* and *Rambling Rector*. But I think my husband will despair if I ask him to dig a hole for *yet another* pink rose!

And, of course, I love spending time with my animals. We have a rescue springer spaniel and four ex-battery chickens who are an absolute delight. A perfect day off for me would be a good book and a cup of tea in the garden, watching my hens dust-bathing amongst the roses!

What is a typical working day like for you?
When a novel is in full flow, I aim to write about 1000 words a day. I suffer from RSI so try to do most of my work using voice recognition software which means I look a bit like someone from air traffic control with my microphone and headphones on!

I don't really have set hours but I work best in the morning and late afternoon and I like to punctuate the day with walking our dog and getting out into the garden. I also like to log in to Facebook and Twitter to connect with friends and readers but I try not to get *too* distracted by it.

Have you ever had writer's block and if so how do you cope with it?
I wrote a novel called *Three Graces* about a woman called Carys who marries a duke and finds herself living in an enormous old house haunted by one of his ancestors. I got about three-quarters of the way through and just came to a standstill. This had never happened to me before and it was very frustrating. So I put it to one side and wrote two children's books. I then went back to *Three Graces* and wrote the ending without any difficulty at all. I think the main problem was

that I only had one viewpoint character in that book – Carys - and I usually have three and so I found that really hard going. I won't make that mistake again!

Do you have any secret ambitions?
Last summer, I entered our village show for the first time. I was absolutely thrilled to win a first prize and the 'WI Shield' for my chocolate cake but, of course, this puts the pressure on for this year and I've set myself the challenge of winning first prize in each of the home baking sections – although not all in one year! So I've got to get to work on perfecting my Victoria Sandwich and bread-making skills now.

On the writing front, I'd *love* to write an action adventure one day – a kind of Indiana Jones but with a female protagonist. And it would be wonderful if one of my books was turned into a film. My first published novel – *Flights of Angels* – was made into a film in Germany but I'd love to see one made in English and, if somebody could cast Henry Cavill or Richard Armitage as one of my heroes then that would be absolutely wonderful!

Follow Avon on
Twitter@AvonBooksUK
and
Facebook@AvonBooksUK
For news, giveaways and
exclusive author extras

A V O N